Second Chances in Serendipity

Serendipity Sunsets Book Two

Liza Lanter

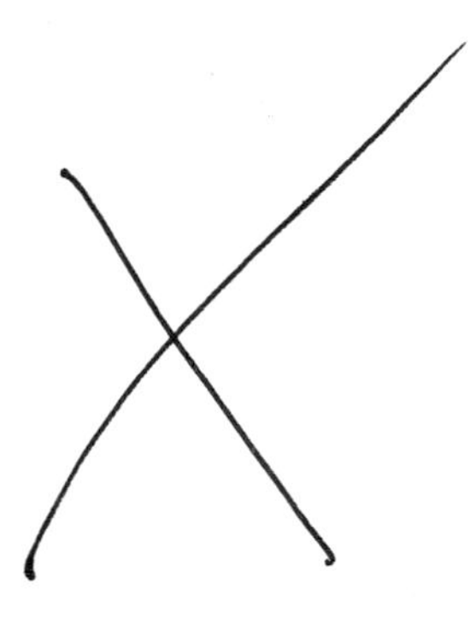

Copyright © 2023 Liza Lanter

ISBN: 978-1-942994-10-7

Published by Ink On My Fingers Publishing

All Rights Reserved

Cover Design by Cassy Roop / PinkInkDesigns.com

No part of this book may be reproduced in any form or by any electronic or mechanical means including information storage and retrieval systems, without permission in writing from the author. The only exception is by a reviewer, who may quote short excerpts in a review.

This book is a work of fiction. Names, characters, places, and incidents either are products of the author's imagination or are used fictitiously. Any resemblance to actual persons, living or dead, events, or locales is entirely coincidental.

Printed in the United States of America

Also By

SERENDIPITY SUNSETS

Return to Serendipity

Second Chances in Serendipity

Miracles in Serendipity

Revelations in Serendipity

Wedding in Serendipity

New Beginnings in Serendipity

Happy Endings in Serendipity

Contents

Chapter One

Jenn

"No wonder Mel calls it Serendipity's welcome mat—the sunsets are out of this world."

It had only been a month since Jenn Halston returned to her beloved hometown of Serendipity. Yet, in some ways, she felt like she'd never left the small coastal town of her childhood. Sitting in a high back Adirondack chair on the sand in front of the beachfront house she inherited a few months earlier, the crashing of the ocean waves was a simultaneous sound of loud and quiet with a never-ending view of tomorrow.

"The sunsets sneak up on you." Gladys, Jenn's neighbor, sat beside her in a matching chair. The eclectic woman was draped in a mustard-yellow kaftan and wide-brimmed straw hat. "You spend the day looking at a seemingly endless haze. Then, out of nowhere, there's a downpour of color like the angels are painting the sky."

Jenn smiled at her friend's creative description. Watching the sun set over the ocean was relaxing on a level that she never realized during her youth or on the short visits to her parents' home throughout her adult life. The evening view was a breathtaking display of incredible colors. The skyline put on a show before saying goodnight.

Life had been amazing during her short time back in Serendipity. Repeatedly, circumstances had proven that the town's name was accurate. So many 'happy accidents' were crossing her path. Jenn could only imagine what the next six months, or a year, would reveal.

Prior to returning, Jenn's life had not been without stress and concern. Jenn was recently divorced from her husband of thirty years. Simon was starting a new family with his young wife. As the divorce was finalizing, Jenn's beloved mother, Paisley, passed suddenly leaving a hole in Jenn's heart like she'd never imagined. To Jenn's surprise, the family's long-loved beachfront property was willed to her. Deciding to move back to her hometown and live on the family property, Jenn learned that the local newspaper, the *Serendipity Sun,* where she had her first job as a young reporter, was for sale. She fulfilled a lifelong dream and bought the business, clinching the deal that she should return home. It was all a whirlwind, a roller coaster of happy and sad.

Moving 'home' also offered the opportunity to reconnect with old friends. Despite living hours away from each other in adult life, Jenn and her best friend, Mel Snow, remained close. Only a few days after Jenn's return, both were coincidently reconnecting with the boys, now men, who once held their young hearts.

Growing up in the same neighborhood as Randy Nave, he and Jenn were close friends, like siblings, all through school. Randy was an all-around athlete and the most popular boy in their class. Jenn never thought she stood a chance with her handsome neighbor, especially since he often dated a different girl each week. After a career in the U.S. Army, divorced Randy returned to Serendipity, and began working in the police department. Now the Chief of Police, Randy was one of the first people to stop by the newspaper to welcome her home. Soon thereafter, he confessed that he regretted not dating Jenn when they were young. Jenn was shocked to learn that her first crush had similar feelings, then and now.

Jenn's best friend Mel and local baseball star, Sinclair Lewis, were high school sweethearts. On a senior beach trip, Sinclair cheated on Mel with a fellow classmate named Dana, resulting in a pregnancy. Forced by his parents to marry Dana, Sinclair left Mel brokenhearted. A few months before Jenn returned to Serendipity, newly divorced Sinclair bought a car dealership in the neighboring county, also moving back to their hometown. Like Randy, Sinclair's heart was set on rekindling a romance with his long-lost love.

Like the name of her beloved town, the 'happy accidents' kept happening in Jenn's life. Every day, she wondered what new surprises were around the corner, hoping that none of them would add any more stress to her life.

"Renee, you sound so much stronger."

Jenn's older sister answered the phone on the first ring.

"I feel the best I have since my days in purgatory began."

Renee was recovering at home after an abscess related to colon cancer resulted in her having emergency surgery. Jenn hoped to convince Renee to stay with her during recovery.

"Have you given any more thought to spending some of your recovery here in Serendipity?"

"I think about it every day. The ocean waves. The sand between my toes. My little sister at my beck and call. The prospect makes me feel better than the morphine." Renee's laugh was followed by a moan of pain. "I have a follow-up appointment with my surgeon in a few days. If he says everything is okay, I will welcome the opportunity for my healing to occur with my butt in the sand and my face in the sun. Will there be wine?"

"Paisley Halston never let her stock get low. You'll have to ask your doctor about your ability to consume it." Jenn was happy to hear Renee joking.

"Wine has healing properties, I'm sure of it. Enough about me. I've missed at least a week of updates about your new adventures. What's going on in Serendipity?"

"I hired a new Editor for the newspaper. He held the job several years ago. You might remember him from your high school days. He's probably about your age. His name is Lyle Livingston."

"Lyle the Smile." Renee laughed. "Mom used to share some of his editorials when he was there the first time."

"She used to send me some, too. I never connected his name with the guy from our high school days."

"He looked like Shaun Cassidy. I think one of my friends dated Lyle for a while. Is he still handsome?"

"He wasn't afraid to tackle tough issues when he worked for the newspaper before. I want someone in this role with strong journalism skills who can lead the editorial team. It's important that we carry on Mr. Sebastian's legacy of providing unbiased news coverage. I also want the newspaper to be a proactive part of any growth the town might experience in the future. Growth means more advertisers. A better financial situation will allow me to run a more responsive newspaper." Jenn paused. "And, yes, Lyle is still handsome."

"My little sis is going to conquer the world. She is single, too. Eligible men will be swarming. Have you run into the handsome police chief again who used to hang around our house?"

Jenn knew Renee had a sixth sense when it came to Jenn keeping secrets. Maybe if she played it cool, Renee wouldn't pick up, in her medicated state, on anything else happening in Jenn's life.

"Yes, Randy came by to meet the new Publisher during my first week."

"I have heard that story already. Mom used to say Randy was even more handsome than when he was young."

Jenn remained silent.

"Would you agree with Mom's opinion?"

"Randy is a handsome man."

"I hope he decides to finally act on those long-concealed feelings he's had for you."

"I don't know what you're talking about."

"You can deny it all you want, little sister. Don't forget, I lived in the same house. You thought Randy hung the moon. I think Randy always had a thing for my little sister. It was a look in his eyes or the sound of his voice when he was talking to you. You had his full attention. I think you might have been like a porcelain doll to him. Randy could gaze upon you, sitting quietly close by. Getting too close wasn't an option. He was afraid you might break."

"Randy is still the kind soul we knew growing up."

"So, you have spent some time with him."

There was that radar of Renee's.

"We've eaten a couple of meals together. Mostly with Mel and Sinclair."

"What? A couple of meals, you say. Since you've only been there a month that seems significant. Wait! You are trying to distract me. Mel and Sinclair? I haven't heard those two names in the same sentence in decades, at least three decades, maybe four. I'm out of commission for a couple of weeks and I miss a whole season of Serendipity. You better have recorded the episodes I missed."

Jenn chuckled under her breath. She was hearing the personality of the sister she knew. It was a welcomed sound. Even though the interrogation was directed at her, Jenn was thrilled to hear the real Renee coming through. It gave Jenn hope that her sister was conquering the illness.

"You'll have to come to Serendipity and find out for yourself. Things are changing daily. The whole Mel and Sinclair saga could be its own show."

"Well, if that's not incentive to come and stay a while, I don't know what is." Renee was silent for a moment. "Sinclair better not hurt Mel again. Seriously, I sure hope that story finally gets a happy ending."

"Me, too."

"I took the liberty of rearranging the office. I thought I might get into the groove quicker if I put it back to the way I used to have it."

Jenn looked around the Editor's office. Newly hired Lyle Livingston obviously spent some of his weekend making changes to the arrangement of the furniture and adding personal touches. There was a bookcase that she didn't remember being there before as well as an old-fashioned desk lamp. On one of the walls was a large framed front page from Lyle's first time being the newspaper's editor. It reminded Jenn of her time at the newspaper years ago.

"Certainly, you can change your office any way you like. Is that a fresh coat of paint on the walls?"

"I really should have waited and asked your permission. I talked to Doris about it on Friday afternoon. She showed me a couple cans of paint in the maintenance closet. She said that it was purchased to repaint your office before you arrived. I assumed that you picked out the color."

Jenn looked at the medium shade of gray on the walls. It was identical to her own office.

"I'm so glad my office was painted this color. It's a lovely, soothing shade."

"The walls were previously a dull dingy white with outlines of where pictures once hung." Lyle pointed at each wall. "I remember those old white walls. I had a dartboard in here once."

"Making your space comfortable helps you be more productive. The whole building could probably use a fresh coat of paint." Jenn looked around Lyle's office, thinking about how the color might look everywhere.

"That would actually be a good team-building activity to do one afternoon." Lyle leaned against his desk. "Maybe close the office to the public for a few hours and let everyone paint their space. Order some pizza. There would be some good stories afterward, guaranteed."

"That's an excellent idea. Maybe we could then have an open house sometime afterwards." Jenn felt excited about a special event. "It would be a great way for us to reintroduce the newspaper to the community."

"The weekend of the annual Christmas parade would be a good time."

"Absolutely! Then, it would be less likely to interfere with events that are geared to visitors."

"Your friend, the tourism director, would approve of that." Lyle's grin lit up his whole face.

Seeing his famous smile took Jenn back to their youth when Lyle was the slightly older athlete with blonde hair that touched his shoulders and a smile that could have adorned a magazine cover. Jenn shook her head at the memory. *Lyle the Smile.*

"I like the idea of the newspaper being part of community activities. Perhaps we can also find a local charity that we, as an organization, can support." Jenn felt a surge of renewed energy. It was exhilarating.

"One thing I've been thinking about for the news and editorial side of the paper is that perhaps we can run a series about local nonprofits and their impact on the community. After the series runs, we could put the articles into a special edition that Mel could get into the hands of some of the folks who have long-term rentals here, those who are seasonal citizens. It might be a great way for the nonprofits to tap into some potential funding sources."

"Another great idea. Keep them coming, Mr. Livingston." Jenn turned to exit his office. "After you get acclimated to your new schedule, let me know when might be a good block of time that you and I could have a weekly meeting. There's much planning to be done."

"Will do, Boss."

Jenn took one final glance at Lyle's million-dollar smile before walking away.

"I need to find a way to use that smile to our advantage." Jenn mumbled while she walked down the hallway toward the lobby.

"Use what?"

Jenn cringed, not realizing someone was behind her. Thankfully, it was Shaun, the sportswriter.

"Hello, Shaun, I was thinking aloud about how I can best use all of this talent I'm surrounded by every day."

Jenn briefly glanced behind her before continuing to walk toward her office. She noticed that Alice Ziegler, the company's bookkeeper, was at the front desk. Turning around, Jenn returned to the desk to speak to Alice.

"How are you feeling, Alice?"

"Stronger every day, Ms. Halston."

"Please, you must call me Jenn. Where's Doris?"

"Oh, I thought she mentioned to you that a neighbor of hers passed away a few days ago. Doris is attending the funeral."

"That's right. I forgot. Thanks for the reminder."

"She's been gone most of the morning. I believe she will be back after lunch. I think the woman who passed was a member of Doris' church." Alice nodded. "I told Doris that I would move into her desk area while she was gone. I've got some invoices that need to be sent out."

"That sounds good, Alice. Happy to see that you are getting stronger. We need you here."

Jenn heard a beeping noise. She'd forgotten that her cell phone was inside the notebook she was still carrying. Checking the screen, she saw that the call was from her son, Foster.

"Hello, favorite son."

"Hello, favorite mother. It's been several days since we talked, so I thought I better check in. Claire told me about Aunt Renee. I called her last evening. She sounds terrific."

"I'm sure she enjoyed hearing from you, Foster. Renee sounds better each time I talk to her. Did she tell you that she may come and camp out with me while she recuperates?"

"She mentioned that. It made me wonder where Michelle and I will sleep if we head in that direction." Foster laughed. "I'm kidding. Michelle has already scoped out several real estate options. We are now leaning toward purchasing a condo. That's one reason I was calling. We are planning to rent a moving truck this weekend and begin loading up.

Because my wife is such a brilliant salesperson, our condo here sold in less than forty-eight hours."

"Wow! That's incredible. I didn't realize that you two were motivated to make a change so quickly."

"We weren't. Michelle knew our condo would sell but had no idea it would do so that fast. We even got more than our list price for it as there was a bidding war."

"Excellent! That gives you more cash to begin your next chapter."

"Exactly! Michelle wanted me to ask if the sales position with the newspaper was still open."

"It is. We haven't begun interviewing yet."

"Would it be okay with you if Michelle applied? She doesn't expect any special treatment."

"I would love for her to apply. There will be a team interview with two of my existing advertising staff. I won't have a majority vote anyway. Tell Michelle that the application is on our newspaper website. I'll text you a link."

"Awesome. She'd like to submit her application before we get too deep into packing."

Foster paused. Jenn could hear papers rustling.

"Sorry, Mom. I dropped a pile of papers that I was trying to organize with one hand. Bad idea. I also talked to Dad the other day."

Speaking of bad ideas. Jenn rolled her eyes. "How's Simon?"

"In a word, my normally calm father is freaked. He told me his news. I could hear a tremble in his voice. It wasn't a happy and excited emotion; it was pure fear. I remember how you were the one who got most things done in our lives while we were growing up. Looking back, I always thought that was because Dad was so busy with his job. I didn't realize that maybe he wasn't interested in doing the hard parenting stuff. Thank goodness we had you."

Jenn's heart swelled. She raised good kids.

"Thank you, son. My life would be so empty without my three amigos." Jenn laughed, remembering that it was on a summer trip to Serendipity when that nickname was coined. "Your father loves his children, but he preferred being part of the fun activities."

"I'm sure there were times when you would have rather experienced things that were more fun than us all having the stomach flu at the same time."

"That was one of my tougher weeks of motherhood. But I would have dealt with that every week rather than what your Aunt Renee and Uncle Neil are still going through."

"Yes. I was telling Michelle about Jonah last night after I talked to Aunt Renee. She'd only heard bits and pieces of the story. It must be the worst thing that a parent can go through."

"Foster, it is worse than a child's death. As horrific as that would be, not knowing what happened to him is worse. If Jonah is missing, they still have a little hope, but that is a torturous place to live."

"They have always been good to us and interested in what we were doing. That must have been hard for them. I hope I can spend some time with Aunt Renee when she stays with you."

"I think that would be good for her."

"As I said, I wanted to check in for a few minutes. We really hope to be able to get everything packed up in a few days. We sold our condo furnished. It worked out that the man who bought it is transferring to Atlanta for a new position and was going to have to buy furnishings. It will make the move so much easier for us."

"Absolutely. Maybe you can find a furnished condo here."

"We are thinking we should be able to since there are so many furnished rentals for visitors. We've even thought about perhaps buying multiple condos, so that we could have our own rental business. It would be a good investment and something I think both of us would enjoy operating."

"Another great idea. We are becoming quite an entrepreneurial family." Jenn looked up. She saw the shadow of someone at her door. "Foster, I need to go. I have a visitor. Thanks so much for updating me. Please let me know when to expect you and Michelle. There's plenty of room at my house for you to stay while you transition to your own place."

"Thanks, Mom. We'll keep in touch. Love you."

"Love you, son."

Jenn began walking toward her doorway, looking at a text message from Emily. When she looked up, she was inches away from Randy.

"Oh, sorry, I wasn't paying attention to where I was going." Jenn was a little flustered being so close to him. Randy's cologne was intoxicating.

"As police officers, we learn to stand our ground. Especially when a beautiful woman is about to run over top of us." Randy's eyebrows rose with his smile.

"Well, I need to be more careful." Jenn willed her pulse to slow down. Randy was enjoying her reaction too much.

"I'm here to serve and protect, ma'am. And, maybe, take you to lunch."

"Lunch, I forgot about that." Jenn looked at her watch. It was almost two.

"That's what I figured. I've been busy myself. I needed to bring in a payment for a classified ad that's been running for several patrol officer positions that are currently open. I thought I'd stick my head in and see if you might be interested in grabbing a bite. If you haven't tried La Siesta down the street yet, it's delicious. I know you like Mexican food."

"That sounds great. Let me get my purse." Jenn took a few steps back to her desk and quickly grabbed her purse.

"I thought we'd walk." Randy stepped out of the way for Jenn to go ahead.

"Good idea. I will probably need to walk off an obscene amount of cheese and guacamole." Jenn stopped at the front desk, speaking to Alice. "I'm going to have lunch with the Chief."

"Hey, Randy, great to see you, man." Lyle walked up from the back of the building.

"Hey, Lyle, welcome back! Happy to hear you've returned. You'll be a valuable part of this new Publisher's team."

"That's my plan." Lyle turned to Jenn. "Looks like you're heading out."

"Yes, I stopped in to see if Jenn had eaten lunch yet."

"She stays very busy. It's easy to do in this business. Maybe we can grab coffee one day soon, Chief."

"I'll give you a shout, Lyle. I'd like to give you an overview of the new police-related situations our community is currently dealing with."

"I want to hear about them. Enjoy your lunch."

It was a short walk to the restaurant. Jenn could see the sombrero on the building a block before they arrived.

"This location has been a Mexican restaurant for a while, hasn't it? I don't remember this name though." Jenn looked at the design of the storefront before they entered the building.

"It opened during our senior year, I think, as 'The Mexican Restaurant.' How's that for an original name? It was owned by the Lopez family. Remember Marc?"

"Well, of course, he was the valedictorian of our class. Do his parents still own this?"

"They used to. Marc and his sister, Joella, and their families own it now. It's still a family operation. The food has an authenticity that you don't find at your average Mexican restaurant. Marc and Joella spent a lot of time developing dishes that have flavors from their family's culture combined with a modern twist. They have created some amazing entrees."

"I'm glad I didn't eat lunch."

Walking into the restaurant, Jenn's mouth immediately began to water as her nose took in the incredible aromas coming from the kitchen in the rear. The interior design was an eclectic combination of old furniture painted in deep vibrant colors with unique pieces of art. After being seated in a corner booth, Jenn began reading the menu.

"How in the world will I ever decide? The choices are endless."

"My mother always said that you should choose the first thing on a menu that catches your eye. It's usually what you are craving the most. Fortunately, this doesn't have to be your only visit, you live here now." Randy grinned before putting a tortilla chip loaded with homemade salsa into his mouth.

"That's right! So, I should start at the beginning and work my way through the menu."

"I still say take my mother's advice. Pick the first thing that makes your mouth water. In my case, that would be the fiesta burrito with calypso rice."

"That sounds delicious, but my eyes are drawn to the seafood fajita salad with mango guacamole dressing."

"It's wonderful." Randy motioned to the server. "I think we're ready to order."

One basket of tortilla chips later, Jenn was laughing until her sides hurt from stories Randy told of his time in the military. The antics he and his Army buddies got into during their time off reminded Jenn of the same shenanigans a younger version of this man used to tell her about with the fellow players on his sports teams.

As Jenn began to chew the first bite of her entrée, a feeling of pure bliss filled her taste buds. She hoped she wasn't moaning, but it was that delicious.

"Oh, Randy, you should arrest these people, this food is criminal."

"My goodness, Jenn, you've made a joke. I was beginning to wonder if you'd lost your sense of humor in Atlanta."

Jenn frowned, finishing her bite before taking a sip of water. *I lost a lot of myself.*

"Please forgive me." Randy reached for Jenn's hand. "I shouldn't have said that."

"It's fine. I admit I'm not as carefree as I once was. Decades of responsibility sort of wrung it out of me."

Jenn felt the warmth and strength of Randy's hand. It was a comforting feeling. A feeling she knew she could get used to, if she would allow herself.

"Sometimes I get caught up in our conversations and forget that we've spent most of our lives apart. Some moments feel so familiar, I think we are sitting under that old tree in your backyard, and you are trying to teach me geometry."

Jenn saw a faraway look in Randy's eyes when he finished speaking. He released her hand, to resume eating his meal.

"I hope you didn't need any geometry skills in the Army. It wasn't your strong suit."

"No, thankfully, they didn't assign me any jobs that required geometry. I did benefit from the English skills you made me hone. I feel like I've been writing one long report since my first days in the military. Everything about police work requires a report. They like the words to be spelled correctly and the grammar clean and clear."

"English skills come in handy."

Jenn looked around the restaurant. A woman, seated a couple of tables away, seemed to be watching Randy.

"I bet Lyle is jumping back into his old job with both feet. I don't think he wanted to leave before. The woman he was living with seemed to have a powerful grasp on him."

"He's quickly making himself right at home. He painted his office over the weekend and rearranged the furniture. Lyle has some good ideas that we can build on to make the newspaper better, more focused on real issues in our community."

Jenn glanced back to where the woman had been sitting. She was walking toward them.

"I think there is someone approaching our table."

Jenn watched Randy glance up as the woman stopped in front of their table.

"Hello, Randy." The woman did not smile.

"Oh, hello, Vivian. How have you been?"

Randy appeared to tense up.

"I've been great. I'm getting married." The woman extended her left hand, flashing an engagement ring.

"Congratulations, Vivian. I'm happy to hear it. I'd like you to meet my girlfriend, Jenn."

Jenn gave Randy a wide-eyed look. His expression seemed to be asking for her to go along with it.

"Hello, I'm Jenn." Jenn flashed a smile. "Congratulations on your engagement."

"Good luck trying to get one of these out of Randy." Vivian flashed her hand. "He's hung up on some girl he grew up with who lives in Atlanta. Or at least that's what his sister told me. Don't worry, Randy, I won't be bothering you anymore. I've got a man now who is ready to settle down. You take care of yourself. Good luck to you, Jenn."

Without another word, Vivian walked away, joining another woman who was waiting for her near the entrance.

"Well, that was awkward." Randy rubbed his forehead. "I apologize for how I introduced you. I think you can tell that she had some designs on me. I was trying to throw her off that."

"Old girlfriend, I presume."

"I wouldn't call her a girlfriend exactly. One of my officers fixed us up on a blind date about ten years ago. Vivian is a nice lady. We didn't have a lot in common. After going out a couple of times, I said we should part as friends. She had another plan. It made matters worse that my sister, Juliet, works with Vivian's grown daughter."

"Who's this girl in Atlanta?" Jenn smirked. It was her turn to enjoy Randy's embarrassment.

"She's the most wonderful woman I know, who despite my best efforts doesn't seem to want to believe I'm interested in her."

There she was again, back in the hot seat. Jenn looked into Randy's sad eyes.

"Maybe she doesn't want me to have those feelings." Randy broke eye contact, returning his attention to his food.

The girl who always had plenty of words running through her head was having difficulty coming up with the right ones.

"Would you all like anything else?" The server interrupted the lull in conversation. "Perhaps, a box for you, ma'am?"

Jenn's plate was still over half full. "Yes, thank you."

"We're probably ready for the bill." Randy handed his plate to the server.

The server pulled out a small notebook from his apron pocket and retrieved the bill. Jenn tried to grab it, but Randy was too quick for her.

"I invited you to lunch."

By the time the server returned with Jenn's box, Randy was ready to hand the bill with cash back to the server.

"Keep the change, John. Tell your mother and uncle that Chief Nave says the food was great."

Jenn quickly filled the box with the leftovers, closing the lid. She tried to think of something to say to ease the tension between them.

"Are you ready to go?" Randy stood up.

"Certainly. Thank you."

Jenn rose and began heading to the front of the restaurant with Randy behind her. Once they reached the outside, she was about to say something to him when his phone rang.

"Chief Nave." Randy immediately answered the call. "Yes. I'll stop at the courthouse on my way back to the station." Randy returned the phone to the holder on his belt. "I've got to head over to the District Attorney's office."

"Sure."

It took less than five minutes for them to walk quickly back to the newspaper office. Jenn asked Randy a couple of questions about the buildings they passed. He gave her short answers.

"I'll see you later, Jenn."

"Randy, wait a second."

Jenn put her hand on Randy's arm. His eyes went from her hand to her eyes. Jenn saw more sadness. She took a deep breath.

"I didn't respond well back there. Honestly, I don't know how to do this. I met Simon in college. I barely dated anyone before that. I feel like I've been married my whole life. Before that, the last time I dated someone more than once was Brett Nelson during our senior year."

Jenn watched Randy sneer.

"You didn't like him very much, I remember."

"He was a jerk."

"I hadn't thought of him in years. I hope I don't run into him."

"You won't. He's dead."

"I'm sorry to hear that."

"Brett dropped dead of a heart attack about five years ago. I'm sorry for his family. But he was still a jerk." Randy's tone was very matter of fact.

"I don't want to hurt your feelings. I don't want to run you off. I just can't fathom why the Randy Nave I used to know would be interested in me."

Before Jenn knew what was happening, Randy's hands were on each side of her face. As he pulled her into a kiss, Jenn felt an electrical charge from the top of her head to the tips of her toes and music playing between her ears. The kiss was soft and firm, gentle and passionate, long, but all too short. Her eyes were still closed when she felt him pull away. A symphony inside her head began to quiet, Jenn opened her eyes to find Randy watching her, a sweet smile on his face. In her peripheral vision, she could see people standing on both sides of the street, watching them. Jenn could see that Doris had returned to the office and was standing behind the office door smiling.

"This is Chief Nave speaking." Randy glanced around to the people nearby, raising his voice. "I want everyone to know that I would like to date Jenn Halston. I hope that today is the beginning of our relationship. People can stop whispering about us because this is not a rumor, it's a fact."

Still clutching her plastic box of food, Jenn stood still. She was too shocked to speak.

"I hope I've not embarrassed you too much. I'm going to teach you how to do this dating thing. Remember, I'm an expert." Randy lowered his voice, winking. "You've got to promise me one thing."

Still numb from the experience, Jenn managed to shake her head affirmatively.

"You've got to believe me."

Chapter Two

Randy

"That's correct, Edwin. Officers Patton and Fairfield worked that call. Officer Fairfield has since left police work."

"We're going to need Fairfield to testify."

District Attorney Edwin Greer had summoned Randy to his office to discuss an upcoming trial.

"That may be difficult. Fairfield has gone off the radar."

"We need both testimonies if we are going to convict this guy. They need to corroborate each other's testimony. The defense attorney is saying his client was framed. If we can't find Fairfield, that's only going to add fuel to the defense's fire."

"Okay. We will look for him. Maybe Fairfield is keeping in touch with some people locally."

"He's not from here, is he?"

"No, I think it was the lure of the beach that brought him here. Lots of people vacation at the beach while growing up and think they'd like to live at a beach year around. After he completed the police academy, I believe this was his first job."

"Why did he leave police work?"

"A couple of weeks after the arrest in your case, Fairfield responded to a call at one of the vacation rental properties. Apparently two children disappeared while on vacation with their mother. From talking to Fairfield's partner, I don't think he handled the situation too well. He hadn't been an officer long; maybe he couldn't cut it emotionally. Situations that involve children are some of the worst incidents we face as officers."

"Working cases that involve children are tough. Were the kids found?"

"Yes, the following day. They were with their estranged father at a hotel about ten miles away."

"Score one for a happy ending." Edwin closed a folder on his desk. "Do what you can to find him, Randy. I'm going to file for an extension; hopefully, that will give us a few extra weeks to get Fairfield back here."

"I'll do my best."

Randy sat in his vehicle for a few minutes after leaving the courthouse. Thinking about who he would assign to look for Fairfield; he knew his team was short-staffed as it was. They had two openings for patrol officers and one of the detectives was out on medical leave after surgery.

"Maybe I should handle this one myself." Randy mumbled, watching people go in and out of the courthouse. "I found plenty of AWOL soldiers back in my early years in Army investigation. I've never had to find one of my patrol officers before, thank heavens. I learned in the Army though, nine times out of ten, if you could find the girl, you could find the boy."

Randy's phone beeped. Smiling, he opened a text from Jenn. "Thanks for lunch. I'll work on believing."

"After all these years, I found *this* girl; maybe my skills are good enough to find the girl Fairfield left behind."

"Hey, Randy, what brings you to the Visitors Bureau this afternoon? I thought you might have been arrested earlier for kissing in public."

Randy rolled his eyes. He should have known that if Mel wasn't on the street to witness his public display of affection with Jenn, she had an informant who probably took a photograph.

"I think I'm going to save this photo for your and Jenn's engagement announcement." Mel turned her phone around so that Randy could briefly see what was on her screen. "Doris and I will conspire with Lyle to make that happen."

"I'm willing to take all forms of harassment about the incident. It was worth every single moment of kidding that I will receive in the days and weeks to come." Randy flashed a big smile. "That's not why I came here though. I'm on official business."

Mel's expression turned serious. "Is everything okay?"

"Yes, no worries. I'm looking for Imogene. I need to ask her a few questions about a friend of hers." Randy didn't see Mel's assistant at her normal spot at the front desk.

"She's in the back. We received a shipment of brochures this morning. She's opening the boxes and putting the inventory away. I can get her, no problem. Have a seat. I just made a fresh pot of coffee over in the corner, if you'd like some." Mel pointed at the coffee pot on a small table. "For the record, I would be the *last* person to complain about you kissing Jenn, in the street, on the roof, on the field of the Super Bowl. I'm as happy as I can be about this latest development."

Mel did a little dance while walking to the back of her office. Randy laughed, pouring himself a cup of coffee. A few moments later, Mel's twentysomething assistant Imogene returned to her desk.

"Hello, Chief Nave, Mel said that you wanted to talk to me. How can I help you, sir?" Imogene looked a little apprehensive.

"Hey, Imogene, first, there's nothing for you to be concerned about. I'm trying to locate one of my former patrol officers and I believe that he used to date one of your friends."

"Oh, you must be talking about Megan. She was dating Officer Fairfield before he moved away."

"Yes. I need to find Fairfield. Do you happen to know where he moved to?" Randy took out a small notepad he kept in his pocket.

"I'm afraid I don't. Megan's been heartbroken since he left. She really liked him. They didn't date for too long."

"Did he tell Megan why he left so suddenly?"

"All I know is that Megan said one night he worked a call that involved children. It upset him. He told her that he didn't think he could handle police work. Megan assumes that he may have gone back to where he was from. I think it was a small town near Asheville."

"Fairfield hasn't communicated with Megan since he left?"

"No. It was kind of weird, Chief. He didn't have a personal cell phone. When he asked Megan out, he'd either stop by where she worked or call her from his police phone. I probably shouldn't be telling you that."

"It's okay, Imogene. Fairfield isn't in trouble. Where does Megan work? I'd like to talk to her."

"Megan is a teller at the main branch of First Bank of Serendipity."

"I bet I knew her then and didn't realize it. I appreciate your time, Imogene. Fairfield worked for me for such a short time; I didn't have much of a chance to get to know him. I know his initials are J. H. What did he go by?"

"Joe, that's what Megan called him."

"Joe, right, I remember now. Thanks again, Imogene."

Randy looked through the glass into Mel's office. She was on the phone. She stood up and waved as Randy headed for the door.

His next stop would be the institution that held all his money. Maybe Megan would have some information that would help him find Joe Fairfield.

Brady Mountcastle had been the President of the First Bank of Serendipity since Randy was a teenager. A distant cousin of Randy's mother, Brady worked his way up through the banking ranks before helping launch the company's venture into becoming a coastal banking chain. While the name of the brand included Brady's hometown, the reach of the bank franchise extended a couple hundred miles north and south.

Randy wouldn't have any difficulty talking to Megan privately, if Brady was in the office. Luckily, Randy could see Brady sitting at his large mahogany desk in the rear of the bank, next to the safe. After Randy knocked once at the open door, Brady motioned for Randy to come inside while he ended a phone call.

"Yes, Lester, I think it's time that we hired a new marketing firm for a redesign of our logo. This is the twenty-first century; we've had the same logo since the 1990s. I'll trust you to solicit some proposals from reputable firms. We'll talk next week. Good-bye."

Before the phone hit the cradle, Brady was up from his desk and reaching to shake Randy's hand.

"Chief Nave, to what do I owe this pleasure?"

"Good to see you, Brady. Hope Cecile is well."

"She was talking the other day about your sweet mother. I think she was making one of the family cake recipes for our grandson's birthday."

"That family made some good cakes." Randy looked at the clock on the wall of Brady's office. It was four o'clock. The bank's end of the day rush would begin shortly. "Brady, I'm sorry to stop by at the end of the banking day, but I need to talk to one of your employees for a few minutes, if possible."

"Certainly, Randy. I hope none of my staff are in any sort of trouble." The lines in Brady's forehead deepened when his expression turned serious.

"Absolutely not. I'm trying to locate someone for an investigation. The person was a friend of Megan's. I don't think I even have Megan's last name."

"Whitman, Megan Whitman. She works at Booth Three, over there in the middle."

Brady and Randy walked to Brady's doorway where Brady pointed to the row of teller stations.

"How about I go get her and you can use my office to talk? It's the most private spot since I have the blinds of the windows down."

"That would be great, Brady. I promise it will only take a few minutes. Thank you for your help. Let me reassure you again, Megan is not in any trouble. I'm hoping she can tell me where I can find someone."

Brady shook his head affirmatively. Randy knew the man must be in his mid-seventies, but he showed no signs of slowing down or retiring. It didn't take the tall man but a few seconds, with his long strides, to cross the large lobby and stop in front of Megan's booth. Randy watched a look of concern cross the young woman's face before she nodded and began leaving the teller area. Randy waited in the doorway of Brady's office for the young woman to arrive.

"Hello, Miss Whitman, I'm Chief Randy Nave." Randy stepped out of her way when Megan entered the room. "I hope that you won't mind for me to ask you a few questions."

"No, sir. I'm a little nervous though. I've never been questioned by the police before."

"There's no reason for you to be alarmed. Please sit down." Randy pointed to a chair a few feet away. "I would like to ask you some questions about a friend of yours."

Megan sat down, nodding her head. "Oh, I bet I know who you want to ask me about. I dated one of your officers for a little while."

"Yes, Megan, that is exactly who I would like to talk to you about, Joe Fairfield." Randy sat down in a chair across from Megan. "Joe is not in any trouble, yet, but he might be if we can't locate him."

"Did Joe do something wrong while he worked for you?"

"Not that I am aware of, but, as an officer of the law, he sometimes needs to testify in court regarding cases that he worked. There's a court case coming up that Joe needs to be in Serendipity for. That's why I'm trying to find him. Do you know where he is?"

"No, sir. I do not. I've not heard from him since he left town." Tears escaped Megan's eyes. She quickly brushed them away. "Joe and I only dated a little over a month, but I thought we were getting along well. I was surprised when he quit the police department. He said that was all he ever wanted to do since he was a little boy."

"Do you remember anything unusual that happened before he quit and left town? Did he seem upset about anything?"

"Well, there was this one incident that he and his partner worked. He probably shouldn't have told me about it." Megan bowed her head for a moment. "We went out on a date the night after it happened. It was all that Joe talked about. It wasn't so much that he told me details about it. He talked about the case involving children. He kept saying that their mother couldn't stop crying. I was so happy when I heard a couple of days later that the children were found and were going home with their mother."

"It was a tragic case with a happy ending." Randy looked at the clock. He didn't want to take too much more time. "Did Joe ever talk about his family?"

"No, other than saying his father was dead and his mother had health problems. I don't think he has any brothers or sisters. He mentioned that they moved several times during his childhood, but he graduated high school in a small town near Asheville. I don't remember the name of it. I think it might be one of those skiing towns in the western end of the state."

"Okay, that's helpful. I appreciate your time, Megan. I'm going to let you get back to work." Randy stood up, reaching into his front shirt pocket. "Here's my card. It has my cell number on it. If you think of anything else, please give me a call. If Joe should happen to call you, please give him this number and tell him that the Chief needs him to call as soon as possible."

"I certainly will do that."

Megan stood up, taking the card from Randy's hand. Randy followed her out of Brady's office. She turned back to him right before they reached the middle of the foyer.

"Chief Nave, if you find Joe and talk to him, would you please tell him that I hope he will call me sometime?"

Randy saw sadness in the young woman's eyes, the sadness of unrequited love. He knew that feeling.

"I certainly will, Megan. If he's smart, he will hightail it back here and take you on another date. I'll tell him that, too."

The comment made Megan smile. She extended her hand for Randy to shake before she scurried back to the teller area and a long line of customers.

Randy waved to Brady from across the room before tipping his hat at the woman he knew in the loan office and exiting the building.

"Looks like I'm going to have to make a trip to Asheville." Randy jumped into his vehicle, taking off his hat. "Finding a young man in all those little skiing towns is going to be like finding a needle in a haystack. I sure hope I can find some connection to Joe Fairfield before I work my way around Western North Carolina."

"I had two people call on my way home to tell me that you were seen kissing Jenn on Main Street. Believe it or not, neither one of them was Mel."

Randy sat across from Sinclair in a booth at O'Reilly's. They were developing the habit of meeting there a couple of nights a week for a beer.

"I expect there to be an article in the *Serendipity Sun* about it. Mel has a photograph."

"I know. She sent it to me when I asked her if the rumors were true. I decided that was as good of an excuse as any to contact her." Sinclair scrolled through his phone, finally showing the photo to Randy. "Have you ever kissed Jenn before?"

"Only in my dreams."

"And you picked somewhere romantic like the sidewalk of the business district. I now understand why you had so many first dates in high school."

"It's a good thing that you didn't pursue comedy as a career, my friend. Your family would have starved."

"Okay, Romeo, what's your next move?"

"I don't have a plan, Sinclair. Today was an innocent occurrence. I stopped by the newspaper office to see if Jenn had time for a late lunch. We went to La Siesta."

"Oh, that's some good eating there, buddy. We need to all go there one night."

"Maybe we can wait awhile. The food was fabulous, as always. Our overall experience went a little south when a woman I briefly dated a decade ago decided to give Jenn dating advice about me."

"Oh, this I've got to hear."

Randy ordered an appetizer for them to share and began to tell him about dating Vivian and the conversation she had with Jenn.

"Stories like this are why I am even more thankful to have found Mel again. I don't want to date a bunch of women. It's hard to tell these days who the crazy ones are."

"I'm sure they feel the same way about us. I see a lot of nut jobs and worse in my line of work."

"No doubt, Randy. People really should do a background check before they go on even one date."

"I think I almost blew it, Sinclair. I was trying to get Vivian to leave us alone. I got a little cocky when I introduced Jenn as my girlfriend. Jenn got that 'deer in the headlights' look of fear. I didn't think about the fact that she's been married a long time. Dating is a foreign country to her."

"I'm right there with her. I was married to Dana for thirty-five years. I don't have a clue what it's like."

"I guess that makes Mel and I professional daters. I'm sure she would agree that she would not miss it." Randy paused, drinking the last sip of his beer. "Sinclair, since you are a business owner now, does that mean you can take off anytime you want?"

Sinclair howled with laughter.

"Randy, since you are the Chief of Police, does that mean you can take off anytime you want?"

"Point taken. Here's why I'm asking, I've got to go out toward Asheville to do a little investigative work. I thought you might want to ride shotgun."

"Will there be a shootout? Are we going to capture a bad guy?" Sinclair made gestures like he was shooting guns with his fingers.

"Not hardly. I need to find one of my former patrol officers who is needed soon in court to testify. I've got to sharpen my detective skills."

"I think I could swing a couple of days away. It will give me an opportunity to find out how good my staff is without me."

"Excellent idea. What days would work best for you?"

"How about Thursday and Friday?"

"Works for me. That will give me time to do some background work and narrow the search."

"I sure do wish we could take Mel and Jenn with us." Sinclair sighed.

"I think you better concentrate on getting her to go on a date with you before you take her away for a trip." Randy shook his head.

"I know. I can dream though. It sure would be nice to spend a long weekend in the mountains together."

"Well, maybe we can check out some places in the area that we can talk to them about later." Randy winked.

"That sounds like a plan, my friend. It sounds like an excellent plan."

Chapter Three

Jenn

"I WANT TO REPORT the news, not *be* the news." Jenn smacked her forehead with the palm of her hand.

"It was darling, Jenn. I felt like I was watching a Hallmark movie." Doris giggled.

The day ended with little fanfare. After 'the kiss that stopped Main Street,' as Doris dubbed it, Jenn retreated to her office with the door closed, pretending to have a conference call.

Jenn's heart finally stopped racing an hour after the surprising occurrence. She certainly was several decades younger when her first actual kiss occurred. Sadly, she knew that she was today days old when she received such a passionate one. Up until now, she had no idea there was a difference in the passion a kiss could include.

Those early years with Simon were full of lots of kisses that led to engagement, marriage, children, and what she assumed was wedded bliss. She loved him. He loved her. She thought it was forever. Simon forgot how long forever was.

She'd never felt her knees get weak, like Elvis had sung would happen. She hadn't felt time stand still. Proper, controlled Jenn always cared who was looking and what they saw. That Jenn would never have kissed a man on Main Street, stopping traffic.

All Jenn could think about now was doing it again, several times, every day, for the rest of her life. Did she dare have such a dream this late in life? Somehow, the 'new' Jenn thought it was possible. Perhaps with Randy Nave, she could live happily ever after...the beginning.

"Jenn! Speak to me, dear!"

Doris was yelling. Jenn had no idea for how long. *This is getting embarrassing.*

"Yes, Doris. Is it time to go home?" Jenn thought it was a reasonable question. She hoped so anyway.

"Yes, Jenn, that's what I've been trying to tell you for the last five minutes. It's time to go home. You've still got 'great kiss brain.'"

"Is that a thing?" It was Jenn's turn to giggle.

"I've not experienced one myself in quite a few years. Decades, truthfully. But all the wonderful romantic movies have characters who have 'great kiss brain.'"

"You are the sweetest, Miss Doris." Jenn pulled the woman into a quick hug while the two of them walked out of Jenn's office.

"I suppose that an employee should not talk to her boss about her love life." Doris began locking the front door after they walked out. "But I've got to say that it fills my heart with such joy to see you and Randy together. I hope you don't mind me telling your Aunt Rachel about today's surprise event. Rachel and your mother wanted you and Randy to get together when you were young."

"What? I never knew that." Jenn took Doris' arm while they crossed the street to the parking lot.

"Rachel and Paisley both thought that Randy was the sweetest young man. Your father thought highly of him as well. I don't think that they ever wanted to interfere in their daughters' love lives. I think they only would have done so if they thought the young men were not suitable. Your mother and father thought Simon was fine. He was your choice and they respected that. They would have been dancing a jig on Main Street if they saw what I did today. So, on their behalf, I must say this. I know that it has only been a short time since you were officially divorced, but, my dear, you are as divorced as you are ever going to be. Take a chance and grab onto love. Don't let it slip away. I made that mistake many years ago. I've regretted my decision almost every day since. Good night, Jenn. See you in the morning."

Jenn waited for Doris to pull away before she moved her own vehicle out of the parking lot. Doris' words hung in Jenn's mind, both for their wisdom and the revelation that Doris had given Jenn about her own experience. It reminded Jenn that it was past time for her to visit Aunt Rachel. Her mother's last living sibling had been Doris' lifelong best friend. There was much Rachel could tell Jenn about this important person at the *Serendipity Sun.*

"Hello, Randy, how are you this evening?"

Jenn had only been home long enough to walk Jasper before she answered Randy's call on the first ring. There was no sense in being bashful after what happened earlier.

"Haven't you heard? I'm the talk of the town. I guess you are, too. Since I was the one who initiated the incident, I'm going to claim most of the talk on my head."

"It's been an interesting day. I don't think I will soon forget it." *For as long as I live.*

"I probably should apologize to you for creating such a spectacle. The thing is that I don't have the habit of apologizing for things that I'm not sorry about. I've waited my whole life to do that. I could probably have picked a better location though, some place more romantic."

"I don't know. I've watched plenty of romantic movies in my life. Many of them take place in a small town and the couple kiss in the town square. Sometimes it's in front of a shop owned by the female heroine. I would say my newspaper counts as a shop." Jenn giggled.

"I like your attitude, Jenn Halston. I'm going to be a little longer at the office but was hoping that maybe I could bring some takeout and spend the evening with you. No pressure about what transpired today. I've got to go out of town for a couple of days later in the week. I want to see you and tell you about it."

"That sounds fine." A momentary feeling of apprehension passed over Jenn that Randy was already including her in his daily plans. She shook the feeling off. "Takeout sounds good. I need to go to the grocery store. Eventually, I need to stock this house like I'm going to stay here."

"Staying here is your only option. How about I pick up a pizza and a salad?"

"That works. I do have several types of beverages. My freezer is also stocked with ice cream."

"I wonder why?" Randy laughed. "I'll be there in about ninety minutes or so."

"Great. That gives me a little time to get some laundry and other chores done. See you then."

When the call ended, Jenn noticed that a text message was waiting from Mel. Jenn shook her head, imagining what teasing comment her friend was going to make.

"Dana called me."

The message surprised Jenn. She opted to call Mel rather than text her.

"Hey, Mel. Are you okay?"

"Yes, I'm just stunned. I never expected for Sinclair's wife to call me."

"Ex-wife."

"Yes. She called the office while Imogene was helping a visitor. I picked up the call. I always say my name when I answer. She told me her name and immediately started talking. I was so stunned that I listened in silence."

"That's shocking. What did she say?"

"She started off by saying that she owed me an apology. That she should have known better than to steal someone else's boyfriend. Dana said that Sinclair was a good father and provider for their family, but she knew now that he never really belonged to her."

"Wow! That's a powerful statement. I'm amazed that Dana would admit that to anyone, especially you."

"Dana said that one of her children told her that Sinclair had reconnected with me."

"That was fast. Does that surprise you?"

"I'm not sure. You've seen how anxious he is. He did mention the other night that he talks to both of his children every day, either by phone or a text. I get the impression that he is quite close to them."

"If that is the case, I would imagine that they have been wondering about his new life in Serendipity. They might have heard some excitement in their father's voice."

"It's still weird for Dana to call."

"I agree, especially this soon. What else did she say?"

"She rambled on about how we all make our own happiness. That she thought she was doing that back then and she has done that again with this new man of hers."

"How long did this conversation go on?"

"Longer than I would have liked. I was too stunned to interrupt her or even hang up. I just let her talk. Finally, she thanked me for listening and apologized again. Her last statement was chilling and quite accurate."

"What did she say?"

"Dana said, 'I'm sorry I took your chance for happiness. I hope you get it back now.'"

"That's like a line out of a book. I have goosebumps."

"Do you think I should tell Sinclair about it?"

"How can you not? Dana may tell her children that she called you, or she might even tell Sinclair himself. You wouldn't want him to find out that way. I'm assuming this means that you are going to see him again."

"I have been thinking about it. I don't think I will be able to live with myself if I don't at least try to get to know him again. Honestly, Jenn, I'm excited and terrified, at the same time. But I don't think my heart can be broken anymore by him. Since I can't turn back the hands of time, I can give him a chance at friendship, if nothing else."

Jenn could hear the emotion in Mel's voice. She remained silent, giving her friend an opportunity to gather her thoughts.

"It's going to seem strange to be having dinner with Sinclair and casually tell him that the person who wrecked our relationship called and wants me to be happy."

"There's nothing normal about anything that has happened between you and Sinclair. Maybe Dana is truly sorry for what she did. Maybe she wanted to see how you would react. It really doesn't matter. One thing you do know is that she never got his whole heart because you had it all along."

"Why doesn't that make me feel better?"

"Because Dana had all those years with him. You were robbed of that. You've got the future to look forward to, if it works out, but it doesn't change what you've lost in the past. I know that's a hard statement. But there's no way to sugarcoat it."

"You're exactly right, Jenn. I've got to go forward at this point. Think happy thoughts." Mel paused. "I'm thinking some happy thoughts right now. I'm picturing my best friend in the whole world locking lips with the best-looking police chief I've ever met in the middle of the downtown district. I think I might use that photo in a tourism ad for Serendipity. The headline could be, 'Find Love on the Streets of Serendipity.'"

"That would be funny if I didn't think you might be serious."

"I wish I could come over for a complete play-by-play of the entire incident. But I agreed to allow Sinclair to bring pizza and visit. I agreed to this before Dana called. Now, I'm a nervous wreck."

"That's ironic. Randy is coming over with pizza, too."

"We should be doing this together. Sinclair says that he would like to talk to me again before he goes out of town later in week."

"Really? That's exactly what Randy said."

"Do you think they might be going somewhere together?"

"Oh, that doesn't seem likely since I would imagine both are working, but who knows? I'm still amazed that we are even talking about them in the present tense."

"Good point." Mel took a deep breath. "Thanks for listening, my friend. I'm glad I talked it out with you before Sinclair came over. The story will sound more coherent now that I have gotten it out of my head. Hope you and Randy have a lovely evening."

"Not sure how it can top earlier today."

"That's something to hope for. We can call these wishes, love goals."

"I like that. I like that a lot. I'm going to let you go. I'm going to try and get a few chores done before Randy gets here. Let's text later once we find out where each of them is going."

"Sounds good. Talk to you later."

By the time Jenn finished a load of laundry and a quick vacuum of the living room area, Randy was pulling into her driveway. Jenn watched him from the window as he got out of his vehicle, opening the back passenger door to retrieve the food. She felt her heart catch in her chest. She could not believe that she was potentially beginning a relationship with this wonderful man. The man, if she was truly honest with herself, was the one she had dreamed about since she was a little girl. Jenn's heart was full of anticipation.

"Knock, knock." Randy opened the sliding glass door.

For a moment, Jenn considered running up to Randy and throwing her arms around him. She decided to restrain herself. *Baby steps.*

"Hey, there. Let me help you." Jenn shook the thought out of her head, taking the food out of Randy's hands while he came inside. "The pizza smells delicious."

"You can't go wrong with pizza. I got a deluxe version with a little bit of everything. Hope that's okay."

"I'm not picky about toppings. If I don't want something, I can just take it off."

"I'm the same way. There's something else we have in common."

"I'm starving."

"I'm not surprised. You didn't finish your lunch."

"That's a shame, too. What I did eat was delicious."

Jenn led the way into the kitchen area, setting the food down on the table there.

"There are several different beverages in the fridge. Please help yourself. I'm having some iced tea."

"Thanks, I'll do that."

Randy stepped over to the kitchen sink. He quickly washed his hands before opening the refrigerator and choosing a bottle of soda.

Grabbing some plates and utensils, Jenn joined him at the table. They began serving themselves while they talked.

"You mentioned that you are going out of town. Is this for business or pleasure?"

"It's business. One of my former patrol officers needs to testify in an upcoming court case. He quit suddenly and we're not sure where he moved. The District Attorney needs him to be found. We think that he is from a small town near Asheville. I'll do some preliminary investigating tomorrow with plans to head in that direction early Thursday and hopefully return Friday evening. I've asked Sinclair to go along."

"Oh, that explains it." Jenn took a bite of pizza, pulling a long string of cheese. "This is so good."

"Explains what?" Randy took his first bite.

"Mel mentioned that Sinclair was taking a trip, too. We thought it was ironic that you both were going at the same time."

"I didn't realize that Sinclair would have already told Mel."

"He was headed over to her house with a pizza tonight, too."

"Are we all living parallel lives?"

"It would seem so." Jenn poured dressing on her salad. "Except I've not received any calls from your ex-wife."

"What?" Randy almost choked on his pizza.

"I'm sorry. I didn't mean to make you choke. You may hear this story while you and Sinclair are away. Dana called Mel today. From what Mel said, it was sort of a backhanded apology. Dana told Mel that she knew that she'd never really had Sinclair's heart."

"That's an amazing admission for someone like her. Dana was 'the other woman.' Other women don't normally take the high road."

"Maybe Dana's had some epiphany since she's broken up her own marriage. There's nothing normal about any of this."

"That's true. I hope the phone call didn't upset Mel."

He has such a good heart. Jenn's heart swelled at Randy's caring attitude.

"Mel was stunned at first. I think she's okay. She's going to tell Sinclair about it."

"So, Dana knew already that Sinclair had seen Mel?"

"Yes, we think that Sinclair told one or both of his children. I would suspect that the child told Dana."

"That must have been an interesting conversation. I can't wait to hear what Sinclair has to say."

"That will give you something to talk about on your drive across the state. Did you say you plan to be gone for two days?"

"Yes, I hope that I learn where to find my former officer before we get there. That will make it a shorter trip. I don't have any reason to think that he is hiding. Sometimes officers just up and quit. Police work is not for everyone."

"If this officer was single, have you considered trying to find out if he was dating anyone here?'"

"I like how you think, Ms. Halston. I've already gone down that road. He was dating a young lady who works at the bank. She's a friend of Mel's assistant, Imogene. I've already talked to the young lady. She was as shocked as we were that he left. She could tell me the general area where his family lived. I guess their relationship hadn't been going on long enough for her to know too much."

"It's the reporter in me." Jenn smiled. "There are probably more similarities between a reporter and a detective then most people would realize."

"I think you are right." Randy took another bite of his meal. "Enough about me. What's going on with you? We didn't get too far in our conversation at lunch. Since I brought it up, I want to apologize for you having to encounter a woman that I used to date."

"I would imagine that since we live in this small town, if I am going to continue to see you, I need to be prepared to meet women you've been involved with. You've lived here as a single man for over a decade. Since you haven't gotten married, you've probably racked up a long list of old girlfriends."

"I can assure you the list is nothing like when I was in high school. Like I said earlier, most of the encounters were short-term. Probably many of the women were glad to be rid of me. I know that several of them are married. I was even invited to a few of the weddings."

"Sounds like those relationships ended on good terms. That is always a desirable thing. Maybe Vivian will invite both of us to her wedding." Jenn winked. "On to another topic. Did I tell you that I've talked to my son, Foster? He and his wife are getting ready to move here."

"I believe that you told me that was a possibility. I didn't know it was a sure thing."

"It is now. Michelle, Foster's wife, is a real estate agent in Atlanta. She's been quite successful, always winning awards in the field. Apparently, almost immediately after they put their condo on the market, it sold. The buyer is also purchasing quite a bit of the furnishings. They are planning to load up a moving truck this weekend and head this way as soon as they can. Foster can now work remotely. Michelle's excellent sales skills make her ability to find a job easy. She even plans to apply for the new sales position we have at the newspaper. I will remain neutral. She would be fabulous though."

"Sounds like you think a lot of Michelle."

"I do. She's a lovely girl. Foster met her in high school. Her parents are great people. Foster and Michelle have been married several years. They may be thinking about starting a family. I'm not sure."

"I don't believe that I've heard you mention any grandchildren. Do you have any?"

"No. Claire and her husband have been married several years. She's never mentioned children. I'm not entirely sure how she feels about having any." Jenn took a deep breath, twirling her fork through her salad. "I'm a little concerned about Claire's marriage. I don't always get the impression that she is happy. It's not what she says; it's what she doesn't say."

"That must be hard for you. Sensing something is wrong."

"I've always tried to not interfere in my children's lives. Even when they were teenagers, I only stepped into decisions that a parent needs to be in. My father used to say that we all need to learn our own lessons."

"I remember him saying that. He was such a great man. I miss him."

"He thought a lot of you, Randy."

"That feeling was mutual." Randy set down his fork. "I am so full. I should have stopped at three slices of that pizza."

"They were big slices, too."

"Don't rub it in. I'll probably be up half the night with heartburn." Randy looked at his watch. "I didn't realize it was getting so late. I better get going."

"Once again, we're not eating ice cream. I think the next time we eat together here, we should start with ice cream."

"Works for me. We're adults. We can do that." Randy rose from the table, rubbing his stomach.

"Thanks for bringing dinner." Jenn picked up the plates while Randy walked toward the door.

"Thanks for allowing me the pleasure of your company this evening."

"I promise that I will try to be more open to the idea of there being an 'us.'" Jenn joined Randy at the door.

"That would be great. It's going to take me a while to figure out how to top today's grand gesture."

Randy reached over and slid one finger down the side of Jenn's face. Like the kiss earlier, she felt it all over. It was like electricity.

"It's time for me to say goodnight." Randy leaned over, kissing Jenn on the cheek. "I'll call you tomorrow evening. I think that Sinclair and I will try to leave as early as possible the following morning."

"Okay." Jenn could still feel the electricity of his touch. It was making her brain mush.

"Goodnight." Randy smiled before turning to leave.

Watching him first go down the steps, then pull out of the driveway a few minutes later, Jenn shook her head in disbelief. *I'm in so much trouble.*

"It's wonderful."

Chapter Four

Mel

"I cannot believe I missed it!"

Mel pulled out paper plates and bowls for the pizza and salad that Sinclair brought for dinner. The food and beverages were already spread out on the counter for self-serve dining that they would then eat in the living room. Maybe Sinclair could find a sports game to watch, and they wouldn't have to stare at each other all evening. After the shock of Dana's phone call, Mel needed their interaction to be more casual.

"It certainly sounds like it caused a commotion. It must have taken social media by storm. A couple of my employees were talking about it. They met Jenn recently when she brought us the advertising proposal."

"I was only a few feet away, but on a boring conference call. Thankfully, someone got a photograph."

"I spit out a mouthful of coffee when I opened that text message from you. It will be a long time before Randy lives that one down." Sinclair chuckled, filling his plate with pizza. "You know, in some small towns, there are ordinances prohibiting kissing in public. Not sure if there's still one on the books for Serendipity. At the minimum, his officers are going to have fun with him, I'm sure."

"All joking aside. What could be more wonderful than the two of them finally getting together?" Mel took a deep breath, feeling a wave of happiness for her best friend.

"The two of us getting *back* together." Ever so gently, Sinclair leaned over and bumped shoulders with Mel.

"That's a sweet thought, Sinclair, but I don't want to be rushed." Mel raised her eyebrows, filling a bowl with salad.

"I'll keep having sweet thoughts." Sinclair winked before he carried his food into Mel's living room.

Mel stopped in her tracks, watching Sinclair. Remembering the boy of her youth, she could still see him behind the blondish-brown hair that was now streaked with gray. The deep brown eyes seemed lighter in color, but still sparkling. Never in a million years would Mel have believed she would ever be in the same room with Sinclair again, much less be having dinner with him. Her heart still hurt for the lost years. It raced with the hope that they could potentially have years together into the future.

"What's wrong?" Sinclair asked, chewing his first bite of pizza. "I know it's not this pizza. I'd forgotten how good this joint was."

"I'm amazed and thankful to be here with you. My arms are probably black and blue from where I keep pinching myself." The sentiment poured out of Mel while she approached Sinclair, balancing her pizza, salad, and a beverage.

"It's like a dream." Sinclair scooted down the couch to make room for Mel. "As I've said before, I took my responsibility seriously. As much as I wondered how you were doing and what your life was like, I wouldn't have interfered. I wouldn't have done what Dana did."

"I wonder if she had the affair on purpose."

"Well, I don't think it was an accidental affair." Sinclair scowled. "Dana knew what she was doing."

"That's not what I mean. I wonder if she intentionally gave you a way out of your marriage. Your children are grown and on their own. Maybe Dana had regrets about how she got you. Maybe she wanted to make it right."

"How would having an affair make anything right?" Sinclair shook his head.

"It made her the bad guy. It gave the man who had 'done the right thing' a way out."

"What's got you thinking about this? Why are we talking about Dana's affair?" Sinclair took a sip of his drink.

"Mainly because Dana called me today."

"What?!" Sinclair spewed his drink, beginning to choke.

"Are you okay? Are you choking?" Mel started to pat Sinclair on the back.

"I'm choking on those words I think I just heard you say. Dana called you. Is that true?"

"Yes."

"I can't believe you took her call."

"I didn't have much choice. Imogene was helping a visitor. I answered the phone. Dana was on the other end."

"What did she say? I'm terrified to hear your answer. She can be a piece of work."

"She was quite gracious. She told me that she'd heard that we reconnected."

"It must have been from one of the kids. I told them. They've been asking me if I've seen any of my old friends. I never dreamed they would immediately mention it to their mother."

"Dana apologized for what happened years ago. She also said that she knew you never stopped loving me."

"That's an amazing statement. Guess I didn't hide that too well. After the first year or so, your name was never brought up between us."

"I'm not taking up for her by any means. Dana messed up my future horrendously. I'm sure her actions on the senior trip were intentional. Dana wanted to take you away from me." Mel took a deep breath. "But she was young. She's probably discovered through the years that you really can't take something that doesn't belong to you and expect to live happily ever after."

"That's true. Our home was pleasant. We enjoyed raising our children. Looking back, I can see that she didn't receive the kind of love from me that she probably wanted. For the first ten years, I was too mad to do anything but go through the motions. By the time I started to mellow some, it was too late. We lived in the same house. We were never in love."

"I think that's why she called. It seemed important to her to say, in so many words, that she was sorry. I guess Dana understands a little about what I lost. I listened to her. I didn't really respond. I was too shocked, for one thing."

"Well, I don't know if I should say I'm sorry that she called or not."

"I'm not sorry. I'm beginning to understand how much you loved me, once upon a time. Honestly, I'm happy that you kept some of it tucked away. I always thought that Dana won. Today, I found out she really didn't. It may not be a good feeling for me to have, but I have a little satisfaction in that knowledge, even after all these years."

Mel watched Sinclair first set his food down on the table in front of them, and then he did the same with her plate. Something about his movements made her feel like she was watching it happen in slow motion. While this thought was still in her mind, she felt Sinclair pull her into an embrace. The hug was so tight, she thought he truly might be putting some of her broken pieces back together again. Overcome with emotion, Mel felt tears well in her eyes. A few moments later, Sinclair pulled back, their faces inches apart.

"Try as I might, I never stopped loving you, Mel. I loved you then and I still do."

Sinclair leaned in, gentling kissing Mel. Tears began to stream down her face. Her emotions were raw, feelings from long ago mixed with today. When the kiss was over and they were once again looking eye-to-eye, Mel saw tear stains on Sinclair's face as well.

"Maybe we should think about starting over." Mel whispered. "And write a new ending to our story."

"No endings this time, Mel. We've had our share of those."

"We're both on a rocky road of emotion, aren't we?"

Jenn spoke while pouring Mel a glass of wine. A couple of days came and went in the busyness of life. It was Thursday evening before Mel and Jenn had a real chance to talk.

"It would seem so. I'm continually thankful that we are both in the same zip code for this point in our lives. As happy as I'm hoping this is going to turn out, I'm not sure that I could go through it without my best friend close by."

"Ditto to that. Randy and Sinclair seem to need a similar type of bonding and support."

"Yes, I find it quite interesting how quickly they have become buddies again. This adventure to the western part of the state seems more like something they might have run off and done when they were much younger." Mel looked at her phone, laughing under her breath. "In other news, Mom and Dad just got on their cruise ship."

"Where are they cruising to this time?"

"It's a two- or three-week trip through the Hawaiian Islands."

"Oh, I would have imagined they had already made that trip."

"They went to Hawaii for their twenty-fifth anniversary. Don't you remember? It was right before our senior year in college."

"Oh, yes. They brought us shell necklaces." Jenn lifted the lid on her outdoor grill. She was cooking shrimp and veggie kabobs for their dinner.

"Once they retired, they didn't want to have any repeat trips for a while. Mom says on this trip they will immerse themselves in Hawaiian culture. I think there are cooking classes and hula lessons."

"That sounds like fodder for some good stories. Maybe I should have one of my reporters interview your parents for an article about their travels. Better yet, your folks could have their own column and write about their adventures. I bet a lot of people who've known them for years would find that interesting."

"It's not a bad idea. Dad would enjoy writing them. He keeps a journal for each of their trips. I keep telling him that he needs to start a blog."

"Oh, I like the idea of a blog." Jenn smiled. "He might even be able to monetize it, get sponsors, or go on some complimentary trips. As I'm sure you know, travel journalism is serious business."

"Yes, my office hosts several travel writers every year."

On the side table beside Mel, Jenn's phone buzzed. Mel looked at the screen.

"It's Emily." Mel picked up the phone, handing it to Jenn.

"Hi, Emily." Jenn answered the phone with one hand, while closing the grill lid with her other. "I'm grilling some dinner for your Aunt Mel and me." Jenn listened. "Okay, I'll put the phone on speaker."

Jenn pushed a button before laying the phone back on the side table that was between two deck chairs.

"Hi, Emily." Mel yelled, before taking a sip of her wine. "How's college life?"

Mel pictured the young woman in her mind. While Jenn's oldest daughter, Claire, was a carbon copy of her mother, Emily's features more resembled Simon. In fact, Emily's black hair and blue eyes were almost identical to Simon's older sister. Mel could never remember the woman's name.

"Hi, Aunt Mel. It's fine. I'm counting the days until it's over. I think I'm ready for real life."

"Enjoy college life while you can. You have a lot of years of real life ahead of you."

"I know. I'm just tired of school. I've been going since I was three or so. That's over twenty years. I feel like I've had a book in my lap my whole life."

"What's going on with you, dear?" Jenn sat down next to Mel. "I normally only get texts from you during the week."

"I talked to Foster yesterday. He told me that he and Michelle are moving in your direction. I couldn't remember how many bedrooms are in the house."

"There are five, with a couple extra couches. It seems like I remember we had about fifteen people sleeping here one Christmas. Why do you ask? Are you thinking about coming for a visit?"

"Not right away. But Foster also told me that Aunt Renee might stay with you through her recovery. And I know something else that I'm not supposed to tell you."

Mel smiled, listening to Jenn's youngest. Emily always had trouble keeping secrets. The age difference between her and her two older siblings caused conflicts. Emily had been nicknamed 'Tattle' from as soon as she could talk.

"It sounds like you're about to tell me anyway." Jenn rolled her eyes, shaking her head.

"I don't want to."

Mel could hear the drama in Emily's voice.

"Then, maybe you shouldn't." Jenn's motherly tone kicked in.

"You always said that if one of us was in trouble, we should tell you.'

"Emily, are you in trouble?"

"No. It's Claire."

Mel watched Jenn sit up straighter in her chair, looking at the phone as if it might reveal something.

"Did something happen? I've not heard from her today. What's going on?"

"We met at Foster's last weekend. There was a piece of furniture that they offered me. When I got there, I overheard Claire talking to Foster. I think Claire is going to leave Derek."

Mel locked eyes with Jenn. Her friend didn't seem shocked.

"I don't know anything about the situation, Emily. We need to be supportive of her, no matter what." Jenn's 'mother voice' was back. "If that is true, let's give her space to tell us when she's ready."

"Absolutely, Mom! I didn't want you to be blindsided. I heard her tell Foster that she didn't want to bother you with all the change you've had in the last few months."

Mel watched Jenn's expression change. Closing her eyes, Jenn rubbed her forehead, frowning.

"Okay, baby girl, I know you're worried about your sister. Everything will be okay. All three of you can come live with me if you need places to stay."

"I've got two extra bedrooms, too." Mel chimed in. "Of course, my house isn't on the beach. Maybe, I need to come live here as well."

"The more the merrier." Jenn laughed.

"Thanks, Mom. I've got to go. My study partners are here. We've got an exam tomorrow."

"Study hard, sweet girl. Call me on Sunday, like you normally do."

Jenn clicked off the phone, walking back to the grill.

"You told me a while ago that you knew something was going on with Claire." Mel followed her.

"I did. You know, Claire holds stuff in. You can tell more by what she doesn't say than what she does."

"She and Derek have been married how long?"

"Four years. I've always liked Derek. They dated all through college, you remember?"

"Yes."

"It always seemed to me like they made better friends than husband and wife."

"I don't ever remember hearing you say that."

"I've never said it aloud before. Somehow, my mother radar knew this day might come."

"What are you going to do?"

"Wait for her to tell me. Claire is strong-willed. She does things in her own way and time."

"It would be an interesting turn of events if over the next few years everyone you loved followed you here."

"It would be an awesome turn of events. But I want them to move here for good reasons, not because they need to escape something."

Jenn pulled the kabobs off the grill, placing them on a platter Mel was holding.

"The food smells delicious."

"It's a 'tried and true' marinade recipe. Would you go inside and get the pineapple rice that's in the microwave? I've already heated it."

"I haven't had your pineapple rice in years. Yummo!"

"There's also a small bowl of salad on the counter. I think everything else is already on the table."

Mel walked into the kitchen with Mia and Jasper following her. Even though her little dog was used to being alone, Mia had quickly warmed up to Jasper, seeming to enjoy their visits. Mel forgot that she'd left her phone in her purse until she heard a beeping noise. Retrieving her phone, Mel saw that she had a text from Sinclair. Balancing the items that Jenn asked her to bring on a tray, Mel rejoined her friend on the deck.

"Will you believe that I've been so relaxed sitting on your deck, listening to the ocean, that I forgot my phone? It was beeping with a text from Sinclair."

"Happy to hear about the relaxation. If it wasn't for missing calls and messages from all the people I love, I would be tempted to turn mine off every evening."

"It's tempting, no doubt." Mel held up her phone so that Jenn could see the photo Sinclair sent. "Apparently, Sinclair and Randy have found a well-known steakhouse in the area that serves huge porterhouse steaks. I think our guys are in steak heaven."

"Oh, my goodness. That steak looks big enough for all four of us. I think I'm happy we are having shrimp." Jenn sat next to Mel, handing her the plate of kabobs.

"Me, too. At least they are having fun."

"I hope they've had success finding the former officer Randy is looking for. It sounds like an unusual situation. I hope nothing is wrong with the young man or he hasn't gotten into any trouble."

"I only met the officer once or twice. I remember him coming into the office one day with the girl he was dating who is friends with Imogene. He also helped with crowd control for the Fourth of July parade. I'm not sure that he was on the police force more than a year." Mel took a serving of pineapple rice before offering the bowl to Jenn.

"I imagine there is a percentage of officers who go into police work and then discover it isn't for them."

"Probably so." Mel took a bite of shrimp with the rice. "This is so delicious. It's amazing to me that even though I've lived here all my life, I rarely take advantage of the great weather and eat outdoors. When I do, I'm reminded that it makes me feel like I'm on vacation."

"That is one of my favorite aspects so far of living here, everything I can do outside. I've been meaning to ask you how the recent winters have been. I'm sure Mom told me. I didn't retain it."

"The winters have been mild, in the fifties most days. About three years ago, we had a freak snowstorm on Valentine's Day. We got a whopping two inches. Everyone freaked out." Mel took another bite of food.

"I remember how we used to long for snow growing up. I loved it when we would go visit your grandparents in Virginia. Sleigh riding was so much fun. We didn't see much snow in Atlanta either. The occasional ice storms were freaky though."

"I bet those make Downtown Atlanta a parking lot."

"Exactly."

Mel and Jenn ate in silence for a few minutes, enjoying the ocean breeze and delicious food.

"We've spent so much time recently talking about these new men in our lives." Mel winked. "We've barely talked about how things are going at the newspaper. I guess you've had time to get to know some of the staff. I see Lyle walking up and down the street frequently. He seems right at home in Serendipity again. How is he doing?"

"Lyle is changing many aspects of how the newsroom is operating. Helen has loved having him back. I think he makes Tyler and Shaun nervous. Lots of red ink on their stories. Lyle refuses to edit their work electronically. He says that is too easy for them to correct. They need to type the words themselves and learn."

"He's got a point."

"I agree wholeheartedly. I've got to say that I think it's a little funny. He's kind of like a drill sergeant. They 'sir' him to death."

"Mr. Sebastian wasn't exactly a warm and fuzzy fellow. He could be tough and gruff."

"That's true. I wouldn't say that Lyle is gruff. He's quite comical and sarcastic. He doesn't give the staff much room for error though. They need to be able to defend their stories and editorials. I've hovered outside the newsroom door a couple of times and listened to his lectures, with a whiteboard to prove his point. We already had a good team. They will now be a well-oiled machine."

"They may need to be with Town Council's proposal to annex three miles of oceanfront in each direction. Those are going to be some tough council meetings coming up."

"I've heard a little about this issue. Do you think there's going to be resistance?"

"Certainly. The annexation will open more property for development and change some of the land use."

"Is my property in the proposed annexation?"

"I believe it is. It probably will not affect you much, outside of maybe changing your tax rate a little, because you plan to keep the property long term. Parker Bentley, on the other hand, will probably want to pay close attention."

"I'll mention that next time I see him. I've not seen much movement at his house in the last few days. He may have gone out of town."

"Have you talked to him much since you reconnected?" Mel took another kabob from the platter. "The encounters I had with him left me feeling like he could peer into your soul. He's made comments to me that were completely spot-on to my situation."

"That's an interesting way to describe him. Our conversations have been short. I think he seems a little lost. Sort of like he wants to belong here, but he doesn't know how. It's so sad that his family situation kept him away from his grandparents for so many years. They were wonderful people. It must feel haunting for him to wander around that grand empty house."

"Walter and Zella Bentley were fabulous. They helped start half of the non-profits in our area. They supported the arts, abuse victims, the homeless, education. The list is endless."

"Mr. Bentley was a powerhouse businessman. It's like whatever he touched was successful." Jenn laid her silverware on her plate, pushing it away from her. "I'm stuffed."

"It was delicious. Thank you." Mel folded her arms, leaning back in her chair. "I've restrained myself all through dinner. Now, it's time for you to spill it. Tell me about the kiss that everyone is talking about."

Mel watched Jenn's expression go from the blush of embarrassment to a contentment that she'd never seen her friend have. It made Mel happy.

"It was the best kiss I've ever had. Honestly, Mel, it's heartbreaking to have to admit that kiss was better than my wedding kiss."

"I remember your wedding kiss. Simon seemed uncomfortable kissing you in front of everyone."

"Up until the other day, I would have given that kiss high marks. Now, I know better." Jenn shook her head. "I don't remember any of those girls that Randy dated back in high school talking about him being such a good kisser."

"Maybe it depends on who he is kissing." Mel reached over, jabbing Jenn in the arm.

"I don't know. I think the Earth might have tilted on its axis."

"Oh, my goodness, girlfriend, you have got it bad."

"I can't help it. I've never felt this way. It's different than those normal first feelings of love. It's not like a crush. This is a serious feeling. It is scaring me to death."

"You're a grown-up falling in love. There's none of the pressure that goes with it when you're younger. You get to enjoy every little aspect of it this time without any fears of what your future might include."

"That seems like a first-person description there, friend. I'm betting you are feeling this way, too."

"I do believe that I am, Jenn. I've got to be cautious. I know this may not work out. I intend to enjoy every second of it while I can. I've waited my entire life to have this experience. You should do the same."

"Another part of our lives that we can enjoy together." Jenn hugged her friend.

"I cannot imagine in our wildest dreams we could have predicted what has happened to us. It's like we've walked into an alternative reality where our deepest dreams are coming true."

Chapter Five

Randy

"You really lucked up finding that young man so quickly." Sinclair took a bite of his salad, looking around the restaurant. "This is really a creative idea, turning an old bank into a restaurant. The online reviews I read gave 'The Vault' high marks."

"I can't believe we each ordered the largest steak on the menu. We're not young bucks anymore."

Randy looked around the crowded restaurant. The room still held the character of an old downtown bank combined with the aroma of charbroiling. It still smelled like money.

"Speak for yourself. I feel like a teenager again every time I see Mel." Sinclair snorted. "I've got the photo to prove that it's the same way when you see Jenn."

"I'll be a hundred before I live that down." Randy shook his head. "I don't care. That kiss was worth every comment I will endure. I hope to have lots more of them."

"I hear you, my man. We are two lucky guys. We've got to concentrate on not blowing this opportunity we've been given." Sinclair took a hot roll from a basket between them, slathering butter on it. "How did you find the kid? What's his name again?"

"Joe. I made a call to the local police department. I figured they might know something since Joe grew up here and entered the academy shortly after completing a criminal justice program at a nearby community college. Turns out that he did an internship with the department. He was easy to find then."

"Stop watching your girlish figure and have one of these rolls, Randy. They are something else. That's honey butter next to them, too." Sinclair took another bite of his roll. "Maybe I shouldn't be asking this, but how did the meeting with him go?"

"There's nothing about this trip that's top secret. I'm just trying to find an officer to testify in a case. The meeting was okay. Joe was agreeable and will return to Serendipity to testify. He wasn't an officer long enough to understand that sometimes it can take a while for the cases you work to get to court. The lawyers for the defense have gotten the case postponed a few times." Randy took a bite of his salad, thinking about his conversation with Joe. "There's something about that young man that bothers me though. He seems so troubled, as if something is weighing down his thoughts."

"Does he have family here?"

"He's living with his mother. He said that his father passed away quite a while ago. The Sheriff here told me that Joe's parents have lived in the area for at least a decade but have always been reclusive. It really surprised most people that Joe pursued police work."

"Maybe he had a desire to not be so reclusive. I can't imagine growing up like that. I know you can't either. Our families were in the middle of everything in our town. Church activities, sports, and civic events are the main things I remember from childhood. We took that for granted.

You might long for it if you only saw it from the sidelines. Being a police officer would certainly put you into the middle of a community."

"That's true. I'm going to try to get to know him a little better when he comes to testify in a couple of weeks. I've offered to let him stay at my house. Maybe I can find out why he left my team so suddenly and help him find his way back to police work, if he still has the desire. He left in good standing."

"That's the Randy I remember, always wanting to help someone out. I guess that's why you gravitated toward the military and police work."

"Even though I don't have any family members that have done either, I think this public service thing is in my blood. I sleep better when I've helped someone that day."

The two men became lost in their individual thoughts for a few minutes, digging into their food.

"So, Romeo, what are you going to do to top that romantic gesture on Main Street?"

"I should have thought that through. I'm surprised that Jenn didn't slap my face." Randy laughed under his breath. "Honestly, I felt like I was in one of those time travel movies. I can't tell you the number of times I stood somewhere with Jenn when we were teens, wanting to kiss her, but lost my nerve."

"That was never my problem. I was too hyped up on hormones and stupid to think that any girl would turn me down."

"There weren't many girls before Mel that I remember." Randy smiled, thinking about the younger Sinclair.

"Not really. The ones I did date were just practice. I had my sights on her for a while before I made a move."

"It's amazing how life has a way of working out, Sinclair. Both you and I made mistakes with Mel and Jenn back then. In some ways, my reluctance to tell Jenn how I felt was as life changing as your stupid fling with Dana. Neither one of us got to be with the woman we loved. They didn't get the love they deserved either. It's a blessing that we are being given a second chance to do it the right way. Maybe, if we are lucky, you and I will live to be old coots and have thirty or forty years with these wonderful women."

"From your mouth to God's ears, my friend. I pray every night for that exact chance."

The server appeared at the table with two huge plates. Randy's and Sinclair's eyes bugged out when they saw the size of the steaks.

"Can I get you gentlemen anything else?" The server stepped back after placing the plates on the table.

"I think you might better go ahead and call 911." Randy blew out a deep breath. "This looks like a heart attack on a plate."

"I hear that a lot." The server chuckled, walking away.

"We will not live another thirty years eating like this, Randy." Sinclair stared at his plate.

"I think this is one time that our eyes were bigger than our stomachs. With all due respect to my late mother, I don't think I'm going to clean my plate." Randy cut a small bite, slipping it into his mouth. He barely had to chew before swallowing. "This has got to be the most delicious steak I've ever tasted. It's like butter."

"I'm not sure either of us can eat our money's worth." Sinclair closed his eyes while chewing his first bite.

"Doesn't matter. This is a meal of celebration for two stupid kids who are going to make better decisions going forward. The first ones are to win back the girls of our dreams. The second better decision is to not eat this whole steak." Randy laughed.

"Here's to us, old friend." Sinclair picked up his glass, clanking it with Randy's. "May both of us live happily ever after with the women we don't deserve."

"And may our friendship continue. Because we know that there's nothing coming between Jenn and Mel."

"Indeed. We both need to stay on their good sides."

"I have a feeling we can do that." Randy smiled at his friend.

"Yes, Edwin. I met with Joe Fairfield yesterday. I don't see any problems with him returning to Serendipity to testify."

Waiting for Sinclair to load his luggage into the vehicle, Randy called the District Attorney, Edwin Greer, to give him an update about his meeting with Joe.

"I sent you an email this morning with Fairfield's contact information. He'll be expecting a call from you to confirm the court date. If you'd please confirm that with me, also, as I've told Fairfield he can stay at my house when he comes to testify. We can talk when I get back to town, if you have any questions."

Randy ended the call, putting his phone back on his belt while Sinclair put his bag into the back of the vehicle.

"I know this shouldn't be possible, but I'm actually hungry." Sinclair frowned. "At a minimum, I've got to have about a pot of coffee."

"I hear you, buddy. We are going to blame our hunger on this clean mountain air." Randy looked around them at the beautiful views in every direction. "The man at the front desk said that there's a great pancake house on the road leading out of town. I say we eat us a good breakfast and make tracks back to Serendipity."

"Sounds good. I do think we need to stop at some shop and buy the girls something pretty. While you were talking to your former officer yesterday, I wandered around downtown a little. Someone told me about a shop that may be near that pancake house, which sells local art. Maybe we can find something there."

"You are smarter than you look, Sinclair. It can't hurt our chances with the ladies to bring back presents."

Randy climbed into the driver's seat while Sinclair did the same on the other side. A few miles down the road, they were surprised to find the gift shop Sinclair mentioned shared a parking lot with the pancake house. After both ate a hearty sampling of the restaurant's signature pancakes, a quick stop in the shop led to both finding handmade necklaces created by the store's owner.

"Why don't you go back over to the restaurant and get us each an iced tea?" Randy pulled out his cell phone. "I'm going to check into the office before we get on the road."

Sinclair nodded, walking across the parking lot toward the restaurant.

While he was chatting with one of his sergeants, Randy saw Joe get out of his vehicle in the same parking lot and begin to walk toward the restaurant. He was wearing a restaurant uniform. Joe recognized Randy, walking toward him.

"Hello, Chief Nave." Joe's expression was somber.

"Good morning, Joe. I didn't expect to see you again so soon. I just had breakfast and am getting ready to head home."

"Yes, sir. This is a good place to eat." Joe looked down. "I've been working in the kitchen a few mornings a week to help supplement the security job I got at a department store nearby. Trying to help Mom with the bills until I can figure out what I'm going to do next."

"Maybe we can talk about that a little when you come back to Serendipity. I'd like to understand what made you leave police work. You left in good standing. There's no reason why you can't get back on a force somewhere if you are still interested in the work."

"I appreciate that, Chief. I've thought about that a lot." Joe looked up; a slight smile crossed his face. "I don't really know what happened to me. Maybe it would do me good to talk to someone about it."

"We will plan to do that when you come stay with me—get to the bottom of what's bothering you. Keep an open mind about the future, Joe. I've seen many young officers go through tough spells. Dealing with the reality of police work can be hard. It's never easy, but it does get easier. You've got to focus on how you are helping people. That's what keeps you going."

"I want to help people." Joe looked at his watch. "I've got to get to work. You have a safe trip back to Serendipity, Chief. If you happen to see Megan, tell her I asked about her."

"If it was me, Joe, I'd tell her myself. Megan seemed mighty sad about you leaving. I think there's still time for you to mend that relationship, if you are interested."

Joe smiled, waving as he walked away. Randy watched Joe stop when he opened the door, letting Sinclair come out carrying two cups. The irony of those two crossing paths did not escape Randy. *Sinclair could teach Joe a thing or two about letting the right girl get away.*

"What are you smiling about, Randy? I didn't expect you to hear good news when you called into the office."

"I'm laughing about life. That young man who opened the door for you was Joe Fairfield."

"You don't say." Sinclair looked back in the direction of the restaurant. "How about that?"

"He's working here part-time, supplementing a department store security job he's doing. When I saw you two crossing paths, I couldn't help but think that Joe could learn a thing or two from you about leaving a girl behind. He was dating a girl who works at First Bank of Serendipity. She's friends with Mel's assistant. Joe asked about her yesterday and mentioned her again just now."

"I could save that boy a life of heartache for sure. He needs to hear from the both of us about long-lost love."

"I'm hoping to help him in more ways than one when he comes back to testify. There's something eating at Joe's soul. If he doesn't get to the root of it, he might make some unfortunate decisions about his future. Going through the police academy and becoming certified is a lot of hard work and dedication. I don't want to see him throw that away just because he had a bad night of police work."

Sinclair opened the passenger side of the vehicle, putting the two cups of tea into the beverage holders in the console. Both climbed into their seats.

"You're a good man, Randy Nave. You might turn that young fellow's whole life around."

"We do what we can, Sinclair. I learned a long time ago that police work will eat you alive, body and soul, if you let it. We see plenty of the ugliest aspects of life. I've tried to concentrate on the good. If I work a heinous crime scene today, I try and go visit a nursing home the next day or work a school crossing. You've got to balance out the bad with as much good as you can find. I think that most officers, the good ones, at their core, love people. You must have that in you, or you'd quit long before retirement."

"I'm sure that is true. I have a buddy back in Raleigh who retired from police work a couple of years ago. He told me once that even working the worst crimes, he tried to focus on the victim or the family and find a way to make a difference."

"He's exactly right. There's always a way to make a difference, even if the ultimate victim is not around any longer to receive your help. I look at Joe and I see a good kid. Maybe his heart is a little tender now and he thinks he can't overcome that. Or maybe he's experienced something in his own short life that makes parts of police work a little painful. That's even more of a reason why he would make an outstanding officer. Those who are the best never lose their empathy. They see a child who's been abused, and they shed a tear. They feel the pain of a mother whose daughter has been murdered. They teach officers at the police academy to have a tough exterior. I teach the men and women on my team to not forget that the people we serve are our neighbors and friends. It's okay if we care about them. It's the preferred emotion in my book."

"I'll say it again, you're a good man. I hope that a year from now you are telling me that Joe is back on your team, doing a fine job."

"There's something about that young man that has touched my soul, Sinclair. I think there's more to the story than I know yet. I'm hoping for a happy ending."

"Randy, this necklace is beautiful." Jenn pulled the piece of jewelry out of the gift box, holding it up to the light. "I've never seen anything quite like it."

Randy and Sinclair returned from their trip on Friday afternoon. That evening, Jenn invited Randy to have dinner on her deck.

"It came from a little shop next to where Sinclair and I had breakfast this morning before we left. The owner does all the glass blowing herself.

I imagine that it is quite a process to add the precious stones into the glass."

"I would say so. The glass is so hot at that point. She is quite the artist. I love the color of this."

"I remember growing up that your favorite color was purple. I hoped that you still liked it."

"I love it. It's still my favorite." Jenn leaned toward Randy, kissing him on the check. "It's very special. Thank you."

"You're very special."

Jenn handed the necklace to Randy, turning around so that he could put it around her neck. Randy's hands shook a little as he reached around her to place the necklace, then clasping it at the nape of her neck. It was a personal gesture, often reserved for a husband to do for his wife. *I hope that's us one day.*

"I hope that Sinclair got Mel something pretty, too."

"He did. We were united in our pursuit of pretty things. He picked out a necklace for Mel as well. Instead of a large stone, as yours has, he picked one with three smaller stones because it was a beautiful swirly teal bluish green."

"Oh, she will love that. You both are quite thoughtful."

Jenn turned back to face Randy, touching the pendant part of the necklace between her fingers. Randy had seen enough women do that to know the gesture indicated that it was something special.

"We both have lots of 'thoughtful' to make up for. As old men, we have more of an appreciation for what is important."

"Don't call yourself an old man. We're the same age. That makes me old, too."

"You're not old. My old comes mostly from life experience. The things I've seen and done. My body feels like it's lived two lifetimes already."

"Eating the biggest steak in the state isn't going to help that."

"I know. I think it's time to get a few of these pounds off. I should probably resume jogging on the beach in front of my cottage."

"You could also come some mornings or evenings and jog with me."

"Have you fallen into a schedule of doing that already?" Randy was happy to receive such an invitation.

"I'm not sure I would call it a schedule yet. I do attempt to jog a couple of mornings a week. If I don't jog in the morning, I try to take a long walk when I get home. Let's do that after we eat."

"That sounds great. Something smells delicious."

"I thought you might like a lighter dinner. I've made baked salmon with roasted vegetables and risotto."

"Great." Randy rubbed his stomach. "I don't think I'll be interested in a steak dinner anytime soon. It was delicious, probably the best steak I've ever eaten. You will be happy to know that I did not clean my plate, neither did Sinclair. The two of us together barely ate the equivalent of one steak."

"After you sent the photo, I remembered that I have been to that restaurant. Simon and I spent a long weekend in the Asheville area with some friends several years ago. The food was delicious. It was an interesting atmosphere with the restaurant being in an old bank."

"Yes, I think it is one of the area's most popular restaurants. Maybe we can take a trip there sometime."

"Maybe." Jenn got up from her seat on the couch next to Randy.

He wondered if his comment made her uncomfortable. He decided to not pursue the topic further since she was already in the kitchen, checking on the food.

"I thought that your son and daughter-in-law would be here by now. Weren't they packing last weekend?" Randy followed Jenn into the kitchen.

"That was the plan. Right before they were ready to sign the closing papers with the new buyer, the buyer had a death in his immediate family. They had to postpone the closing for about two weeks. I think Foster and Michelle are now living out of the boxes they packed."

Randy watched Jenn peek at the salmon and vegetables in the oven.

"That's a shame, for everyone."

"Yes, I think it was the buyer's father who passed suddenly. I believe that Foster said the man lived in Arizona. Nothing has changed with the sale, only the closing date."

"Are you excited that your son is coming here?" Randy took the plates and silverware that Jenn held out to him.

"Yes and no."

Jenn picked up a couple of glasses, leading the way to the deck. Randy caught up with her, opening the sliding door before they both walked outside.

"I will be thrilled to have Foster and Michelle close by. The only downside is that so much has changed in my life in the last year or so, it's overwhelming. I'm finally starting to get used to living here again as well as owning and building a business. Two things that I never thought I would be doing. Add to that, the reconnection with so many wonderful old friends. My head spins every morning when I wake up and realize that this is really my life."

"That's a lot of change."

"Yes, and that change is on top of the painful change of divorce and Mom's sudden passing. On that same spectrum, there is Renee's illness and the possibility that within the next few weeks she will be coming here to recuperate."

"Oh, did I know that?" Randy closed his eyes a second, trying to remember.

"I'm not sure if I've told you that or not. There's been so much going on."

"I remember you telling me about Renee's illness. I don't remember the recuperating here part. You are going to have a full house soon."

"Well, there are plenty of bedrooms, which is good. I believe that Michelle may have already found a condo for her and Foster. She's quite a successful real estate agent in Atlanta and has lots of connections with other realtors across the South. I don't expect that they will be staying here long, if at all. With this delay in the closing, they might be able to move directly into their new place when they get here."

After placing the plates, silverware, and glasses on the table, Jenn turned back toward the house.

"I'm going to put the food on a platter and bring it out here. Would you like to have wine with dinner?"

"I'm on call this evening. Well, being the Chief, I guess I'm always on call. But tonight, we have someone out sick, and I may need to take some calls. I'm sorry that I forgot to tell you that. It just came up before I arrived. I'll just have water. I could use a little extra hydration anyway."

"Sounds good. Come back to the kitchen with me. You can fill up a pitcher with iced water while I get our platter of food ready."

Randy followed Jenn to the kitchen. After a few minutes of both completing tasks, they were back outside and seated at the table. In the distance, Randy could see the sun beginning to set on the horizon. Despite the many years he lived on the coast, the views never got old.

"It's beautiful, isn't it?" Jenn voiced the thoughts in Randy's mind.

Randy took his gaze away from the sunset and focused on Jenn. Smiling to himself, he reached out and took her hand.

"It certainly is."

Chapter Six

Jenn

The feeling of peace that Jenn felt on her deck enjoying a simple meal with Randy was unlike any contentment she'd ever known. The knowledge that this might be how she could feel for the rest of her life made her heart skip a beat.

"You look relaxed." Randy put his silverware on his plate, scooting his chair back a little from the table and stretching his legs. "I bet I look full."

"I am relaxed. I remember being surprised that my parents moved into this house after my grandparents passed. We certainly spent a lot of time here while I was growing up. I never saw my parents as 'beach people.' Our families lived inland on Danner Street for so many years. It was hard to imagine them living anywhere else."

"Your father was ready to enjoy retirement. I hadn't been back long from the military when they moved in here. I remember running into him at the home improvement store over in the next county. I was trying to do some repairs at Mom's house. Marshall was planning to add something on here."

"That would be the sunroom, a room I haven't even touched yet. He told my mother that he would build on to this house one more time. Supervised by my grandfather, he'd taken this house from three to five bedrooms, plus a couple of bathrooms and this deck, while my grandparents were still living here. Mom chose to have a sunroom added when they took the house over. You know how she loved her plants."

"Indeed. I believe I remember reading in your newspaper about her winning some prizes at the Annual Garden Show. That was one thing that our mothers had in common. I believe they stayed in touch up until my mother's death."

"I think you are correct. I remember hearing Mom mention Mrs. Nave now and then." Jenn took a long drink of water. "We've talked a lot about me and my world. You mentioned that your trip to Asheville was successful."

"Yes. I found the former officer I was looking for. He will be coming here in a couple of weeks to testify in a court case. He's mighty young. I think he may have made a hasty decision leaving the force. He probably witnessed something that spooked him. I've offered him a place to stay while he's here. Maybe I can talk to him and figure out what is making him think he can't do police work."

"Wow. I didn't realize that you offered counseling services. You've got a mighty big heart, Chief." Jenn breathed in a deep breath of ocean air. *I'm so lucky to have found him again.*

"Each generation needs to help the next, don't they? He wasn't on my team long enough for me to get to know him. What I saw of his work though showed me that he was a young man with a good head on his shoulders. Even if he's not meant to be a police officer, I want to make sure he stays on the right road. I don't get the impression that he has too much family support and direction. His father is deceased. I believe his mother is in poor health."

"Is this the same young man that Mel mentioned was dating a friend of Imogene's?"

"Yes. Megan works at the bank. She's a sweet girl from a good family. I think she's already quite smitten with this young man."

"Randy doesn't want to see another case of young love gone wrong." Jenn winked, patting Randy's hand as she picked up the dishes to take to the kitchen. "How about we take that walk I mentioned earlier?"

"Sounds good. Let me call into the office and check on things."

After Jenn put the leftover food away and loaded the dishwasher, she quickly checked her own phone. She was surprised that she didn't find any messages or missed calls.

"Everyone must have plans tonight." Jenn laughed to herself.

"What did you say?"

Jenn jumped when Randy spoke from behind her.

"I don't know why I jumped. I know you are here. I was talking to myself. I didn't find any texts or messages from anyone on my phone and said that everyone must have plans tonight."

"They do, including us. I was looking forward to that walk in the sunset with you."

"Oh, that sounds like the beginning of a cancellation."

"It is. Apparently, there are some criminals who had some plans for tonight, too. I've got to go help my team."

"Duty calls and you must answer. I'm glad we were able to have dinner together. I really do love my necklace." Jenn fingered her necklace while walking toward Randy. She gave him a brief hug.

"I like this new level of comfortable I am starting to experience from you." Randy put his arms around Jenn, pulling her back toward him. A mischievous smile crossed his face.

Jenn's heart skipped a beat. Randy's smile was a dangerous weapon.

"After that quite public display of affection, I guess I'm feeling a little differently."

"Know this, Jenn, that was not meant to rush you. It was spontaneous. While I don't regret the kiss in any way, I am sorry that I let my feelings get ahead of my good judgment. I shouldn't have allowed our first kiss to be in such a public place."

"It could have been worse. It could have been on one of those big boards at baseball games."

"Oh, the 'kiss cam,' that's an idea. Sinclair was asking me the other night how I was going to top kissing you on Main Street."

"Okay, mister, this doesn't need to become a game that you and Sinclair play to one-up the other."

Jenn poked Randy's chest with her finger, noticing how muscular it was. She closed her eyes, shaking off the thought.

"Yes, ma'am. Sometimes Sinclair and I forget that we are grown men."

"I sort of feel like the four of us are reliving our teen years."

"I know. I caught myself thinking something similar a couple of times while Sinclair and I were on our trip. Back then, he and I would sometimes ride around together after our dates were over, talking about stuff. I wish both of us could talk to those young fellows, maybe we would have made some better decisions."

"All of our decisions have contributed to who we are today. Who knows? Sinclair and Mel could have gotten married back then and be divorced by now. You and I might have dated and broken up with hard feelings."

"So, you wouldn't have married me?"

"What?"

"You had Sinclair and Mel getting married and us not getting past dating."

Randy's lips, the ones that kissed her the other day, were only inches away from her, curled up in a devilish grin.

"I said that we might have broken up if we dated. Sinclair and Mel were far ahead of us in that department. Don't try and put words in my mouth."

"I'm teasing." Randy looked over Jenn's shoulder at the clock she knew was in his view. "I better get going. This is Friday, right?"

"Yes."

"That means, in theory, you are probably off this weekend."

"Being the owner of the newspaper, I'm not sure that I am technically ever really off."

"Yes, ma'am, but perhaps you are not planning to go into the office tomorrow or Sunday."

Randy pulled her a little closer. Jenn's heart began to race again.

"The only newspaper work that I am planning on doing is on my laptop."

"I'm not sure what tonight is going to hold for me or whether I will need to work tomorrow, but I was thinking that maybe we could go out on my boat on Sunday and then I could cook dinner."

"That sounds wonderful. I'm glad you said Sunday. I am planning to go to Raleigh and visit Renee tomorrow. I will probably stay overnight but can come home early on Sunday."

"If you had plans to spend the weekend with Renee, I don't want to keep you from doing that. I hope she's doing better."

"Renee is home and beginning her recovery according to her husband. I feel like it's time that I see for myself. I need to take her a little sisterly love. I wasn't planning on staying longer than Saturday afternoon to Sunday morning. I believe she has a follow-up appointment with her surgeon the latter part of next week. By then, she may be able to come stay with me for a couple of weeks. That's one thing we are going to discuss."

"I know it will ease your mind to see her."

"Yes, and it will also give her husband a little break. Neil can go play some golf on Saturday or something. I will look forward to a Sunday afternoon on the boat with you."

"It's a date. I've got to run. Text me when you head to Raleigh."

Jenn held on to Randy's forearms while he moved away from her. She breathed in his rich cologne, remembering their kiss.

"You may be out all night fighting crime, I wouldn't want to wake you."

"You're the best reason I've had to wake up in a long time. I'll also appreciate a text when you get to Raleigh." Randy kissed the top of Jenn's head before he began to walk away.

"Yes, sir, Chief."

"I'd rather you called me Honey or Sweetheart or anything less official."

"How about Randy Poo?" Jenn giggled at the name she called him in middle school.

"Believe it or not, that's not the worst nickname I've ever had. I'd forgotten about that one though. Why don't you come up with one that better reflects our advanced years?"

"Speak for yourself, old timer. I'm still a young chick."

"Yes, you are. You make this old fogie feel young again, too. Have a safe trip and a wonderful visit. Please give my best regards to Renee and her husband."

Before Jenn could say anything else, Randy was waving and out the door.

Following him out to the railing on her deck, she looked down the steps, watching him drive away.

"I don't know how I've gotten so lucky." Jenn hugged herself, remembering the feeling of Randy's arms around her. "I'm going to shake off this fear of what could go wrong and embrace this chance at a new life."

"Please tell me that little cooler you are carrying contains something rich in calories. Hospital food sucks!"

Before Jenn could reach the couch where Renee was lounging, her sister began talking.

"I'm following the tried-and-true remedy that our grandfather prescribed for anything that ailed us."

"Yippee! It's Dippers ice cream!"

Jenn looked over her shoulder to see her brother-in-law Neil's laughing reaction to Renee's excitement about the ice cream. It was good to see a smile on his face. The conversations Jenn had with him over the past few weeks were anything but light.

"I hope I got some of your favorite flavors. Yours, too, Neil."

"There are no bad flavors at Dippers." Neil gave Jenn a thumbs up. "I'll get some bowls and spoons."

"Sit down here next to me, my darling sister." Renee moved on the couch, making room for Jenn to sit.

Jenn paused a moment to take a good look at her oldest sibling. Since her mid-teens, Renee had been tall and slender. Jenn always thought that her sister had a glamourous look, no matter the occasion. Her long, auburn hair seemed to match her vibrant personality with a little flair for the comedic. The loss of her son had certainly put a dent in Renee's jovial personality. Over the years, Jenn had seen slivers of that personality return. Today, Jenn would say she looked exhausted.

"You're in good humor for someone who grimaced when she just moved." Jenn gently sat next to her sister.

"I've worked my way down from yelping in pain to grimacing. I call that progress."

"Renee's not exaggerating. Her first couple of days at home were full of little screams that scared me to death." Neil returned with a tray of bowls, spoons, and an ice cream scoop in a glass of warm water. "Would you like some iced water?"

"Yes, please." Jenn responded while she pulled out four pints of ice cream.

"Oh, my goodness. It's been too long." Renee smiled. "What are my flavor choices?"

"Key Lime Coconut. Strawberry Cheesecake. Raspberry Chocolate, which I think is Neil's favorite."

"You're exactly right." Neil returned with a tray of glasses of iced water. "Thank you, Jenn."

"Want to guess the final flavor, sis?" Jenn held the name on the carton away from Renee's view.

"I'm afraid to say. I don't want to make either of us disappointed."

"Well, I've been your sister for a long time. We've eaten lots of Dippers together. I think I've passed this test. To cinch the deal, I called Dippers yesterday and asked them to save me two pints of this one. There's a spare still in the cooler."

"I feel like I'm ten and it's report card week." Renee moved her arms in a cheering motion. She quickly stopped, making a face indicating discomfort. "I hope it's Peanut Butter Banana."

"Otherwise known as—"

"Elvis ice cream!!" Renee and Jenn yelled simultaneously.

Neil shook his head while he took the ice cream from Jenn. He immediately filled a bowl with two huge scoops of his wife's favorite flavor, handing the bowl to Jenn to pass to Renee. Jenn pointed to the Key Lime Coconut. Neil prepared a serving for her.

Taking her first bite, Renee closed her eyes, tilting her head back in pleasure. "Oh, sister, I can't imagine what you could have brought me that I would have enjoyed more. I can't believe you came all this way to bring me ice cream."

"So says the sister who stocked my kitchen before I moved into my new home. I lived off those supplies for quite a few days. It was a wonderfully caring gesture. You deserve nothing less."

"Food is love."

"Our mother's words were true in our childhood, and they are true today."

"I'm so glad you came, and not just because of the ice cream." Renee winked, taking her second bite.

"I've wanted to come since Neil first called me." Jenn nodded to her brother-in-law as he re-entered the room after putting the ice cream away. "I knew that you needed time to get through your hospital recovery and settled at home. I believe you mentioned that you have a follow-up appointment on Friday."

"Yes." Renee made eye contact with Neil. "The surgeon mentioned, before we left the hospital, that there was a possibility I would need to have another procedure. It seems that since the surgery ended up being an emergency procedure, it affected the way the surgery was carried out. They might not have done everything needed."

"Wouldn't the surgeon know that one way or another already?" Jenn furrowed her brow, looking from Renee to Neil.

"The surgeon thinks the procedure is complete. He wants Renee to have another scan to get more views of the overall area. It may only be a formality." Neil finished his serving of ice cream.

"We hope so." Renee smiled at Jenn. "I talked to both of my doctors about your suggestion that I come stay at the beach while I'm healing. Neither one of them had any issues with that. I believe they will recommend a doctor in the area who I could go see if needed. I told them that my father and grandfather built most of the homes of the doctors in the area. He said that connection might come in handy."

"Jenn, I'm going to take you up on your offer and go do a few things while you're here." Neil stood up, holding his now-empty ice cream bowl. "I'm going to go by the office and then see if I can get in a little golf."

"Absolutely. You take as long as you need. Don't make it all about work though. Renee's caretaker needs a little relaxation."

"She's been a good patient, mostly." Neil winked at his wife. "I think she's ready for some sister time though. Don't let her eat a whole pint of ice cream. I've got some steaks marinating in the fridge. I can grill those and some potatoes when I return and pair that with a salad."

"That sounds great, Neil. Text me when you are starting to head home, and I'll get a head start on the cooking."

Jenn watched Neil lean down and kiss Renee. Her sister gently caressed his face while he whispered something to her. The strength of their bond always amazed Jenn. They had experienced the worse thing a couple could endure, the loss of a child. In the almost two decades since their son was abducted, Renee and Neil had fervently held onto each other. While Renee rarely spoke of her son in recent years, Jenn knew that the worst part was not knowing what had happened. Never having closure was worse than burying a child, Neil often said through the years. There was a guilt associated with giving up. You couldn't go through the stages of grief properly without closure.

"Don't make her giggle too much, Jenn. She's still got plenty of stitches, inside and out." Neil nodded at Jenn. "Thank you for coming."

Jenn took her and Renee's empty ice cream bowls to the kitchen while Neil gathered up his belongings to leave.

"I'm going to bring in my suitcase, Renee." Jenn yelled over her shoulder, leaving the door open so she could get back inside.

Neil was waiting by her car. His expression was serious.

"You need to know something, Jenn. The main reason the doctors want to do an overall scan is because they suspect there may be more cancer. The infection that was beginning to spread because of the abscess threw them off the original plan for the surgery. Her bloodwork had indicated something else suspicious. It could be something from the infection that, at the time, they didn't know was there. We're hoping for the best but preparing for other possibilities. Renee doesn't really want me to tell you all this. I think you need to know."

Jenn pulled her brother-in-law into a hug. *Neil is such a good man.*

"I'm glad you've told me. It will stay between us. Renee needs to be the tough one. I'll give her that. I know that's how she's survived all these years. Please let me help you. I'm so much closer now and since I run my own business, I have more leeway with my time."

"I hope the doctor will release her to come stay with you. I think spending some time in that house, on that beach, with you, is probably the best medicine she can have. I think it will be much better for her than being cooped up in this house. We've got a Jonah anniversary coming up. Twenty years is going to be a hard milestone."

"I can't believe it has been that many years."

"It never gets easier, Jenn. We've learned to live with it. We've had no choice. But it's a pain that's always there."

"I'll take care of her, Neil. Here and at home. You go take some stress out on those golf balls. Soak up the sunshine. Laugh with your buddies. You need some medicine, too."

"Thanks, Jenn. I'll text when I'm getting ready to head back." Neil started getting into his vehicle. "Normally, Renee would be taking a nap soon. I'm not sure if she will after that sugar high."

"I'll encourage it. Might take one myself."

Jenn waved, turning toward her vehicle to retrieve her suitcase from the back. She also got her laptop. Closing the door as she got back inside, she peeked into the living room. Renee pointed in the direction of Jenn's purse.

"Your purse has been beeping."

"Sorry about that."

"No bother to me, but now you'll have to tell me who it is."

Jenn rolled her eyes, digging her phone out of her purse. There were two texts and a phone call.

"I guess I'm in trouble. I was supposed to text Mel and Randy when I arrived."

"Randy? Now I know what our main topic of conversation will be while you're here. Spill it, sister."

"How about I unpack and return some messages? Then, you can interrogate me."

"Oh, good! I'll take a short little cat nap to work up my energy."

"That sounds good."

Jenn made her way to the rear of the house, finding the door open on one of the spacious home's guest rooms. She sent Randy a brief text letting him know that she arrived a little earlier. She did the same with Mel before sending a group text to her three children telling them that their Aunt Renee was in good spirits and ate a hearty bowl of Dippers ice cream. Only Emily responded immediately with a surprised emoji followed by a heart.

After hanging up the outfit she brought to wear home, Jenn returned to the living room, finding Renee sound asleep. Jenn decided to use the time to prep the food for dinner. Finding the ingredients for a green salad, Jenn began washing and chopping the assorted vegetables. A few minutes into the process, she heard the buzz of a text message from her phone on the counter. Since it was Mel, Jenn decided to go through the sliding doors to the patio and call her.

"That was fast." Mel answered on the first ring. "I figured that you and Renee would be in deep sister chat by now."

"Renee is weaker than she would want to admit. After a bowl of Dippers ice cream, she was snoring in no time."

"Bless her heart. Her poor body has been through a lot in the last few weeks."

"Yes, her poor soul has been through too much in the last twenty years."

"Has it been that long?"

"Yes. Neil mentioned it to me earlier. It's one reason that he hopes she will be visiting me by the time the anniversary rolls around. I am still amazed there haven't been any leads or new information in probably ten years. Whoever took that precious boy knew how to cover their tracks."

"If Renee is staying with you when the anniversary date rolls around, that means Neil will be by himself. Does that concern you?"

"A little. Maybe they will do better without each other for this. They can each cope in their own way without worrying about the other one. Neil's brother lives just outside of Raleigh. I think they are close. Neil's business partner was also his college roommate. They are like brothers."

"His name is Peter, right?"

"Yes. I forgot that you two dated a couple of times while we were still in college."

"Peter is a nice guy. There just wasn't any chemistry between us. I enjoyed going out with him though. Is he married?"

"He was. I believe his daughter is grown now. His wife died from a brain aneurysm when their daughter was a teenager. That's one reason I know that Peter will take care of Neil, if Renee is with me. Peter understands loss."

"I'm glad he has a good support system. We will do our best to keep Renee busy. I love being around her."

"Her adopted sister, Mellie Bellie."

"You don't have to remind her about the nickname."

"I know I don't have to. Renee has a memory like a steel trap. She'll make sure everyone knows how much she loves her Mellie Bellie."

"Great. I can't wait." Mel's voice was monotone, with a snort at the end. "I almost forgot why I called you. Sinclair dropped a big bomb on me."

"What? Did he propose?"!

"No! It wasn't that shocking but close. He wants me to meet his children."

"He's not wasting any time. Somehow, I don't find that too surprising. Since you heard from Dana, his kids must know of your existence. If your relationship is going to grow and continue, you are bound to meet them."

"I know. I guess I wasn't expecting it to happen so soon."

"Does he have a time in mind?"

"Tomorrow."

"Oh, that is soon."

"Apparently, his children's birthdays are in the same month. He's been so busy with the dealership that he hasn't had a chance to go see them. Both of his children live in Goldsboro. They have jobs related to Seymour Johnson Air Force Base."

"Were they in the military?"

"I think his son was for a few years. His daughter's husband is on active duty. They are stationed there."

"That's not too far. Are you going?"

"Do I have a choice? It's not like I can say I don't want to meet them." Mel paused. "I do want to meet them. My head is spinning. Everything is happening too fast."

"Sinclair is trying to make up for lost time."

"We can't make up for thirty years in thirty days."

"I understand. He may have a little apprehension that if he doesn't keep things moving forward, they might stagnate."

"I want things to move forward. At least, I think I do. I'm just starting to feel a little whiplash at the speed."

"Maybe you should tell Sinclair that."

"Sinclair's so excited. He's like a kid about everything he plans for us. He barely stopped to breathe while he was talking about meeting his kids. He says they are anxious to meet me. I wonder what Dana's told them. I can't imagine that 'anxious' is a word they used. Sinclair is anxious."

"It took a lot for Dana to make that call to you and apologize. I would bet that she's told her children the truth. Kids are smarter than we give them credit for. They know when things aren't right in their home, especially as they get older and start experiencing relationships themselves. I'd let them lead the conversation."

"This is exactly why you are my best friend. You always know the right answers."

"I wouldn't be sure about the 'always' part. Sometimes I feel like I'm making a mess of my relationship with Randy."

"I'm thrilled to hear you use the word 'relationship' to describe you two. This is a huge step. It's as big as Chief Romeo kissing you on Main Street."

"Chief Romeo? Please tell me that you made that up just now."

"Oh, no. That's the talk on the street, sister. Randy's got a new name."

"Good grief!" Jenn hit her forehead with the palm of her hand. "I'm going to pretend I don't know that."

"That's probably a good idea. For the record, Sinclair didn't coin the name. It came from one of Randy's coaching buddies. Randy is a good sport. He'll take it in stride. I don't think he's the least bit ashamed of what he did."

"No, he's not. I think he's a little concerned that he might have overstepped his bounds with me. It's not exactly the first kiss location I dreamed of, but it's hard to imagine a more romantic one."

"From what Doris says, it looked like a scene right out of a Hallmark Channel movie without snow falling or Christmas lights."

"I think I heard a choir singing."

"I bet you did." Mel howled in laughter. "The last month for the both of us could have been the plot for a romance novel."

"One of those fun quirky ones where the heroine owns a newspaper or operates a visitors bureau."

"Hey, Jenn, you may be on to something. Perhaps you need to pull out those fiction writing skills you used to have. With the way our lives are going, you might have enough material for a book series."

"Truth is stranger than fiction, or is it?" Jenn paused, listening for sounds from the living room. "Listen, Mel, I'm going to hop off here and check my emails before Renee wakes up. I want to spend as much time with her as possible."

"Absolutely. If you have time, text me tonight in case I need any more pep talks in anticipation for tomorrow. When do you plan to head home?"

"I will probably get on the road right after breakfast. Randy invited me to go on his boat tomorrow afternoon. I told him I would try to get home around midday."

"That sounds like fun. I'd forgotten that he had a boat. I'm surprised him and Sinclair haven't gone fishing yet."

"Don't forget Sinclair has a new business as well and a new lady in his life."

"More like an old lady. Wait! I don't like the sound of that. Maybe I should call myself a rerun."

"Maybe you should call it what it truly is, a second chance at happiness."

"Amen, my friend. Amen. Give Renee my love."

Ending the call, Jenn pulled out her laptop. While she waited for it to power up, she went back to the living room, checking on her sister. Renee was still resting.

Returning to her laptop, Jenn quickly scrolled through her email, looking for anything pressing. An email from Betsy Lawson, the newspaper's Advertising Director, provided a list of potential candidates for the new advertising representative position. There were six potential interview candidates, including her daughter-in-law, Michelle Young. Betsy's message asked if Jenn would like her to begin scheduling interviews. Jenn replied affirmatively, suggesting that the initial interviews be conducted virtually with in-person meetings for the final candidates. Since several of the candidates lived an hour or more away from Serendipity, that seemed like a fair way to handle the process.

Another long email was from Lyle Livingston. Her new editor outlined a yearlong plan for revamping the editorial side of the newspaper, including a new look for the front page, some new column suggestions, and a plan for some revenue-producing special sections.

"Lyle has certainly taken my assignment seriously."

Jenn was pleased she'd decided to bring back someone who already had a long history with the newspaper. After briefly glancing at a few more messages, Jenn closed her laptop, picked up her phone, and headed back to the living room.

"You're awake." Jenn found Renee sitting up on the couch, rubbing her eyes.

"That nap came on quick. It was a serious one." Renee yawned, stretching her arms up. The action made her wince in pain. "I'd probably still be asleep if my phone didn't keep ringing. It's just far enough away that I couldn't easily get to it." Renee pointed to the other end of the couch.

"I'll get that for you." Jenn retrieved Renee's phone, handing it to her.

"Uh oh." Renee looked at the screen. "We may be in trouble."

"We? That's a phrase I've not heard since we were teenagers. Who could I possibly have heard from?"

"The next best thing to Paisley Halston." Renee looked Jenn in the eyes.

"Aunt Rachel!" Jenn and Renee exclaimed simultaneously.

"I've not called her since I moved back to Serendipity." Jenn bit her bottom lip.

"I've not told her about my illness." Renee shook her head, scowling.

"We are definitely in trouble." Jenn sat down next to Renee.

"There's been an informant."

"I bet I know who. It's got to be Doris."

"Well, of course." Renee shook her head affirmatively. "Her lifelong best friend is the lifeline of your newspaper. Doris sees and hears everything that you do practically."

Jenn smirked to herself, thinking about the kiss in front of the building. *She sure does.*

"I guess it's time to face the music. She's left a message."

Renee slowly hit the buttons for the voicemail to play. Jenn noticed that her sister almost seemed afraid to touch them.

"Hello, Renee, dear. I was so sorry to hear that you have been ill. I was not able to send up prayers of healing for you until now, since *no one* in this family saw fit to let me know that something was wrong. I don't know why that surprises me, since your sister Jenn moved back to Serendipity over a month ago and *still* hasn't even called me. I know you are there listening, Jenn. Aunt Rachel is quite disappointed. Your mother would not be pleased. I would appreciate if someone would call me back before I die. Kiss. Kiss."

"She ended with kisses. The kiss of death." Renee sat up on the couch, grimacing. "I have an excuse. I've been in the hospital. You, my dear sister, are in deep trouble."

"Crap. It's crossed my mind several times to call her. I just never seemed to get it done. I'm really surprised that Doris didn't send me an email about it, like she sends all my messages and appointments. I guess she thought I would know better than to go this long."

"Quite frankly, I've only talked to her a couple of times since Mom passed. I never noticed this when Mom was living, but she and Rachel sound quite a bit alike."

"I know. I noticed that when I talked to her the last time. I think it's because we can't hear Mom's voice anymore. The similarities are more pronounced." Jenn felt a tinge of sadness, missing her mother's voice. "Maybe we could call her together."

"You are trying to use me as an excuse, aren't you? Make her focus on hearing about what's happened to me and deviate attention from the prodigal sister."

"That's exactly right."

"Played like a true Halston. I would have done the same thing. We'll put the phone on speaker between us." Renee motioned for Jenn to sit next to her on the couch. "Are you ready?"

"It's time to face the music." Jenn took a cleansing breath to calm her nerves.

"It's time to face 'the Rachel.'" Renee laughed. She frowned with pain from the movement. "I've got to learn that laughing hurts. I need to gently laugh. Here we go."

Renee hit the button to dial. The phone rang one-two-three-four-five times.

"Hello."

Rachel's voice almost sounded sultry, like Joan Crawford in one of those old black-and-white movies. *Auntie Dearest.* Jenn bit her bottom lip to keep from laughing.

"Hello, Aunt Rachel. This is Renee. Thank you so much for calling to check on me."

"I've been so worried about you, my dear, for about three hours now. Doris came to visit this morning. How are you?"

"I'm recovering nicely. I still have more healing ahead."

"Doris said something about emergency surgery."

"Yes. Well, it started a while back. I had some bloodwork that didn't seem quite right. That led to some tests, more bloodwork, and more tests."

"It sounds like this has been going on for a while. I know about tests and bloodwork. Doctors never seem to be able to do those on the same day. You must make a visit for every little one and the results are weeks apart."

Jenn thought that Aunt Rachel was making a good point. Renee must have known something was going on for weeks, if not months.

"That's true. It seems to take longer to get a diagnosis then it should." Renee pulled the pillow, which she clutched when she got up or down, closer to her. "Anyway, they finally decided that I had a tumor in my colon, a cancerous one."

Rachel gasped.

"It's not the diagnosis that anyone wants to hear, but I've faced worse things."

"Yes, my dear, you have."

Jenn heard a gentleness in Rachel's voice. In that moment, Rachel sounded just like her sister, their mother, Paisley. Jenn could feel tears forming in her eyes. She dared not look at Renee.

"They scheduled for me to have surgery to remove the tumor. In the meantime, though, something went wrong inside there, and an abscess formed. They had to do emergency surgery. I have great doctors. They saved me."

"That's wonderful. I'm so happy to hear it. Did they remove the tumor while they were taking care of the abscess?"

"Yes, they did."

"Does that mean you are cancer free?" There was a hopeful lilt to Rachel's voice. Another telltale Paisley trait.

"That I do not know yet. My doctors are hoping they got all the cancer through the surgery. It was a rushed job though. They want me to have a scan next week to check that out. If the scan comes back clear, I'm planning to spend some of my recuperation time with Jenn in Serendipity."

"That would be wonderful, Renee. Maybe then I might be able to see your sister, the newspaper owner. I know you're there, Jenn. You can breathe now. I'm relieved that Renee is okay, so you are partially off the hook."

"Hello, Aunt Rachel. I'm so sorry that I haven't called you. I've been so—"

"Busy. That's what everyone says. I know that you've had a lot of change in your life, young lady."

Young lady. No one called Jenn a young lady. It was all about perspective. Someone in their fifties was young to someone in their eighties.

"Yes, ma'am. Change seems to find me. It's no excuse. I should have called you. I'm surprised that Doris hasn't questioned me daily about that very thing."

"I told her not to do that. She's told me how much you've been working. I understand that it's a lot of responsibility buying a business and learning how to run it. I thought I would have heard from you by *now* though. Especially since you seem to have time to start a new romance with our esteemed Police Chief."

Busted. Jenn could feel the color rising on her face. She could also feel Renee's eyes boring holes through the side of her head.

"What have you heard about that, Aunt Rachel? Little Jenn has not been keeping her sister up to date regarding that aspect of her life."

"Well, Doris says that the Police Chief kissed her on Main Street, right in front of the newspaper!"

"You have got to be kidding me!" Renee reached over and hit Jenn on the shoulder. "I sure hope someone got a photograph of that."

"Doris did. She sent it to me on my phone. I'll send it to you when we end our call." Rachel made a clicking sound with her tongue. It was the sound of disapproval. "Don't feel bad, Renee. I had to hear all this secondhand as well. If it wasn't for Doris, I wouldn't know anything either."

"I'm sorry, Aunt Rachel. I promise I will do better."

Jenn glanced at Renee. Her sister was clutching her pillow, laughing. The pained-laughing expression was not a good one for Renee.

"I know you will, Jenn. I've used the proven guilt-inducing regret formula that was perfected by mine and Paisley's mother when we were teenagers."

"Grammie Elana was good at that." Renee responded, now calm from her laughing fit. "I remember how easily it worked on Mom."

"Our mother was the master. It is my job to carry the torch now."

"Seriously, Aunt Rachel, I did not mean to slight you or leave you out of the loop regarding Renee. Everything with her health scare happened so quickly. She has kept most of this illness to herself. It was only when the emergency arose that I learned the real details."

"I didn't want to worry anyone until there was something to worry about." Renee scowled at Jenn, hitting her on the shoulder again. "If it makes you both feel better, you can worry now."

"We shall indeed worry about you, darling girl." Rachel cleared her throat. "Since my beloved Paisley is not here to carefully watch over her girls, I must do so. Truthfully, I would have regardless. Neither of you are normally the ones who need the extra prayers. What do we know about Amber?"

"Neil called the rehab facility after we returned from the hospital. They told him that Amber is doing quite well and might be released early. The counselor who Neil talked to is the one who worked with Amber during her previous stay. He thinks that Amber has made some positive progress this time. Apparently, she has responded well to the medications they are giving to help with her addiction."

"It's strange to think that one drug could help a person overcome another one." Jenn pondered the concept.

"It is. Neil did some research on the matter. Certain medications can mimic the effects of addictive drugs, which relieve withdrawal symptoms and cravings."

"Science is amazing. Do you know the whereabouts of Amber's son?" Rachel spoke up.

"Willis is in California. Neil reached out to Willis' father when Amber went back into rehab. He arranged for Willis to fly to California and stay with him."

"Amber was married so briefly to the man. I cannot remember his name."

"Willis' father's name is Dawson Hyder." Jenn answered Rachel. "Dawson was playing professional basketball when he and Amber met. You probably remember that it was quite a whirlwind romance. They barely knew each other when they eloped. The marriage didn't last long after Willis was born."

"Dawson has been the one who has paid for Amber's rehab, both times." Renee continued telling the story. "Dawson told Neil that he feels responsible for Amber's addictions since he was the one who introduced her to the life where she picked up the habits. Amber told us that some of the other basketball wives were into all sorts of addictive substances. She might have been in worse shape sooner were it not for her becoming pregnant. We've told Dawson that only Amber should be held responsible for her actions. He insists on still taking care of her. From what I understand, Dawson also pays the bulk of Amber's regular bills."

"It's a shame it didn't work out between them. He sounds like a good man. I only met him once. He was so tall and handsome."

"Dawson is a fine man." Renee responded. "Neil has gotten to know him quite well through the years. After Dawson retired from playing basketball, he started a contracting business in California. They have long conversations about construction."

Jenn was not sure she knew that Dawson now had such a business. "It's a shame the marriage didn't survive. Dawson would have fit right in with his interest in construction. Dad would have enjoyed having another son-in-law to work with in the family business."

"It's true. From what Neil understands, Dawson has grown his company into a wonderful business. His professional basketball connections led to many multi-million dollar homes that his company has built throughout California."

"Did Dawson remarry?" Rachel asked.

"No."

"Interesting. I'll have to ponder that some more. Girls, it's about time for my afternoon beauty nap. I'm happy that I was able to reach you both. Please don't forget your Aunt Rachel. She loves you both very much."

"We love you, too." Jenn and Renee replied.

"Hopefully, I will be in Serendipity in a few weeks. I will visit and bring the prodigal niece with me." Renee poked Jenn in the ribs.

"I promise to not be a stranger, Aunt Rachel. A visit will be on my calendar pronto."

"Goodbye, my darlings."

The call ended. Jenn breathed a sigh of relief.

"That was a close one." Jenn rose from the couch.

"Oh, you think you've gotten off easy, don't you?" Renee pointed at the couch. "You've got some explaining to do, little sister. I want details about Chief Randy. *All* the details."

Chapter Seven

Randy

"Renee wasn't happy until she'd heard every detail of the time we've spent together."

Randy listened to Jenn talk about her visit with her sister as he pulled in another fish. He was amazed at how well the fish were biting. He already had two beautiful flounders that he would grill for their dinner. The remaining fish would go into his freezer for later meals.

"Did you really think you could keep anything secret from Renee?"

"I thought that since she was a couple of hours away and had been hospitalized that maybe I might have a little time to prepare for her interrogation. Within a few minutes after our conversation with Aunt Rachel, Renee received a copy of the photo that Doris took of us."

"That Doris, she seems like a nice older lady. I think it's a front." Randy took the fish off the hook, placing it into a cooler. "Sometimes, my officers go visit her at the newspaper to find out information for their investigations. I wouldn't be surprised if she didn't have a Secret Service-like earpiece that she wears every day. Have you ever caught her speaking into her sleeve?"

"You're funny." Jenn laughed, stopping abruptly. "Doris does seem to know more than the reporters most of the time. Maybe the *Serendipity Sun* is a front for a covert spy operation. Should I be concerned?"

"You are probably okay until the men in black show up."

"Is that some sort of action movie reference that I should understand?"

"Obviously not." Randy sat down on the bench opposite Jenn. "We have plenty of fish for dinner. How about we start heading back to shore? There's a possible storm coming in. I'd like to beat it home."

"That sounds great. It's been a wonderful afternoon, so relaxing."

Randy watched the wind blow Jenn's hair away from her face. He could see that the sun had kissed her skin. *Lucky sun.* He knew he needed to concentrate on taking it slow. Overwhelming Jenn might not be the best way to win her heart.

"Okay. I'm going back up front to the driver's seat. You can join me or stay here."

"I'll join you. It's been a while since I've been on a boat. I used to be rather good at driving Dad's. That was a long time ago."

"It would come back to you, I'm sure. Want to get behind the wheel on our way back?" Randy stood up, walking toward the front. "The water might be a little choppy since that storm is getting closer."

"I think I'll just watch. Maybe I can try next time."

Next time. The words filled Randy's heart.

"Sounds good. Let's get going."

Twenty minutes later, Randy's dock and cottage were in sight.

"Do you take your boat out often? I've not heard you mention it." Jenn stood beside Randy's driver seat.

"Not as much as I intended to when I bought the cottage. I was under the illusion that a beachfront property automatically came with limitless time to enjoy it. I was wrong."

"I hear you. I've already discovered that. I can't even seem to find enough time to walk on the beach."

"Maybe we'll get to do things like that when we retire." Randy angled the boat toward the dock.

"Retire. I wonder if I will ever experience that term. Here I am in my fifties, and I've bought a business. That makes retirement seem a long way off."

"If you get a good team of people working for you, maybe that will change. The ideas you've shared with me about the direction you'd like to take the newspaper seem like they have the makings of success."

"I appreciate those words of encouragement. Ideas and reality can be strikingly different. You are right though. I am forming a good team. They can make those dreams a reality."

"That's what I like to hear." Randy turned off the ignition, pulling out the key and sticking it in his pocket. "I've learned that if I don't pull that key out before I stand up, the key lives here until I run out of places to look for it."

"Oh, I bet that is an unsettling feeling to find a key in the boat ignition."

"Especially after it's been sitting there for two weeks, and you've been looking for it all that time." Randy jumped onto the dock, extending his hand to help Jenn up.

"I remember that Mom always kept an extra key to Dad's boat hidden. Apparently, her father had to have an ignition re-keyed because of a misplaced boat key."

"That's tough. Was the key ever found?"

"Of course. It was discovered under the seat of my grandfather's truck two days after a new ignition was installed."

"That hurts. I'll remember that story and keep immediately putting my key in my pocket." Randy reached for the cooler of fish to place it in a more accessible location. "I'm going to clean the fish before I head to the house. You can go on up. I think I left the patio door unlocked. There are some fresh towels in the guest bathroom, if you'd like to freshen up."

"I was hoping you'd suggest that. I feel quite sticky after our afternoon on the water. I still have my overnight bag in the Jeep from my visit to Renee's. Do you mind if I take a quick shower?"

"Not at all. I intend to do the same thing after I clean the fish. I'm going to be feeling a little fishy after that."

"I guess so." Jenn smiled.

With a hint of sunburn on her face and her windblown hair, Randy was reminded of a teenage Jenn. His heart skipped a beat thinking about the warm days they'd spent together growing up. His young heart had fallen in love with his cute neighbor. There she was, in front of him, all these years later.

"Randy, did you hear me?"

Randy realized that he was more lost in thought than he realized.

"I'm sorry. What did you say?" Randy wondered what he'd missed.

"I asked if there was anything I could work on in the kitchen after my shower. What did you plan to fix with the fish?"

"Oh, yes. I picked up a small bowl of coleslaw from the diner. I've already made some hushpuppy batter and have some freshly sliced potatoes soaking in water in the fridge ready to make some home fries. There's really nothing else to do except set the table. I thought we would probably eat inside since we've been out all afternoon and that storm might still come."

"It's looking dark back toward town. I'll set the table once I'm out of my shower." Jenn turned away from the boat, and began to walk up the steps to the cottage.

Randy continued to secure the boat, lifting the cooler of fish and setting it on the dock.

"Randy."

He turned to find Jenn standing on the bottom step, facing him.

"What were you thinking about a few minutes ago? You were so lost in thought."

"Honestly. I was thinking about you. I was remembering that teenage girl who lived next door. The one girl who I couldn't summon the courage to ask out."

Randy watched Jenn's look of surprise change to a smile. They locked eyes for a moment. He could feel the emotion in the air between them. Jenn remained silent, giving Randy a slight nod before climbing the steps to his cottage.

"That was a good start."

"That's not the strangest thing I've ever seen as a police officer."

Randy kept the dinner conversation lighthearted with stories from his early days on patrol.

"I can't believe you can top finding a cow sitting on a couch in a garage."

"Sitting on the remains of a couch. That cow broke the couch when he first sat down on it."

"Is that where the term 'cow-ch potato' came from?"

Jenn giggled. With her hair pulled away from her face, Jenn looked even more like a teenager. Randy wasn't sure his heart could stand it. *She is beautiful.*

"Oh, Jenn, please do not give up your work in the newspaper business for a career in comedy." Randy winked. "My weirdest call was finding a cat with kittens in a casket at the funeral home."

"Oh, my, that's sweet and sad, at the same time. Was the cat looking for her deceased owner?"

"No, it was wintertime. I think the cat wandered into the funeral home to get out of the cold. I took the call in the middle of the night because the funeral home's youngest employee was there all night by himself. He kept hearing a strange sound from within a closed casket. He didn't want to call the owners in the middle of the night, so he called the police."

"This is a strange story."

"When I got there, the kid took me to the funeral home's casket display room, pointing to a casket in the corner. He kept saying that it was making noise. The lid was closed so I asked him if there was a body in it. He said there wasn't supposed to be. I lifted the lid. A few seconds later, the cat came walking out of the closed side. When I lifted the other lid, I found four kittens."

"I'm surprised they didn't smother."

"Well, I don't think a casket is airtight until it is sealed. I guess they got enough airflow to survive."

"Was there a story in the newspaper about that incident?"

"There was. The owner of the funeral home ended up adopting that cat. I saw her several times after that through the years when I would attend services there."

"I'm almost afraid to ask what they named her."

"They called her Satin. They had to replace the satin from within the casket where she gave birth. One of the ladies who worked there made her a bed out of it."

"I'll have to look up that story sometime."

"I think it was Helen who wrote it."

"I guess laughing about some calls helps you get through the ones that would only make you cry."

"You're exactly right. I've been thinking about that very thing this week after going to see that former officer in the western part of the state. I think one of the reasons that young man left the force was because of situations he encountered that were a little hard for him to stomach. Police officers see a lot of ugly situations. Officers who last must learn to remember more cows on couches and fewer bodies on stretchers."

Randy watched Jenn's reaction. She was staring at the glass of water in front of her half-eaten plate of food.

"The main reason I left the newspaper years ago was because Simon was offered a great job in Atlanta. At the time, that made the decision easier. But there was something else that happened around that time which left a lasting impression on me. It was a murder."

"Murders will do that. Was the victim someone you knew?"

"No, but my life crossed paths with his life and his family. I had to write the story about the incident. Mr. Sebastian had me interview the family. He wanted to give them a chance to make a statement."

"I can see him doing that. Was the man well known in the community?"

"Sort of. The family operated the first convenience store in the area. Hardworking large family—father, mother, and five children. The man came here from another country to start a new life. Apparently, some old grudges followed him here. This was before convenience stores were open all night. The man would open the store every day at six in the morning and would often be the one to close the store at midnight. He would leave the family vehicle at home with his wife, riding a bicycle to the store. Right after Christmas, he was abducted on his way to the store early one morning. About a week later, he was found, murdered in a manner that was indicative of the culture he grew up in."

"I think I know the case you are talking about now. I don't think it was ever solved."

"He had a lovely family. Beautiful wife and five children ranging from kindergarten age to a senior in high school. I went to their home to do the interview. It was my twenty-third birthday."

"Not the best way to spend it."

"No, but it is one birthday I will never forget. The mother's English was not very good. So, the oldest child, a daughter, answered my questions. We were on a tight deadline. I rushed back to the office and quickly wrote the story. It was on the front page the following day. Late in the afternoon, on the day the article ran, I was sitting at my desk and my phone rang. It was the young woman I had interviewed. Our conversation was brief. All she said was, 'You've honored my father. Thank you.'"

"Wow. I bet that was a chilling moment for you."

"That's the exact right word to describe it. After she hung up, I sat there with the phone in my hand. One of my coworkers came over and took the phone out of my hand, asking who it was. I ran out of the office to the loading dock on the side of the building. I sat there and cried."

Randy remained silent. He could see from Jenn's expression that she was in another time. He would wait until she was ready to return.

"That day has haunted me ever since. I only knew the man in passing, when I would buy something in his store. I never saw the body, or anything connected with the investigation. Still, I was haunted by it. I can't imagine what that would be like for the police officers or medical personnel who worked such an incident."

"You learn a way to cope with what you see that allows you to remain objective, but not turn to stone. That's what I want to do with this officer. I want to try to counsel him. I want to help him determine if he can get past his fear and work on the mental health side of his police work."

"You're a rare breed, aren't you, Chief Nave?"

"Actually no, thankfully, there are more people with this philosophy in law enforcement than there are not. One generation of officers passes it on to the next. You've got to stay human and be humane even when you must see and hear things you could never imagine. It's the only way you can make a difference and stay on the sane side of the equation. It takes a special breed of human to do this work. We've got to keep as many of the good ones as we can. Police work is a calling. If you leave it too soon, you can feel unfulfilled for the rest of your life."

"I hope you can reach this young man. You obviously see something in him that you think is worth pursuing. Do you know much about his upbringing? Maybe that's a factor."

"That is often the case. I don't know much other than I think he is an only child. The father has been deceased for a while. I'm not sure that the man was much of a positive force. The officer speaks more fondly of his mother. He has a protective edge to his voice when he refers to her. That could indicate there was some abuse in the family. If so, that could be a strong factor in why he wanted to go into law enforcement. He may want to be a protector."

"Interesting. When will he be returning to testify?"

"In about two weeks. The case is a little complicated. He will probably be here for close to a week with the witness preparation that the prosecutor will want to do. I hope he takes me up on my offer to stay at my house. I'm betting that he's going to want to see the young lady he was dating before he left."

"I think you might have mentioned her before. Did you say she has a connection to Imogene in Mel's office?"

"Yes, her name is Megan. She's friends with Imogene. You may have met her if you bank at First Bank of Serendipity. She's a teller there."

"That reminds me that I need to open a personal account. The lawyers helped me set up the newspaper's accounts there. I'd like to do my banking there as well. It's the bank my parents always used."

"Yes, it's a hometown bank, for sure. Brady Mountcastle will welcome your business with open arms."

"I've heard that name. The bank is one of our advertising clients. Which is another good reason for me to use them." Jenn took the last bite of her flounder. "Randy, this meal was so good."

"There's nothing quite like fish caught fresh from the ocean. I'm happy that you were able to come and spend the afternoon with me. Tell me a little more about how Renee is doing. Forgive me; I cannot remember her husband's first name."

"Neil. I'm happy to say that he got to go and play a couple rounds of golf while I was sister sitting. Renee seems to be doing well. She still has quite a bit of pain when she moves. That's to be expected since they had to make some long incisions for the emergency surgery."

"I believe you told me that they removed the tumor during the surgery. I hope that means that all the cancer is gone."

"They did get the tumor. I think there was some reconstruction surgery also done on her colon. She did not have to have a colostomy bag or anything like that. The doctors think they removed all the cancer. There was a lot they had to do inside though, in addition to mitigating the abscess. Renee will go back to have an abdominal scan and additional bloodwork on Friday. Everyone is hoping that the scan comes back clear."

"Then, will she be coming here to stay with you?"

"That's the plan. I think she's excited about the visit. While I was there, we heard from Aunt Rachel. I got quite a tongue-lashing for not contacting her since I moved back."

"Jenn, you hadn't even called her?" Randy shook his head in surprise.

"Nope. I kept meaning to, but time got away from me every day."

"I know Rachel well enough to understand that you've got some major making up to do. She has an even stronger personality than your mother had."

"Renee is calling me the 'prodigal niece.' One of the worst parts is that she already knows lots of details about us."

"Us? As in you and me?" Randy gestured between the two of them.

"Yes. Doris is the informant."

"Of course, she is. I'd forgotten about those two being such close friends. I wasn't kidding in our conversation earlier; Doris has some major private investigator skills."

"I think her chair at the newspaper is a hot seat for information. Every person who speaks to someone on our staff usually goes through Doris first. She even gets all the basic emails that come in. They go through her inbox."

"Doris has the power. Stay on her good side."

"I'm hoping Doris will help me get back on Aunt Rachel's good side. I'm a little miffed at Doris for not fervently reminding me to contact

Aunt Rachel. I even got the blame for Aunt Rachel not being properly informed about Renee's illness."

"You better plan something extravagant for Rachel. She is older than your mother was, right?"

"Yes, a couple of years older. I think she might be turning eighty-five on her next birthday." Jenn paused; her eyes grew wider while she was thinking. "There's an idea."

"Rachel never married, did she?"

"No. I really don't know why. It was sort of a taboo topic in the family. I know my mother knew the backstory. She never seemed willing to reveal it. Renee strongly questioned Mom about it once. She told Renee to stop asking."

"You know who is bound to know the backstory?"

"Doris, of course. I'm not sure she would reveal any more than my mother would. It is worth a little prying though. I hope it is not some sad, tragic story, such as Rachel's great love was killed in a war or something like that."

"Everyone has a past. It's usually a mixture of happy and sad." Randy's phone beeped from the spot it was sitting on the table. He looked at the screen. "I better take this."

When Randy returned to the kitchen, he saw that Jenn had cleaned up all the dinner dishes and was putting the leftovers away in the refrigerator.

"Wow. I must have been on that call longer than I thought. Thanks for cleaning everything up."

"It wasn't any trouble. It's the least I could do for such a delicious meal."

"I'm afraid I'm going to have to cut the evening short. I'm going to need to go into work extra early in the morning."

"That's no problem. I need to go by Mel's and pick up Jasper." Jenn walked toward the doorway, picking up the bag she'd left there after her shower. "I had a wonderful time today, Randy. Thank you for inviting me."

"The pleasure was all mine, Jenn." Randy joined her at the doorway, softly kissing her on the cheek. "I'm diligently trying to take this slow, Miss Halston. I know you've had a rocky road for a while. You're going to have to tell me if I am not going slowly enough."

"I appreciate it, Mr. Nave. Spending time with you is wonderful. I've got to admit that it is a little overwhelming though. I'm not quite sure if I'm ready for this. I still can't quite wrap my mind around the fact that it's you who is kissing me. I spent a lot of years only being kissed by one man. I never dreamed the next one would be you."

"It was my dream, Jenn. I'm happy it's coming true."

"I was pleased to get the message that you were able to get in contact with Joe Fairfield so quickly."

After going into work extra early, Randy felt like he'd already worked a full day by lunch time. He decided to swing by the District Attorney's office to see if Edwin Greer needed any further information regarding the pending case.

"Officer Fairfield answered my phone call on the first ring. He apologized profusely for disappearing on us. He seems very concerned that he might have burned a bridge here."

Edwin took a bite of his half-eaten deli sandwich. Randy imagined that, like him, Edwin ate too many meals on the run. Behind Edwin was a bottle of antacids. Attorneys and police officers should own stock in the company that produces the medicine.

"Yes. I got the impression when I visited him that Fairfield's decision to leave law enforcement and the area might have been a hasty one which he is now regretting."

"Were there any red flags in his performance with your department?"

"None that I have found. No issues with his partner. No citizen complaints. His sergeant said he was one of the more dependable ones on his team. I'm hoping that I can get to the bottom of whatever happened that made him decide to leave. It's not too late for him to come back. I've not filled the spot yet."

"You'll get a chance to see his testifying skills, if you come and view the trial."

Edwin's cell phone buzzed. Randy watched him view the screen and hit the decline button.

"I plan on doing that. It's good for me to periodically watch my officers testify anyway."

"I've asked Fairfield to come to my office a couple of days before the trial begins. He should be on the list to testify on the first or second day. He said he was going to contact you today to let you know when he was planning to arrive."

"Good. That must mean he's going to take me up on my lodging offer."

"I wasn't aware that our Police Chief operated a bed and breakfast." Edwin chuckled. "You're a good man, Randy. I hope you can turn this kid's life around and regain a good officer at the same time."

"That's my plan, Edwin. I hope this case will end with the victim getting some justice."

"That's my plan, Randy. Thanks for your help."

On the sidewalk in front of the Courthouse, Randy saw a man who kept looking up and down from his phone as if he was lost.

"Hello, sir, may I be of assistance? You look a little confused."

"Thank you, officer. I think I may be lost. I was looking for a local florist called Petals. My GPS led me to this location, but I don't see any such business nearby."

"GPS is great when it works, isn't it? The reason your GPS led you here is because up until about a month ago, that building across the street was the location of Petals. It has moved over to Main Street, about a block down from the newspaper office on the same side of the street."

"Newspaper office? Well, that's convenient. The person I want to send flowers to happens to own it."

Randy tried to conceal the shock that was certainly showing on his face.

"Jennifer Halston?"

"Yes, do you know her? Well, I guess that a police officer would know lots of people in town." The man looked at Randy's badge. "Oh, the Police Chief definitely would. I'm an old friend of Jenn's. I am about to make a bold move to take that friendship up a notch, if you know what I mean?"

The man leaned a little toward Randy. Perhaps, he thought better of the gesture, as he stepped back and smiled. Randy did not return the smile. Instead, he looked the man up and down. His designer clothes in the beach town shouted wealth.

"I appreciate you stopping to help me, sir. I've recently moved to the area. My name is Parker Bentley." The man extended his hand.

Randy narrowed his eyes for a moment. He didn't often use his tough police expression with a friendly citizen on the street. This wasn't an average citizen though. This man had designs on *his* Jenn. Maybe he should find the man's vehicle and write a ticket. Randy shook off the feeling. Bentley was a name that was well known in the small community. Walter and Zella Bentley were long-term benevolent members of the Serendipity community. The Bentley family had strong bonds with Jenn's grandparents. This man must be their long-lost grandson who returned to the area before Walter passed away.

"Chief Randy Nave." Randy gave Parker's hand a firm shake. "I knew your grandparents. Fine people. I imagine you will be selling their beautiful home soon." Randy released Parker's hand.

"You've got a strong grip there, Chief." Parker shook out his hand, like it hurt. "That all depends on how Jenn reacts to the flowers. It was nice to meet you, sir. Thanks again for the directions."

Randy watched Parker walk up the sidewalk and get into his vehicle, a large expensive looking SUV. Randy racked his brain trying to remember if Jenn had mentioned this man. He had a vague memory that she'd said something about him. Taking a deep breath, Randy turned and walked in the opposite direction toward his own vehicle. He started to call Jenn and see if she wanted him to bring her some lunch. Unfortunately, his phone lit up with a call which took him back to work instead.

Chapter Eight

Mel

"Hello, Parker, what brings you into the Visitors Bureau today?"

Imogene was on her lunch break, so Mel was the one standing at the front desk when Parker Bentley walked through the door.

"Hello, Mel, I came to see you. I need some advice about flowers."

Mel's expression changed from friendly to confused. She wasn't sure she heard him correctly.

"Advice on what?"

"Flowers. I know that doesn't make any sense to you. Let me explain."

Parker leaned on the counter like he was going to whisper, even though no one else was in the office.

"I would like to send Jenn some flowers. You are her best friend. I thought that you could give me some suggestions on what her favorite flowers are. I'm interested in making a grand expression. I want to impress her."

"You do? What's the occasion?" In her mind, Mel was rolling her eyes. *This is going to be interesting.*

"You and I have chatted a few times. I feel like I can confide this in you. I am interested in possibly beginning a relationship with Jenn."

Oh, boy.

"I want to break the ice in that regard, so to speak. In Europe, men often make grand gestures, expressions of interest, with flowers. I don't want to send Jenn roses if she loves daisies."

Mel was relieved that the phone rang, a distraction from the conversation.

"Excuse me a moment, Parker. Imogene is at lunch, so I need to answer this call."

"Certainly." Parker walked over to a display of brochures.

While Mel was helping the person on the phone, Imogene returned. Mel watched the two interact for a few moments before ending the call she was on.

"I hope you had a good lunch, Imogene. I'm going to take Mr. Bentley back to my office for a brief chat. The visitor who just called is planning a large family reunion here next spring. She would like to have our visitor packets sent to these addresses."

Mel laid the clipboard she'd been using back on Imogene's desk as the young woman sat down in her chair.

"Yes, ma'am. We will get those out in today's mail."

"You can come on back to my office, Parker."

Parker followed Mel to her office in the back of the building. He sat down in a chair across from her desk while she maneuvered to her own chair.

"Flowers. You want to send Jenn flowers."

"Yes. I think I'm sensing some hesitance on your part. Does Jenn not like flowers? Does she have allergies, perhaps?"

Parker leaned back in the chair. Mel thought to herself that the man looked like many of the wealthier 'temporary citizens' that the ocean-front community attracted.

"I'm not aware of Jenn having any flower allergies. As far as I know, she loves flowers. She had a beautiful garden of them at her home in Atlanta."

Mel could see an expression of relief cross Parker's face. *Poor guy.*

"Great! I was hoping that flowers were the right choice. Jewelry seemed too extravagant at this point in our relationship."

Oh, boy.

"Have you talked to Jenn at all about your interest in her? You do realize that she is newly divorced?"

"Our conversations so far have stayed on quite neutral and safe topics. I realize that she has had a rough year. I haven't gotten the impression that she was *that* heartbroken about her marriage ending. Maybe I've read her wrong. My impression was that it might have been coming on for a long time."

"That's true, in some respects. Jenn was married a long time though. The divorce has been a serious change in her life. I think you would be wise to talk to her a little before you make a 'grand gesture,' as you've called it. I wouldn't want either of you to be unnecessarily hurt or embarrassed."

Mel could tell by Parker's body language that he might not be used to someone contradicting his ideas or, perhaps, turning down his advances. *His feathers are ruffled.* Mel smirked to herself.

"You're a good friend to Jenn. That's why I came to get your opinion about the flowers. I can't imagine that *any* woman would be hurt by receiving flowers from someone who cares for her." Parker rose from the chair. "I will see what this local florist, Petals I believe it is called, has in stock, or what they can order that would be a beautiful expression of my feelings for Jenn. Thanks for your time. I trust that you will keep this conversation between us."

Before Mel could say another word, Parker was out of her office and quickly on his way to the door. She watched him wave to Imogene as he exited.

"Not tell Jenn. Fat chance, buddy. You'll be lucky if I don't tell Randy."

"It's time for you to tell me. How was it meeting Sinclair's children?"

Mel figured Jenn hadn't eaten lunch, so thirty minutes after Parker left, Mel showed up at the newspaper office with two chef salads. It took a lot of chewing, especially when someone had just asked a question. Jenn watched her anxiously. Finally, Mel swallowed.

"His children were nice."

"Nice? That's it."

Jenn stared Mel down. Mel was starving, but she dared not take another bite of salad before she gave Jenn more information.

"Benjamin and Regina were friendly. Regina asked me a lot of questions. Benjamin mainly talked to his father. I'm sure they were sizing me up."

"As you were doing them." Jenn began eating. "This is a fabulous salad. Where did you get it? I need to know where I can get another one, maybe daily. Yum."

"Don't laugh. It came from the convenience store a couple of blocks away. The salads and sandwiches there are so fresh. They make their own sandwich bread and rolls."

Jenn was silent for a moment. She stopped eating.

"Jenn don't be a food snob. I know it's convenience store food, but it's different. You just said it was delicious."

"It is. That's not why I stopped eating. Do you know who operates the convenience store now?"

"The same family who started it. Oh, I can't remember the last name. I know all of them by their first names."

"Nguyen."

"That's it. How did you know that?"

"When I was a reporter years ago, I did a story about the father."

"Oh, yes. His murder. It was such a sad time. That's still an unsolved crime."

"How did the family manage to keep the business? Most of the children were quite young."

"Someone stepped in and paid the mortgage off. The person gave the building free and clear to Mrs. Nguyen. Others assisted her by working in the store until she could get past the grief enough to go back to work. I'm surprised you don't know that part of the story."

"That's amazing. I guess I had already moved to Atlanta by the time that happened. I can't believe what a coincidence this is. Last night, I told Randy about writing the story about the murder. I hadn't thought about it in a long time."

"I'm surprised you didn't know because it was your grandfather who paid off the mortgage."

"What? Gramps did that? I had no idea. How wonderful!"

"There wasn't any publicity about it, but word got around. Your grandfather had his own quiet way of helping others. As I understand, that's not the only such story."

"We think we know our family. We probably only scratch the surface."

"It's true." Mel continued eating. "This bread is what makes this salad, in my opinion. Zucchini bread with a chef salad. It's a wonderful combination."

"It is. Yummy yum." Jenn took another bite of the bread. "Now, get back to telling me about meeting Sinclair's children."

"There really wasn't anything noteworthy that was discussed. As I said, Benjamin didn't talk to me much. Regina asked what her father was like as a teenager. I told a story or two, mostly about his athletics. They were pleasant, curious. Sinclair downplayed our dating days. I'm sure he doesn't want to diminish his relationship with their mother in their eyes. I get that. Their whole history is based on Sinclair and Dana getting married."

"You're right. I hadn't thought about that."

"Dana was not mentioned. They talked a little bit about their lives. That portion was a little guarded."

"Brace yourself. I'm going to ask one of those hard questions that only a long-term best friend can ask without being rude."

"Your questions have always been stellar, Jenn. It's the reporter in you." Mel winked.

"I'm thinking about how to best word this question to get to the heart of what I'm curious about." Jenn continued chewing her food for a moment. "In light of the circumstances which led to their existence, how did it feel to sit across from Sinclair's two children?"

Mel smiled. Jenn always managed to get to the heart of a situation. She could see all the veils Mel threw up to guard the sensitive part of Mel's soul.

"Surreal." Mel took a deep breath before she said the truth of what was in her heart. "At one point, I looked at each of them and thought, 'you could have been mine.' I quickly stopped myself from that thinking.

That type of mindset is what led me to wasting the first decade after Sinclair and I broke up, dwelling on what might have been. There's no good that can come from it. It's a waste of time and emotion."

"That's some mighty healthy thinking, Mel. I know it's taken you a lot of years to be able to recognize that."

"There's no doubt that I have loved Sinclair since I was seventeen. Despite how heartbroken and angry I was for many years, that really didn't diminish my feelings for him. I did learn to put those feelings away and move on. You might say they sat in a box in the closet. I never expected to take that box out again. Now that I have a second chance, I've decided to not waste it. How many people get a second chance in life for anything? To have a chance to fall in love again with the love of your life, well, shame on me if I waste it."

"I love hearing this." Jenn reached over, squeezing Mel's hand. "It's like a rebirth, isn't it?"

"It truly is. I feel so young, but with an incredible amount of wisdom at the same time." Mel bit her bottom lip, and then smiled. "I do not expect Sinclair's children to immediately warm up to me. They need to be cautious. Their father being with another woman is a big change for them. Despite how guarded they seemed in some ways, I did also see an openness. It was less about what they said and more about their expressions. Several times, I noticed that Regina would look at her father and then look at me. She watched how he interacted with me, and a little smile would cross her face."

"One of the things I've learned about divorce is that if you have raised your children to be good, caring humans, they want happiness for those they love. I'm thankful that Simon and I did not part before our kids were adults. It made the process easier all the way around. Each of my children has talked to me about my happiness and how they understand that I was unhappy for a long time."

"I'm sure that was a meaningful exchange between you and them. I sense that, perhaps, Sinclair's children may have similar feelings. I didn't sense any resistance to the idea of their father having another relationship. I'm sure they are concerned who that person might be and if the person will be good to their father and make him happy."

"I've encouraged the kids to be good to Simon's new wife. Despite all the circumstances that led to him remarrying, Kenzie is the person Simon has chosen. My children should give her a chance and make their own judgments about her as a person based on *their* interaction with her, not on my opinions. If I have a real relationship with someone else, I hope my children will get to know that person and give him the same chance they are giving Kenzie."

"That's quite open-minded on your part, Jenn. No one said that adulting was going to be easy. I never imagined it would be so complicated." After eating the last bite of her salad, Mel closed the lid on the box. "I hope to have the opportunity to get to know Sinclair's children and be a part of their lives. Only time will tell regarding how any of this will turn out."

There was a gentle knock on the door. Mel looked up and saw the door slowly open. She couldn't see who it was because the person was hidden behind a gigantic vase of mostly white and pale pink flowers. Mel cringed, realizing that she hadn't warned Jenn. It soon became apparent that it was Doris carrying the flowers that were almost as big as the petite woman.

"You have a delivery from Petals, Jenn."

"Oh, my goodness." Jenn stood up from her chair. "Who in the world could these be from? The bouquet is huge. You usually don't get arrangements this big until you die."

Mel snorted at Jenn's comment. *It was true.*

"There's a card, Jenn. I'm going to set them here on this table." Doris gently put the large vase down. "Whew! That was heavier than I expected. Someone certainly wants to impress you." Doris left the room.

"I wonder who this could possibly be from?" Jenn leaned in to smell some of the flowers. "It must have cost a fortune."

"Ah, Jenn, I think I may know who sent it."

"Mel, I really hope Randy has not done this. It's way too much money to spend—"

"It's not Randy. You might want to sit down."

Jenn's brow furrowed, slowly sitting down next to the table that held the flowers. "I cannot even imagine what you are about to say."

"Do you want to look at the card first?"

"No, I'd rather let whatever is going to shock me come from you." Jenn scowled.

"I believe they are from Parker Bentley. He came to see me earlier today."

"Parker? Why in the world would he be sending me flowers?" Jenn's eyes darted back and forth. "Oh, I bet I know. He's decided to sell the house. He's trying to cushion the news. That isn't necessary. He certainly has the right to do whatever he wants with that property. It will seem strange for the property to not be owned by his family anymore, but I certainly understand—"

"Jenn, stop! That's not why he sent you flowers. Maybe you should go ahead and read the card. That may help me explain our conversation."

Jenn stared at Mel for a few moments before she rose and took the card off the holder. Sitting back down, she slowly opened the little envelope, still looking at Mel.

"I'm afraid to read this now."

"Stop worrying. It may make more sense to you than it did to me. I don't really know how much you've interacted with him since you've moved back."

"We've only talked a few times. You've been there for some of those meetings. We've basically been friendly neighbors. I've not had much time to have any lengthy conversations."

Jenn pulled the card out of the envelope. Mel watched her face while she read the words. Jenn's expression went from confusion to amusement.

"Surely, Parker is not serious." Jenn looked from the card to Mel.

"What does the card say?"

"'You never answered my question. Will you marry me?'"

"What?" Mel walked closer to Jenn.

"Read it yourself." Jenn handed the card to Mel.

Mel read the card. It didn't make any more sense to Mel to see it in black-and-white then it did to hear Jenn say the words. "Parker didn't mention anything about a proposal. Has he talked to you about his feelings?"

"No!"

"Then what does he mean by 'you never answered my question?'"

Jenn took the card back from Mel, staring intently at it. Mel watched Jenn's eyes dart back and forth again, like she was searching her memory for information. Suddenly, her eyes grew big.

"He couldn't possibly be referring to when we were kids, could he?"

"Did he ask you to marry him then?" Mel shook her head in disbelief.

"Well, I remember the summer I started school, my grandparents and Parker's grandparents had a big party. It was like a luau. The Bentleys hired a caterer who brought in a big pig to roast and there were all sorts of food like you have at a luau in Hawaii. My grandfather found a band to come and play Hawaiian music and teach everyone how to hula."

"That sounds like fun. What does it have to do with Parker asking you to marry him?"

"They dressed Parker and I up like a little Hawaiian couple. We had the cutest outfits. I wore flowers in my hair." Jenn reached for her head, like she was remembering the headpiece. "Did you ever see the Elvis Presley movie, *Blue Hawaii*?"

"Of course, your mother loved Elvis. We watched all his movies growing up."

"Yes, I forgot. Well, the band performed the *Hawaiian Wedding Song* and had Parker and I play the roles of the bride and the groom. We did a little walk into the group, like a wedding ceremony. It was sweet. After the ceremony was over, Parker leaned over to me and whispered in my ear, 'Will you marry me when we get big?' I guess that's what he's talking about."

"That's a sweet story. It seems sort of strange that after all these years, Parker is bringing it up."

"Especially since we haven't had any contact in close to fifty years. He can't be serious. Maybe this is an elaborate prank. He's a wealthy jetsetter. Maybe this is what he does for fun."

"Jenn, I don't think he's joking. He was quite serious when he visited me this morning. He seemed rather sure of himself. He seemed certain that you would be pleased to receive such a display of affection."

"I don't know how he got that idea." Jenn took a deep breath. "What do you think I should do about this?"

"I'm not sure. It's not like he's a total stranger, and yet, he sort of is. You truly don't know anything about this adult version of your childhood friend. He could be dangerous."

"I can't imagine that the Bentleys' grandson would be dangerous. His family has been best friends with my family for generations."

"That's true. But Parker spent the bulk of his life in the company of others. You don't know who Parker Bentley is. He may be a lovesick middle-aged man trying to connect with his first love. He could also be someone entirely different. Maybe the first thing you should do is call Parker. Perhaps you will get an inkling into his mindset."

"I don't think I have his cell phone number."

"I may have that back at my office from when he came in to find a realtor. I must get back to the office anyway; I have a meeting to attend. I will have Imogene do a quick search to see if we have Parker's number." Mel pulled Jenn into a quick hug before she began to exit the room. "If you do call him, I would suggest that you have someone else listen in with you, maybe Doris. Another person might pick up on things you do not. I need to be at this meeting, or I would be right here with you."

"I understand. This isn't a situation that either of us imagined. He's probably harmless. I must say that such a large bouquet makes me uncomfortable. It's too extravagant."

"Like you said, Parker is wealthy. This might not seem extravagant to him." Mel looked at her watch. "I've got to go. Please keep me posted. I'll call you after my meeting is over."

About fifteen minutes later, Mel sat in the board room of the Municipal Building ready to discuss plans for the seafood festival. Imogene texted her that she had sent Jenn the phone number Mel requested. Looking up, Mel was surprised to see Randy enter the room. The Police Chief normally sent one of his lieutenants or sergeants to participate in planning meetings for the logistics of the festival. Randy nodded at Mel as he sat down. Looking at him more closely, she thought that he looked tired and angry. It was not a pleasant combination. Mel wondered what had put her friend in this state. She also considered that his mood would not improve if he knew about the gift Jenn had received. Randy Nave would be a force to reckon with where Jenn Halston was concerned. *I almost feel sorry for Parker...almost.*

Chapter Nine

Jenn

"Hello, Parker, how are you today?"

After receiving the phone number from Imogene, Jenn called Doris into her office and explained the situation. The woman was visibly shocked. She quickly agreed to be Jenn's second set of ears. Alice, the newspaper's bookkeeper, was taking care of the front desk.

"I'm wonderful, Jenn. It's so great to hear from you."

"Parker, the reason I am calling is about the beautiful bouquet of flowers that appeared in my office this afternoon."

"I'm so happy you received the delivery. I was pleasantly surprised at the selection of flowers that Petals had in stock. I imagine they do a fair number of high-end weddings and special events in the area. I was glad to see their quality of flowers was up to par. Beautiful flowers for a beautiful friend."

Jenn looked at Doris. Her head was down. It appeared that she was writing every word of the conversation. Because of the quickness of the conversation, Jenn was glad to see that Doris still knew how to take shorthand. The notebook in front of her was filled with all sorts of squiggly lines.

"That's quite kind of you, Parker. It wasn't necessary though. I was happy to learn that you were able to reconnect with your family in your grandfather's latter days."

"It was meant to be, Jenn. I now understand that I was destined to return to Serendipity so that I could also reconnect with an old and dear friend." Parker's voice was strong and serious.

"That's how I thought you felt, Parker. You really didn't need to go to such an expense to remind this old friend of our little luau adventure. It is a sweet memory from a long time ago."

"I want us to have more sweet memories, Jenn. Perhaps my declaration was daring and too much, but that doesn't diminish my sentiment. I believe that those two little ones were destined to be together. Circumstances that were beyond our control prevented that a long time ago. Fate has dealt us another chance. I hope you will take a little time to consider this idea. In the meantime, enjoy those flowers; they are a symbol of my serious intent. I will give you time to think about it and await your response."

The call ended before Jenn could say another word. Doris looked at her with an expression of confusion that mirrored Jenn's feelings.

"That was strange. I don't know this man, but I certainly know his grandparents. They were not strange, in any sense of the word. You've not asked me my opinion, but I'm afraid you will have to hear it nonetheless."

Jenn smiled. *I love this woman.*

"I don't know this Parker person, but I certainly knew his grandparents. He sounds quite pompous and haughty. Walter and Zella Bentley were the richest people to ever live in Serendipity. They had a beautiful home built by your grandfather. Those two men worked hard together and reaped material rewards from it. Walter was never pompous. He drove vehicles that were at least ten years old, when he could afford to buy a new one each year. Zella altered her own clothes and cooked most all the meals in that big house. She was not haughty. Parker's father, Jearl, was an unusual one, mostly from suffering ill health most of his life. The woman he married, Parker's mother, was only interested in the Bentley money. That was the wedge that drove a son from his parents. Parker spent too much time away from the people who could have given him a grounded upbringing. That's not his fault. It does explain what you are dealing with now." Doris reached across the desk and took Jenn's hand. "I'm still here at this newspaper because you are here. You are family, Jenn. Please be careful."

"I appreciate your words of wisdom and explanation, Doris. You *are* family to me, too."

Doris released Jenn's hand, picked up her notebook and pen. The woman shook her head, muttering under her breath as she glanced at the flowers on her way out.

"I thought these were from Randy. I should have known he has more sense than this. He knows that you express love by your actions, not through things. I'll have this typed up for you before the end of the day. It goes without saying that I shall speak of this to no one."

Jenn rubbed her head. The situation had taken way too much of her day. Glancing at her email, she saw that her inbox was full, and it was almost four o'clock. Checking her phone revealed a text from Mel stating that it would be closer to five before her meeting was over. Jenn was surprised that she did not have any messages from Randy. She hoped that his long day was not still going on. Maybe he'd been able to go home early and was taking a well-deserved nap. She wondered how she would explain the flowers to him.

"There must be close to a hundred flowers in that vase." Jenn stood up and looked at them again. "This is too many flowers to be in this small office. The aroma is becoming overwhelming. It smells like a funeral in here."

Jenn opened her office door and walked toward Doris' desk. The woman was fervently typing. She was so intent on her work, that she didn't notice Jenn standing next to her until Jenn cleared her throat. Doris jumped.

"I'm sorry. I didn't see you."

"You were in your work zone, Doris. Don't apologize. I'm sorry that I startled you. The smell of those flowers is driving me nuts. What can I do with them?"

"Have them delivered back to him?" Doris lowered her voice, looking around.

"I don't think that's a good idea. He is my neighbor, remember?"

"Okay. Why don't you ask Teresa, she's the owner of Petals, to take them back and make smaller arrangements to deliver to the nursing home? I bet she could make at least ten small arrangements out of that bouquet."

"That's a wonderful idea. Her shop is about a block away, right?"

"Yes, on this side of the street."

"I think I will go in the back and get a cart and roll that bouquet back to the shop. That would be way easier than putting it into a vehicle."

"I agree."

"You did what?"

Jenn laughed at Mel's reaction to how she disposed of the flowers.

"It was Doris' idea. I think it was a great one. Teresa was happy to accommodate."

"What are you going to tell Parker?"

"Nothing. He sent me the flowers. They were mine to use as I see fit. There were so many of them, the smell was getting to me. I also didn't want Randy to walk into my office and wonder who sent them."

"That's a good idea. I hadn't thought of that. Randy was at the meeting I was in."

"Oh, I haven't heard from him today. He told me last night that he had to go in extra early this morning. If he was in a late afternoon meeting, he's had a long day."

"Randy looked tired and angry."

"Angry? How so?"

"I don't know. We only interacted regarding the meeting topic. He left about fifteen minutes before the meeting was over. He was a gruff version of the man I know. It could have been that he just had a bad day."

"I hope that's all it was. There must be a full moon this week. Everything seems off."

"Okay. I just wanted to stop by before I head home." Mel picked up her car keys. "Are you planning on working late?"

"Not too long. I need to catch up on some emails. I feel like I lost a couple of hours today with the Parker situation. Would you like to have a transcript of my conversation with him?"

"What?" Mel was almost at the door. She turned around with a confused look on her face.

"I followed your suggestion and asked Doris to listen in on my phone call with Parker. I put him on speaker phone. Doris sat quietly. She took shorthand of the whole conversation and typed it up before she left. I'll email you a copy."

"Wow! I'm impressed. I hope you don't need it for any reason."

"I don't think I will. I think Parker is harmless. He may have some wild ideas about what might happen between us, but I don't think he is dangerous. I'm going to let a few days pass then I'm going to try to talk to him."

"I would suggest that someone is nearby when you do that."

"I've already thought about that and think I will invite him here to my office."

"Plenty of people nearby who want the boss to be okay. Good idea." Mel looked at her watch. "I've got to run. I've let Mia run out of her favorite food. It will be a serious situation if I don't get to the pet store before it closes. Don't work too late. Text me later."

"Will do. Thanks for your listening ear today."

"My pleasure."

Jenn followed Mel to the door so that she could lock it behind her. There were still a couple of employees in the newsroom and in layout, but the front door was locked after business hours.

After she returned to her desk, Jenn spent the next half hour going through her emails. Looking down at her cell phone, she saw a text from her youngest daughter, Emily, asking if Jenn had time to talk. Jenn hit the call button on her phone. Emily quickly answered.

"Hi, Mom."

"Hello, my darling. How's my favorite youngest daughter today?"

"Well, it's been a weird day. I think there must be a full moon."

"You, too." Jenn laughed. "My day has been bizarre as well."

"Does that mean Dad called you?"

Jenn noticed a hesitance in Emily's voice.

"No, I haven't heard from your father. Is something wrong?"

"Good grief. Where do I start? Apparently, there's been a storm brewing in the *new* Young household. Dad asked the three of us to have a group phone call with him last night. We found a time that worked for all of us. I thought that maybe he wanted to talk about us having a quick visit with him before Foster moves. That wasn't it. Dad had news. It was bigger news than the last time he called us."

Bigger news than Simon becoming a father again for the first time in over twenty years. *This I've got to hear.*

"That sounds interesting, Emily."

"Oh, you are going to find it interesting."

Jenn pictured her youngest, rather dramatic, daughter pacing in her apartment, arms gesturing in different directions as she spoke. Jenn stifled a giggle. She was tired.

"Go ahead, I'm listening."

"Dad and Kenzie are splitting up. He says that he will fully support Kenzie and their child. He doesn't want to have a second family."

"It's a little late for him to be making such a decision. That family has already been created." Jenn shook her head in disgust. This was classic Simon. He wanted things his way. For once, Jenn felt sorry for Kenzie. The young woman had no idea what she'd gotten herself into. Jenn hoped Kenzie had a supportive family.

"I know. That's not all. He asked us about you. He wanted to know if the three of us would help him reconcile with you."

Having just taken a drink of water from a nearby bottle, Jenn immediately spewed the water onto the screen of her computer, choking before it was over.

"He wants to do what?" Jenn kept coughing.

"That was our reaction, too. None of us wanted to see you two get divorced, but we also knew that you two weren't happy, especially you. We're grown. It's more important that both of our parents are happy than that they are together."

Jenn smiled. She raised good humans. That knowledge filled her heart with joy.

"I'm glad you feel that way. What makes your father think I would even consider reconciling?"

"Dad has no concept what a sexy vibrant woman you are. I bet you already have a boyfriend."

Jenn remained silent. Emily was the calculating one of her children. She didn't say things unless she knew things.

"It's okay, Mom. We are excited for you."

Still silent, Jenn knew Emily would eventually spill the beans. She also couldn't keep a secret.

"That photo was so cute."

Ugh. My children saw the kiss. Jenn couldn't blame Doris for this one.

"What photo are you talking about, honey?" Jenn held her breath, knowing what the answer was.

"There's a photo of you and Aunt Mel with two hunky older men on her social media page. It looks like it was taken on your deck. You can see the ocean in the distance."

Jenn breathed a sigh of relief. She rarely looked at social media. Even more rarely since she'd moved to Serendipity.

"Those are some old friends of ours. We had dinner with them the other night. We were all in high school together."

"The dark-haired man wasn't looking at you like you were an old friend, Mom. You must have not seen the photo. Anyway, I hope you do find someone wonderful who appreciates you. Dad had a lot of chances.

His time is up. All three of us basically told him that. As usual, he didn't listen. He says he's coming to see you. I wanted you to be warned."

Mercury must be in retrograde. This day was spinning into another galaxy. Jenn could hardly believe that she had three men in pursuit. Thankfully, she was, at least, interested in only one of them. She longed to be sitting next to *that* one on her couch, relaxing with a nice glass of wine.

"Thank you, Emily. Should I expect a call from your sister and brother about this or are you the designated reporter?"

"Well, you know that Foster is busy getting ready to move. Claire is preoccupied. I told them I would inform you."

Jenn was concerned about Claire. She knew that something was off in her oldest child's life. She had suspected for some time that her daughter's marriage was in trouble. Prying was not the way to reach Claire. She came into the world three weeks late. Claire did things in her own time. Jenn would wait.

"Again, I thank all three of you for your concern and worry. I think I can handle this situation, *if* it presents itself. Until then, I'm going to pretend that I never heard this. Maybe it will blow over. For Kenzie's sake, I hope so."

"I don't know. Dad sounds firm. Claire told me this morning that Dad had already moved into a condo downtown."

Jenn knew that once Simon reached a decision, he rarely changed his mind. She could not understand how he expected to be able to walk away from his new wife and unborn child. Simon's midlife crisis was getting out of hand.

"I hope your classes are continuing to go well. Keep in touch with your sister, okay? She's going to miss having Foster nearby."

"Will do, Mom. I'll catch up with you later. Love you, bunches."

"Love you, sweet girl."

Ending the call, Jenn saw that no other messages were waiting. It was almost seven o'clock. Jasper would be anxious for her to come home and let him out. Before she shut down her computer, Jenn remembered to send the transcript of her conversation with Parker to Mel. That would give something for her best friend to stew on tonight. Wait till she heard about the latest development with Simon. It was indeed a strange day.

Lyle was still in his office. She yelled a goodnight to him as she went out the front, locking the door behind her. Looking up, she saw a bright full moon in the sky.

That explains a lot.

"Michelle is excited about her interview, Mom."

Jenn answered a phone call from Foster while she put together a quick bowl of chicken, rice, and veggies from leftovers in her fridge.

"I'm happy to hear that. My Advertising Director, Betsy Lawson, is overseeing the process. I will be in the room for the interview, but Betsy and another staff member are running the show. Tell Michelle that my team knows our connection and have been advised to treat her like any other applicant. They promise me that they will not hold her being my daughter-in-law against Michelle."

"Good one, Mom. Michelle will get a kick out of that. If it works out, it works out. If not, I'm sure my talented wife will find something equally wonderful."

"Absolutely. Are you all packed?"

"There are literally boxes everywhere. I'd love to have a moving truck in our driveway that we could gradually fill with boxes over the next week and a half, but the funny thing is that moving truck companies want you to pay for those trucks by the day, whether they are moving anything or not."

"Isn't that something? The nerve of them!" Jenn chuckled.

"You are in a mighty good mood. Have you had a good day?"

That comment turned Jenn's chuckle to a snort. *I sound like Mel.*

"There's a full moon tonight. I've experienced it all day. Some extremely strange things have occurred."

"That doesn't sound good."

"Nothing life threatening or anything like that. Just bizarre occurrences. Including a phone call from your baby sister, which is probably the same reason you are calling."

"I hadn't heard from Emily. I wondered if she was able to reach you. I guess that news about Dad is on your list of bizarre occurrences."

"Most definitely. I've heard Emily's version. What's your take on your father's sudden change of heart?"

"Honestly, I don't think it's been sudden at all. He's my father and I love him. I do not *like* what he did to my mother. Affairs are for cowards. But he's been the classic clichéd midlife crisis man. It's like he hit his fifties and turned back into a teenager, all hormones and bad choices."

Jenn cackled in laughter, almost choking on the first bite of her food. In her mind, she could see her tall son, running his fingers through his curly brown hair, a serious expression on his face. Foster came into the world ready to be an adult.

"I have raised such a smart young man. You've hit the nail on the head. This may sound strange coming from me. I feel sorry for Kenzie. If you father is serious about ending their relationship, she's going to become a single parent. Granted, your father was not the most helpful of fathers, but he was there and provided some level of assistance with your care once the three of you were each out of the toddler stage."

"I've raised such a wonderful mother." Foster laughed at his repetition of his mother's comment. "I'm not the least bit surprised that you are thinking about Kenzie, even if she was the other woman. I think Dad is serious. He's already moved out. I tried to talk to him about it and get him to reconsider. No luck. He won't listen to reason. Did Emily tell you what he said about you?"

"Emily said he wants you three to convince me to reconcile. He's lost his mind, Foster."

"I know, Mom. We all know. Dad had the best and he let her slip through his fingers."

"I'm going to correct you, son. Simon pushed me away. Little by little, year after year, he made a life without me."

Jenn stopped, thinking about her own words. She never verbalized it before in that way. *It's the truth.*

"We did not encourage him in any way. I'll try talking some sense into him again. He's determined to travel to Serendipity and try to win you back."

"Good grief! What will I do with him if he comes here? That's overstepping the bounds of divorce. There should be laws that keep your ex-spouse from visiting your new location."

"Unless you've got your own police officer to enforce it, I think you are out of luck."

Jenn held her breath for a moment, wondering if Foster possibly knew some of the same information his sister did. When he didn't say anything further, she exhaled. How ironic that he would say such a thing.

"I'm not going to waste any more time thinking about that now. Simon will shake that idea in a few days. He'll remember what it was like to be married to me and he'll run in the other direction."

"For your sake, I hope you are right. I'll tell you though, Dad sounded mighty sentimental the other night. He was talking about your honeymoon and first apartment. He sounded quite sad."

"Simon has backed himself into a corner. He probably thinks that if he turns back time the other situation will go away."

"You're probably right. In a couple of weeks, I'll be nearby. If Dad comes to town, I can run interference."

"I can handle your father, Foster. I will always be his friend, because of my precious three. Our marriage is over. He will have to face that."

After their conversation ended, Jenn finished her meal. She considered texting Randy but thought he might be resting from his long day.

"Maybe I'll call him in the morning and see if he would like to meet for breakfast."

Jenn talked to Jasper while she took him out for his last walk of the evening. Looking over at the Bentley house, Jenn saw lights on in several rooms. With the calls from Emily and Foster about their father, Jenn had momentarily forgotten about her encounter with Parker. She really thought the best idea at the time was for her to ignore the situation. Maybe he would come to his senses. For the first time, Jenn thought that it might be a good thing for him to sell his family home. Perhaps, their friendship needed to stay in the past.

"The interviews begin at nine o'clock. Is that right, Betsy?"

After unsuccessfully trying to reach Randy to meet for breakfast, Jenn grabbed a large cup of coffee and a slice of quiche at The Frosted Goddess before heading into work early. A day of interviewing meant not a lot of time for other work.

"Yes, Jenn. Half our interviews are in the morning, then a break for lunch, then the remainder in the afternoon. Ellie set everything up in the conference room. We have a virtual meeting session for each candidate that is scheduled to begin promptly at the top of the hour."

"That sounds great. I expect for you and Ellie to run these sessions. I will, for the most part, remain in the background. The main questions that I wish to ask are on your list."

"I was quite impressed with the diversity of backgrounds of each person we are interviewing. While two people have media-related experience, all the candidates' resumes include a solid history in sales." Betsy looked down at the tablet she was holding while she stood in front of Jenn's desk. "Ellie also arranged for a boxed meal to be delivered for us. That way we don't have to worry about someone running out to get lunch. We thought that would give a little time to discuss the first three candidates."

"Excellent idea! I'm going to take the next thirty minutes and see if I can get caught up on some of the emails I skimmed through last evening. If you don't see me in the conference room when I should be, come and get me. I might have fallen down an email hole."

"Certainly. I'll see you in about thirty minutes."

After Betsy left, Jenn retrieved her cell phone from her purse to see if Randy had responded to her earlier message. She found a brief response, 'I'm sorry. Busy morning.' Thinking about Mel's description of Randy's frame of mind during the meeting they were both in the previous afternoon, Jenn wondered if something was going on with him.

"This is one of the reasons I was afraid of getting into a relationship with everything else I have going right now." Jenn talked to herself while scrolling through the unopened emails in her inbox. "I'm going to overthink something that is probably simple."

Jenn ate the last bite of her quiche, following it with the remaining coffee in her cup. Looking in the direction of her coffee maker, she decided that another dose of caffeine would probably be good to have with her for the interviews. Throwing the disposable cup away when she reached the coffee maker, Jenn chose a French Roast pod to make a fresh cup for the meeting. While that was brewing, she returned to her desk.

An email from Lyle drew her attention. He was asking if she was still interested in him reaching out to Sinclair Lewis for an interview. While Jenn initially planned to do the interview herself, Lyle was now writing the series about individuals who had returned to Serendipity. The first article would be about Jenn. Lyle already had several people on his list to feature, including Sinclair.

Responding to Lyle with an affirmative answer, Jenn asked when he planned for the series to begin running. Jenn read and responded to a few more emails before glancing at the clock, seeing that it was time for her to head to the conference room. A surge of excitement raced through her thinking that one of the six people they were about to interview would probably soon be a member of her team.

The morning flew by. Jenn was impressed with the caliber of candidates they were meeting. Moments after Ellie hit the 'leave' button for the third virtual meeting, Doris tapped lightly on the door and wheeled in a small cart with their lunch.

"My goodness! Those last two candidates were outstanding. I think either one of them would do an impressive job."

Jenn opened the box that contained her lunch. It appeared to be an antipasto salad with grilled chicken. Taking the first bite, Jenn moaned in delight.

"This is wonderful. Where did this come from? I'm in love."

"It's from a local caterer called More Please." Ellie opened her box. "They only do catered food. They do not have a restaurant."

"I love the name. It's exactly how I feel about their food. I can't imagine that they normally cater for only three people though. How did you get this food?"

"The company is one of our advertising clients. They have a secret service. A select group of previous clients can call when they need a couple of lunches. The owners normally prepare at least ten percent more food than they will need for a catering meal, just in case the numbers go up. If you are willing to accept whatever the meal of the day is, you can purchase a limited number of boxed lunches. We lucked up. More Please was catering a meal for the hospital board of directors that included many of the doctors. This is a great meal choice."

"I totally agree. Their food is delicious." Jenn was over halfway through her salad. She noticed that there were three smaller containers in the middle of the table. "Is that dessert?"

"Oh, yes!" Betsy jumped into the conversation. "Don't tell us you are on a diet, Jenn. You will not be able to resist their desserts. Do you know what it is, Ellie?"

"I do. It's one of your favorites, Betsy."

Jenn reached for a container. Inside, she found a piece of cake surrounded by slices of fresh peaches.

"Jackpot!" Betsy exclaimed when she opened her own box. "It's Fuzzy Navel Pound Cake."

"How creative! I bet these are local peaches." Jenn went back to finish her salad before digging into the dessert.

"Absolutely. Most of the food they use is from local or regional farmers markets or cooperatives."

"This was a great choice, Ellie. I'm also happy that we are using one of our advertisers. I need to take some time to study our list of clients and make sure that I am personally doing business with them as well."

"You can easily access that through the software program I showed you last week." Betsy turned her laptop around so that Jenn could see the screen. "The search function works several different ways including allowing you to search by name or business type. I think you will find it to be a quite useful tool once you play around with it and are more comfortable." Betsy demonstrated the search tool using the name of the caterer.

"That's impressive, but not as impressive as this cake I just put in my mouth." Jenn mumbled. "I don't know how they pulled it off, but this cake tastes just like a fuzzy navel cocktail. We've got to eat all of this before the next interview. It would be rude of us to be eating while we are asking the candidates questions. It would be too tempting having any left."

"You are absolutely right, boss." Betsy laughed, taking her first bite.

"I had to leave a little early yesterday for an appointment. How did the interview process go?"

When Jenn arrived the following morning, Doris was ready to chat.

"It was great. Betsy and Ellie handled the whole process. I listened. They are going to take a few days to check references and discuss each candidate. I will have final approval, of course. But I'm going to go with their choice. Since Michelle is one of the candidates, I want to stay completely neutral. I think the situation has made my overly confident daughter-in-law nervous. She even told us in the interview that she was applying for other jobs in the area." Jenn laughed. "That's not something you normally say to a potential employer."

"Oh, my goodness. Bless her heart. Michelle is a stellar salesperson, isn't she?"

"Record breaking. She was the top real estate agent in Atlanta three years in a row."

"I'm sure she will have no trouble securing a new position, here or with another company. I know you are excited to have Michelle and your son moving here."

"I am. It is quite the surprise. I didn't expect them to leave the Atlanta area. The world has become such a smaller place. Foster's job allows him to live anywhere and primarily work remotely. The travel his job includes can originate from any airport."

"It's truly amazing. It makes us feel closer even when we are thousands of miles apart."

Before the conversation could continue further, the phone rang, drawing Doris' attention. Jenn went on to her office knowing that there were many things for her to catch up on after spending the previous day in interviews. She'd barely reached her desk before Doris buzzed her.

"Jenn, you have a phone call on line one. The man says that his name is Simon Young."

"You've got to be kidding me, Doris."

"I am not. I believe that if I remember correctly, you were once married to a 'Simon Young.' I never met the man so I cannot for a certainty confirm his identity."

"Okay. Put him through. What a way to start the day!" Jenn paused, waiting for Doris to connect her. "This is Jenn Halston."

"I've not heard you say that name since we were dating. Did I know that you were dropping my name?"

Somehow, it didn't surprise Jenn that Simon would immediately mention her name change. He couldn't begin to understand why taking her maiden name back was important to her.

"Good morning to you, too, Simon. I hear that I should be congratulating you and Kenzie."

"Yeah, well, I wasn't going to begin this conversation with that; there's been a change in plans there."

"I don't imagine that you planned to have any more children unless they were those who might call you Grandpa."

"Oh, no, you and I are too young to be grandparents yet. We've still got a lot of *young* fun to have yet."

Jenn rolled her eyes while Simon laughed at his own joke.

"*You* have some *young* fun yet to have. I'll be having Halston fun. What can I do for you, Simon? I've got a busy day ahead. I don't have too much time to chat."

"I heard about that. Congratulations to you. I understand that you are a business owner now. I know that you hated leaving that little newspaper when we got married. It was the right decision though. We had a good life in Atlanta."

As much as she wanted to disagree with him, Jenn could not deny that they did indeed have a good life. Raising three healthy children who were now mature and independent adults was the most positive accomplishment that had come from their marriage. She was proud of that.

"We raised three wonderful children."

"Absolutely. I understand that one of them is moving in your direction. That will give me a great excuse to visit Serendipity. I always enjoyed the time we spent there."

Here it comes.

"I'm sure that Foster and Michelle will welcome your visits."

"What about you, Jenn, would you welcome a visit from me?"

Jenn allowed a few seconds of silence to hang between them.

"Simon, I don't believe that it is customary for ex-husbands to visit their ex-wives. There might have even been something in the divorce decree about that." Jenn closed her eyes, shaking her head. She knew she was stretching the truth. It felt good though.

"That's the thing, Jenn. I've got to confess I think I was a bit hasty with that divorce thing."

Divorce thing. Good grief.

"I disagree, Simon. I think it was the appropriate next step for us. I'm thrilled that you have been able to start a new life. You were so busy when our kids were small, maybe you can really embrace being a hands-on father to your new baby." Jenn wished she had a fresh cup of coffee to get the horrible taste of those words out of her mouth.

"I don't think that's going to work out. Kenzie and I have separated. I'm thinking about making a real change in my life. Maybe leaving Atlanta and starting over somewhere else."

"Simon, you can't be serious. You and Kenzie are still newlyweds. She is expecting your child. This is *your* responsibility." Jenn couldn't believe she was counseling Simon on his marriage.

"I will certainly support Kenzie and the child financially. She's the one who wanted to have a child. I already have three."

"Simon, please tell me that this is not why you called. Get to the point. I have a staff meeting within the next hour."

"I wanted to ask you if it would be okay if I came to see you."

"You mean, you want to stop by my office and say hello when you come to visit your son and daughter-in-law?"

"No, I want to come and see my wife."

"Your wife lives in Atlanta."

"I made the wrong decision, Jenn. I didn't realize what life would be like without you."

Neither did I. It's wonderful.

"Simon, you chose another person and another life, remember?"

"I made a mistake. You know how hard that is for me to admit. We had a lot of great years together. Don't I deserve a second chance?"

Great was a stretch.

"You made a choice, Simon. You've got some real responsibilities to live up to."

"I just want to see you, Jenn. I need someone to talk to about all of this. You've always understood me."

"Simon, I am busy with my new life. I've got a growing business to focus on and a new home to enjoy. Serendipity is my home. I'm sure that Foster and Michelle will want you to visit them some time in the future. I'm not extending the same invitation to my ex-husband who is now a husband and upcoming father to another."

That felt good.

"Surely you must miss me a little. It's been thirty years since you were single. I think I was the only guy you dated in college. You must be lonely."

Jenn closed her eyes, taking a deep breath. She didn't want to play games with Simon. She didn't want to reveal too much about her personal life. But she wanted him to leave her alone.

"I've been seeing someone." Jenn bit her bottom lip, hating that she'd told her ex-husband something that she hadn't even shared with her children.

"Who? Some beach bum?" Simon snickered.

I'm so thankful I'm no longer married to this man.

"Simon, that's none of your business. But I will say that he is an old friend and a respected member of this community."

He's also handsome, caring, and he carries a gun for a living. Be afraid, Simon. Be very afraid.

Jenn chuckled.

"Whoever he is, he doesn't know you like I do."

"Simon, that's the first intelligent thing I've heard you say in this conversation. You are exactly right. He doesn't know the 'me' you knew. He knows, respects, and values the independent woman I am becoming. I've got to go. Please give my best regards to Kenzie and tell her that I hope she has an easy and healthy pregnancy."

"But Jenn—"

"Simon, I'm going to give you one piece of advice. Man up. Go back to your expectant wife and take care of her and your impending child. You've made your bed. You have the chance to do something for Kenzie and your child that you rarely did for me and ours when they were young—be there. I wish you well. Goodbye, Simon."

Jenn ended the call before he could respond.

"That felt good."

"It sounded good, too."

Jenn jumped, not realizing that Doris was standing in the doorway.

"I'm sorry, Jenn. I didn't mean to eavesdrop. Since I knew who you were talking to, I thought you might need a cup of coffee to sustain you through the conversation. I knew you hadn't had time yet to make your own pot. Lyle just brewed a fresh pot for the newsroom." Doris set the steaming mug in front of Jenn.

"I was wishing for that while I was on the call." Jenn picked up the mug, taking a small sip. "That's wonderful. Thank you. Did I sound tough enough?"

"I could almost see you in boxing gloves, hitting a punching bag. Rachel has told me a little about Simon. She said he was 'good on paper.'"

"That's the beginning of an accurate description. I'm sure Aunt Rachel got most of her information from my mother. I can't think of too many times through the years when Rachel and Simon were in the same room. He was a good provider. He was relatively easy to live with, in most ways. Simon wasn't very interested in my life or my dreams. It was all about him. The same situation may be playing out with his new marriage. My children told me that Simon has already separated from his new wife. She is about the age of our oldest daughter."

"I see." Doris nodded. "He went through a midlife crisis."

"You might say that. I think he was trying to recapture his youth. He didn't realize that when you marry a young woman it is like starting over. She is pregnant. I don't think Simon wants that responsibility again."

"So, you said that he has already left this new wife?"

"Yes. Simon thinks the answer to his new problem is to try to get back his old one."

"Goodness, no. My Jenn is smarter than that." Doris paused. "Unless she still loves him."

"I will always love Simon because he is the father of my three wonderful children. He was not a cruel man, in any way. We grew apart. I do not like that he used an affair as a reason to end our marriage. That was hurtful. I do not deny that it was past time for the marriage to end."

"Perhaps you should give me a photograph of him, so that I can be on the lookout."

"That's not a bad idea. He wants to come here for a visit. I'm sure he will do that when Foster and Michelle get settled."

"That settles it. Give me that photo. I will call the police if he comes through our front door." Doris began walking away from Jenn's desk. "More precisely, I will call the Chief of Police. I'm sure he would be happy to escort Simon to Foster's new home, or elsewhere."

Jenn watched Doris leave the room, wondering to herself why she hadn't heard from the Chief of Police herself.

CHAPTER TEN

Randy

"I NEVER MIND HEARING myself talk, buddy, but you've barely grunted a response through this whole lunch. What's going on with you?"

Randy knew he should have made up some excuse to not have lunch with Sinclair. Even though they had barely seen each other since they left high school, Sinclair had 'old friend radar.' He could tell when something was wrong with Randy.

"I'm tired. I've had to pull some long days. It's been one thing after another."

Sinclair stared at Randy, chewing his sandwich. "Nope. That's not it. Try again."

"Okay, Sinclair, I'll come clean, but you must promise not to discuss this with Mel."

"Randy, that's a tough one. I'm trying to be open and honest with Mel. She'll know if I'm hiding something from her about Jenn."

"I didn't say it was about Jenn. If you can't promise me, I'm not going to discuss it."

"But, man, you can talk to me about anything."

"Remember what we said back in the day in the locker room, bros before—"

"Then, it is about Jenn." Sinclair slammed his hand down on the table to make his point.

"It's more about me than her. I think I'm going to step back and give her some space."

"Why? What happened? Did you two have an argument?" Sinclair furrowed his brow.

"Nothing like that. I think I've been moving too fast. I'm assuming too much. Jenn has made a point of reminding me several times that she is recently divorced. She may not be interested in another relationship so soon. She may not want to be tied down to one person. I've spent all these years wondering what it might have been like for us to be together. During those years, Jenn has been living her own happily-ever-after with someone else. She's not been dreaming of me."

"Randy, I don't think you're making this up in your head. I think Jenn has always been interested in you. You're right that she built a life with someone else and probably never imagined that the two of you would ever be living in the same town again. Now that you are though, I think she's opened her mind and heart to the two of you being more than old friends. She is divorced, remember? That means that her happily-ever-after didn't stay that way."

"Maybe. But just because Jenn may have considered the thought doesn't mean that she's excluded the thought of all others." Randy took a deep breath, looking at his watch. "I've got to get back to the station. I've got a conference call with a couple of other chiefs in neighboring communities."

"You're leaving a lot out of this conversation. What's happened that is suddenly making you think Jenn doesn't want a relationship with you?"

"Again, don't tell Mel."

Sinclair made a gesture crossing his heart, followed by holding up his hand in a Boy Scouts symbol.

"We were never Boy Scouts." Randy shook his head.

"The sentiment still applies. I'm giving my oath of silence."

"There's another man who is interested in Jenn. He's making his move and I'm not sure I can compete. It's just like all those years ago. Jenn's out of my league." Randy threw down some money on top of his bill. "I've got to go. I'll catch up with you later."

On his way back to the police station, Randy was caught by the red light at the nearest corner to the newspaper office. Glancing at the parking spots across from the building, he saw the expensive vehicle that he saw Parker Bentley driving the day when Randy met him. He was surprised to see the man get out of his vehicle and walk toward the real estate office that was next to where the vehicle was parked.

"I've got to stop jumping to conclusions."

No sooner had the words left Randy's mouth before he saw Jenn walk out of her building with a young woman who Randy thought he remembered was on the advertising staff. The two of them crossed the street before the light changed entering the same office Parker had gone into.

"Why did I have to see that?" Randy let his foot off the brake when he saw the light change. "One thing probably has nothing to do with the other. But now I have that in my head."

Hearing his phone buzz on his belt, Randy pulled over a block later to check the call. It was a voicemail from Joe Fairfield telling Randy that he would be arriving in Serendipity in a few days.

"This is the sign I needed. I should be focusing on helping Joe prepare to testify while I also try to discover what made him quit police work. I cannot be distracted by someone like Parker Bentley."

Glancing at the clock in his vehicle, Randy looked in his rearview mirror before beginning to pull out. He immediately slammed on the brakes as Parker's fancy SUV quickly passed him. Randy knew that the fault was his, but he was mighty tempted to pull the guy over anyway. His better judgment won out when he remembered the conference call that he was supposed to be on in less than fifteen minutes.

Later that evening, Randy was warming up some leftovers when the dinging sound of a text drew his attention to the phone that lay on the counter. Beside Jenn's name were the words 'Hello Stranger.' In the short time since he and Jenn had become reacquainted, they'd quickly gone from meetings of coincidence in restaurants and grocery stores to, in recent weeks, daily phone conversations or in-person meetings. She was bound to be wondering why he had suddenly become scarce. Randy wasn't sure that he trusted himself to have a phone conversation quite yet. The thought of another man winning her heart was more than Randy could wrap his mind around.

Moments later, Jenn's first text was followed by another one. 'I've talked to my ex-husband more than you this week. That doesn't make me happy.'

Jenn certainly knew how to bait him. He needed to be cautious.

'It's been a busy week. We're still shorthanded.'

Without hesitation, her response came. 'I understand. Duty calls. Hope we can catch up soon. I miss my friend.'

Friend. Randy wanted to be more than friends. Maybe he should pay attention to the words Jenn used. Time passed while he stared at her last message. He hadn't responded when another one came in.

'Take care.'

That was about as generic as you could get. He'd left her no choice.

Randy backspaced over the 'Miss you' that he so desperately wanted to say to her.

'You, too.' Randy frowned when he hit the submit button. He was too old to be playing high school dating games.

A few moments later, Randy was taking his food out of the microwave when he heard his phone ring.

"Maybe she's decided to call me and see what's going on." Randy quickly grabbed his phone from where it still was on the counter. It was a call from Joe Fairfield. Randy had forgotten that he told Joe to call him this evening.

"Randy Nave."

"Hello, Chief Nave. This is Joe Fairfield. Have I caught you at a bad time?"

"Hey, Joe, you just saved me from eating some leftovers of my own cooking. How are you doing this evening?"

"I'm sorry, sir. I can call you back when you get into your office tomorrow."

"No need. This conversation won't take long. Do I understand correctly that you are planning on arriving in town on Thursday?"

"Ah, yes, sir. Mr. Greer said that he would like to spend some time on Friday reviewing the case and preparing me to testify on Monday. I really do appreciate you allowing me to stay at your house, Chief. I hope it's not a problem for me to stay over the weekend."

"Not a problem at all, Joe. I'm going to give you an assignment while you are here."

"Yes, sir. Anything you need me to do, I'll do it."

"That's the kind of response I like to hear from one of my officers. In this case, my assignment involves a local citizen." Randy paused, grinning to himself. "I expect you to call on a lovely young lady who works at First Bank of Serendipity. Maybe, if you are lucky, she will allow you to take her out."

"I'd like to do that, Chief. I don't know if I stand much of a chance with Megan at this point, sir. She wasn't expecting me to leave town like I did."

"None of us were. But the young lady I met a few weeks ago when I was looking for you seemed mighty sad that you had left. Miss Whitman made a special point to ask me to mention her to you. I don't think that sounds like she'll hang up the phone if you call."

"I don't know. It's been quite a while. She's probably got a boyfriend or at least a couple of fellows who are interested in her."

"I'm sure there are some who would like to turn her head. That doesn't mean she's interested in them."

Randy shook his head, hearing his own words. Maybe he needed to apply his own advice to Jenn. Just because Parker Bentley was interested in her, it didn't mean she returned the interest.

On the other end of the phone, he heard Joe rambling about not knowing what to say to Megan and that it would be awkward. It gave Randy an idea.

"Why don't I invite Megan to have dinner with us on Friday evening, and I'll invite one of my friends to join us?"

"Would this friend of yours be a lady? Because I'm not so sure that Megan will want to have dinner with three men."

"Yes, Joe. I will be inviting a lady friend of mine. She and Megan may even know each other." Randy thought for a moment, remembering that Jenn said she wanted to establish a personal account at the bank.

"Okay. That's sounds great. That sure will break the ice. I guess if she doesn't want to see me, she'll just decline the offer."

"Yes. You text me when you know about what time you will be arriving on Thursday evening. Do I need to text my address?"

"No, sir. I remember where you live. We always made sure to patrol by the Chief's house."

"Just like you patrolled by other citizens, correct?"

"Yes, sir. I'll let you know what time to expect me on Thursday. I'll make sure that it isn't too late. Mr. Greer wants me at his office at seven o'clock sharp on Friday morning."

"Edwin likes to play golf on Friday afternoons. I suggest that you don't interfere with those plans."

"Yes, sir. I understand. I can't thank you enough, sir."

"No thanks needed, Joe. You just get to town and be ready to help Edwin with this case. Sometime over the weekend, we'll go out on my boat, and you and I can have a chat about why you left Serendipity."

"Okay, Chief. I'd like to do that. I think I may have been a little hasty."

After ending the conversation, Randy carried his food and his phone into the living room and settled into his recliner. Taking a few bites of his leftover spaghetti, Randy mulled over how he might approach Jenn about the Friday evening dinner.

"Why am I even concerned about this? Jenn and I have had dinner together many times since she returned to Serendipity. Don't act like it's unusual and it won't be."

Randy picked up his cell phone and typed a text to Jenn about the dinner invitation and the special guests for the evening. Randy jumped when a call came in instead of a text. It was Jenn.

"That was fast."

"I'm so happy to hear from you. I had convinced myself that I'd done something horrendous and made you mad."

"I'm not mad."

"Oh, did I do something horrendous?"

"No, Jenn, you've not done anything wrong." Randy closed his eyes, trying to change the way he was sounding.

"You don't sound too convincing, Mr. Nave."

"I've been covered up, Jenn. It's a busy time. It will be good to see you on Friday. It will be an interesting evening to be around these young people, to remember what that was like."

"You won't believe that I met Megan at the bank today. I finally made it there to open a personal account. I also had some newspaper business, and she was the teller who waited on me."

"She's a nice young lady. I believe the poor girl is quite smitten with this former officer of mine."

"Why does that make her a 'poor girl'?"

"Because I think he's one confused young man. He's got some serious soul searching to do about his future."

"Maybe he just needs a strong, sensible mentor to counsel and help him see things more clearly. I know a man who would be excellent at that."

"He can certainly learn from my long list of mistakes. That would apply to some career choices and personal ones." Randy chuckled. *It's so easy to talk to Jenn.*

"We've all made our share of mistakes. I think what's important is what we learn from them. The changes we make to create a better future." Jenn paused. "Randy, my daughter, Claire, is beeping in. I need to take this call. Thank you for the invitation."

"Glad you can come. Take care."

Another call ended. More plans confirmed. Randy wished everything in his day could be checked off as simply as those two phone conversations were. He still felt like he needed to take a step back. Give Jenn some breathing room. Randy was used to being in control of most situations he encountered. Perhaps it was time to let his relationship with Jenn progress naturally. Maybe it would have a better chance of turning out the best for both, if he let nature take its own course.

Chapter Eleven

Jenn

"Claire, I'm so relieved to hear from you. Your text messages and voicemails have been short. It's made your mother worry."

Jenn was not exaggerating with her description of Claire's communications or the level of concern she was having. Her 'mother radar' was on high alert. It had been for some time. She knew her oldest child well enough to realize that Claire needed time and space.

"My mother worries too much. Her oldest knows what she's doing."

Jenn remained silent. Too many questions would hold Claire back.

"I've made a decision about a change in my life."

"Okay. I'm ready to listen and support."

"I know you are. That's why you are almost the first person to know."

In her mind, Jenn could picture her eldest child pacing. Both of her daughters had the 'pacing gene.' It reminded her of a time in Claire's childhood when she had to confess about breaking something she'd been told not to touch. Claire wore a hole in the living room carpet before finally revealing her infraction.

"I'm a keeper of your secrets."

"It won't be a secret for long."

Jenn could hear Claire take a deep breath.

"Derek and I are getting a divorce. Before you say anything, I have thought this out. Derek and I have already had a trial separation for the last three months. It came as a shock to him at first, but since we've had some time apart, I think he also realizes that our relationship wasn't working. There's not another person involved on either side. I would guess that you knew this all along, Derek and I should have remained friends instead of becoming romantically involved. You shouldn't marry someone who is more like your brother than your boyfriend."

"We always thought Derek was a fine young man, but I can't say this news is a total surprise. It was your decision to make; I would not have interfered. The two of you never seemed madly in love. Frankly, I wondered if there was someone else who stole your heart long before you said, 'I do' to Derek."

"No, I cannot say that there has been anyone other than Derek. I honestly thought he was the one for me, until I realized something when you and Dad were splitting up. My relationship with Derek reminded me of what I saw between you and Dad while I was growing up."

Claire's words hit Jenn's heart.

"Don't get me wrong. I'm not saying that I grew up in an unhappy home. We rarely saw you and Dad argue. Looking back though and seeing how your relationship ended, made me realize that just because something isn't horrible doesn't mean that it's good enough. You deserved to be head-over-heels in love and so do I."

"Yes, you do, my dear. You most certainly do." Jenn could hear the strength in Claire's voice. It made her proud. There was a small part of Jenn who wished she herself had been strong years earlier.

"I do have a surprise though. If it's okay with you, I'm going to follow Foster's example and move to Serendipity."

This news was not surprising either. Jenn felt like, at a minimum, an extended visit was on the horizon for Claire.

"I think it's wonderful. Goodness, with both you and Foster here, Emily will be jealous."

"Well, I think that Emily has a surprise of her own brewing. I'll let her tell her own tales though."

"What about your job? You've worked so hard to climb the ladder at the gallery."

"That's the great thing about this new mobile world we live in. You remember Jocelyn, the Executive Director of the gallery?"

"Certainly. Jocelyn has always reminded me of someone who looked more like she should be the headlining model at a Paris fashion show than running an art gallery." Jenn chuckled remembering the young woman who looked like she belonged on a magazine cover.

"I know you must think that she starves herself, but she really has an incredible metabolism. I've seen her eat a cheeseburger with a vengeance." Claire took a deep breath. "Anyway, Jocelyn has been wanting to hire someone to be a full-time buyer for the gallery. We've experienced a lot of growth in recent years, and she wants to build on that momentum. She's one of my closest friends. When I confided to her about my life change, she offered me an incredible job as the main buyer for the gallery. It's a role that she has mainly filled herself. She said that I was who she had in mind when she first thought of creating the position, but she didn't think I'd want to be away from home that much. When I mentioned spending some time in Serendipity with you, she said that Raleigh had an international airport, so I could fly to anywhere in the world from there."

"That's fabulous, darling. I'm so happy for you. Have you put your condo on the market yet?"

"Nope. Derek wants to buy me out of it. He likes the area. As soon as I can get my stuff boxed up, I can head in your direction."

"Now you are surprising me!" Jenn's mind raced counting the number of people who were coming to Serendipity, her son, Foster, and his wife, Michelle; her sister, Renee; and now, Claire. "I may need to turn my house into a bed and breakfast."

"Oh, Mom, are you expecting others? I thought that Foster and Michelle have about closed on their own condo."

"I think they have. They may be staying with me for a little while though as everything is being finalized. Foster mentioned having it repainted before they move in. Your Aunt Renee is also coming as soon as the doctor releases her. No worries though. You know the house has plenty of space. I'm delighted that you want to come here."

"It won't be forever. I will find my own place once the financial transaction of Derek buying my half of the condo is complete."

"You can stay with me as long as you need. Perhaps, Michelle can help you explore your real estate options. There's also a realty office right across the street from the newspaper."

"Foster told me that there are several condos for sale near the one that he and Michelle are buying. In fact, he might have mentioned to you that they are thinking about buying more than one and using it for vacation rentals. It sounds like a good source of income for them."

"Yes, Foster mentioned that idea. Michelle is such a wiz at real estate; I'm sure whatever they do will be successful." Jenn looked at the clock in the kitchen, shocked at how it was almost time for the sun to set.

"I'm going to let you go. I wanted you to hear this news from me before the sibling grapevine got a hold of it, namely Emily."

"Your little sister has always found it difficult to keep a secret. She'd never make a good government spy."

"That's a frightening thought." Claire chuckled. "I feel so relieved to be able to tell you this. Please do not think badly of Derek. He and I are going to part on good terms. I hope someday that we can be friends again."

"It's a mature way to look at the situation. I don't see that happening with your father and I, but—"

"Don't even get me started about Dad. He's bent my ear already about wanting you back. I've told him bluntly that he's delusional. He doesn't deserve another chance."

"Your brother said something similar. I'm seriously concerned that Simon is going to show up in Serendipity, too. I *do not* have room for him at the house."

"I think all you'll have to do is call that police friend of yours."

"Okay. Who have you been talking to?" Jenn rolled her eyes and shook her head.

"I'm not sure I need to talk to anyone. The photos that Mel has posted on her social media show several old friends reconnecting. In those photos, one very handsome gentleman always seems to be looking at my mother instead of the camera. Longingly looking at my mother. I'd be shocked and appalled if I didn't see my mother glowing in those same photos. I know there are a lot of reasons why you are happy now, despite the reasons that led you to this point. I'm looking forward to having a little of that glow myself one day."

Before Jenn could comment further, Claire ended the call. Smiling to herself, Jenn looked at the clock again. She had just enough time to get a walk in before the moonlight hit the ocean.

An hour later, Jenn slowed down her brisk pace as she approached the steps that led back to her house. The relaxed feeling that this evening exercise on the sand and surf always gave her began to leave when she noticed someone come into view from the other side of the steps. It was Parker. She'd intentionally taken her walk in the opposite direction, going by Gladys' house instead, so she wouldn't have to pass his house. It appeared that he was waiting for her return.

"Good evening, Parker."

"Hello, Jenn. I'm happy for our paths to cross this evening. I was hoping that you might have a nightcap on my deck and chat."

"Thank you for the invitation, but I need to turn in. I've got an early day tomorrow."

Jenn took hold of the railing and took the first step. Parker laid his hand on top of hers. A feeling of apprehension came over her. Her gaze moved from Parker's hand to his eyes. He was smiling. She was not. Parker moved his hand away.

"I feel like you've been avoiding me since we talked on the phone the other day. You didn't make eye contact when you and that other woman came into the real estate office earlier."

"Oh, were you in the office?" Jenn tried to sound convincing. She'd hoped Parker had not seen her scurry by one of the agents' offices as she headed to the owner's office in the back. "Ellie and I had a meeting about an upcoming campaign. I guess I had tunnel vision."

"I guess so. We really need to spend some time together."

"Listen, Parker, I appreciate the lovely gesture of flowers. It was a kind expression. I think though that you should consider focusing your attention elsewhere. I don't want to be rude to an old friend, but a lot of time has passed since we were playmates on this beach. You and I have lived quite different lives."

"I guess I was naïve to think that our families' connection could bridge the gap of time."

Taking another step, Jenn closed her eyes and frowned. Parker had to bring their families into the discussion.

"There was quite a bond between our families. I thought we might have it in our genetic makeup to continue that bond."

Jenn opened her eyes, looking at the flight of steps ahead of her like an escape route. In her mind, she heard the voice of her mother praising the benefits of good neighbors and old friends. Slowly, she turned back to face Parker.

"Parker, I would like for us to continue to be good neighbors as our parents and grandparents once were." Jenn chose her words as carefully as if they were to be written in an editorial in her newspaper. "I hope in that process we can also be friends. I am not prepared to be more than that. The ink on my divorce is not dry yet. I was married for a long time. I will be treading carefully in the future."

Jenn looked into Parker's eyes. They were expressionless, stoic, and unreadable. The overall expression on his face was little different. After a few seconds, he nodded his head, and Jenn took that as her cue to leave.

"It's late. I've had a long day. I will say goodnight." Before he would stop her, Jenn turned and resumed climbing the steps. She'd reached the halfway point before she heard his voice.

"I guess that doesn't apply to the Chief of Police. Did you promise to marry him when you were a child?"

Jenn did not answer or acknowledge Parker's comment. She did not look behind her until she was safely inside the house. By then, Parker was nowhere in sight.

A warning bell chimed inside Jenn's brain. Something was not right about the situation. She'd only known Parker when they were quite young, and she only remembered kindness and a sweet disposition. This was a different person she was dealing with now. Ruthless was the first word that came to mind. She needed to be careful.

"Jenn, thank you for making some time to talk to us this morning."

Jenn's current advertising team, Betsy Lawson and Ellie James, sat across from her in Jenn's office. Both women looked quite serious and a little nervous.

"I imagine that you have reached a decision regarding who you think we should hire for the new position. I want to reiterate again, please do not in any way feel like you should recommend my daughter-in-law. We need to find the best person for this position."

"That's not our concern at all, Jenn." Betsy spoke up, glancing at Ellie. "If we look apprehensive, it's because Ellie and I have an idea. It's a big idea. We know that this is a volatile time for the company, especially since you've only recently made the purchase and invested a sizable chunk of your personal funds."

"You've mentioned several times in the last few weeks that you feel like this is a turning point for the newspaper." Ellie was on the edge of her seat. "Sometimes you must be a little daring when you are at such a point. We have an idea that is daring, but it does involve Michelle and her special sales skills and experience. Please don't be mad at us."

Jenn watched the young woman nervously take a deep breath. Glancing at Betsy, she saw a hopeful expression on the older woman's face.

"I can't wait to hear what you have to say." Jenn leaned back in her chair.

"Okay, here goes." Betsy began. "Ellie and I think that we should hire Sutton Berkley for our new advertising position. Just about all the candidates had a level of experience that could be adapted to our situation. What we think gives Sutton the edge is that she did an excellent job when she worked here previously, and she has a great knowledge of the area as a whole and the client base."

"I enjoyed meeting Sutton. She has a great personality. I've read the messages we've received from several of our clients regarding their previous experience with her. She's an excellent choice."

"We are happy that you agree." Betsy turned to Ellie. "It's your turn."

"Our other idea involves Michelle." Ellie stood up, handing Jenn a folder. "I've been thinking about this for about a year. Betsy and I have discussed it several times. We knew that it could not be implemented until there was a new owner for the newspaper. We were hesitant to mention it when you first came because we knew you had a lot to consider and work on. After we met Michelle and learned about her background, we thought this was the sign we needed that it was the right time to approach you about it."

A smile began to cross Jenn's face. She could feel the enthusiasm and determination coming from Ellie. It was like Jenn's own feelings when she found out the newspaper was for sale.

"Are you saying that this is serendipitous?"

Huge smiles crossed Betsy's and Ellie's faces. "Yes!" They answered simultaneously.

"Then, I like this idea already." Jenn patted the still-closed folder in front of her. "Tell me all about it."

"As you know, Serendipity and the other coastal communities around us are undergoing a fairly extensive building and development phase." Ellie reached across Jenn's desk, opening the folder, and taking out several sheets. "The first sheet gives an overview of these developments. There are many zoning changes underway with our Town Council and neighboring towns' local governments as well. All these changes are working toward the goal of growth."

"I know that you've been reviewing past articles and also, more recently, following Lyle's coverage of these meetings and public hearings that are underway." Betsy pulled out a copy of a recent article Lyle had written that gave an overview of the plans.

"I have indeed." Jenn nodded while beginning to study the documents Ellie gave her. "While I've noticed some resistance, primarily from long-term landowners, most of those who I've talked to about the topic are fine with the changes as long as it produces controlled growth and doesn't turn our community into an area that is purely commercial and environmentally hazardous."

"One of the greatest aspects of growth will be in the form of commercial and residential real estate." Ellie pulled out a booklet-like publication from the back of the folder. "That's where my idea comes in. There is going to be a lot of real estate changing hands, not only in our town, but in all the towns surrounding us." Ellie placed a computer tablet in front of Jenn with the screen facing her. "I've chatted with a few of the larger real estate companies in a fifty-mile radius of Serendipity. I've also talked with some of the tourism offices, like Mel's, in that same vicinity. All of them are excited about the potential to be a part of this real estate boom and think that visitors who already frequent our area will likely be some of the first ones to make purchases."

"We can help the real estate agents reach those potential clients through a publication like this brochure." Jenn held up the example Ellie had given her.

"Exactly! And this website." Ellie began clicking on the screen, showing Jenn examples of what it would include.

"Michelle is the ideal person to lead this type of initiative, Jenn." Betsy stood up. "When Ellie and I had a follow-up conference call with Michelle, we asked her if she had any ideas on additional ways for the newspaper to generate revenue. She asked if the area had a real estate guide. Ellie and I had both already considered Michelle to be ideal for such a product. Her answer confirmed what we were thinking."

"It's all a wonderful idea." Jenn took a deep breath, frowning. "I don't think we currently have enough revenue to bring on two salespeople though."

"We've thought of that." Betsy pulled her chair closer to Jenn's desk before sitting back down. Ellie did the same. "We've come up with a plan that we think might work, especially with someone of Michelle's caliber and understanding of the real estate market."

"I'm all ears!"

"Marella Yarnell, our graphic and layout designer, already handles our current issues of the printed newspaper and our website." Ellie began to explain.

"Yes, she's fabulous. I'm amazed at what she can already juggle, seemingly so easy. Marella never looks stressed out."

"She's a cool cat, for sure. What I don't believe you may know is that she doesn't do all the web work." Ellie turned the tablet back toward herself and began typing.

"I remember in my review of the financials that we do have a company who was paid to design our website that also does periodical updates."

"Correct. It's not really a 'company' though; it's a one-person show. That one person is Marella's twin brother, Wyatt."

"The newspaper was one of Wyatt's first clients, so he has a soft spot for us and Marella." Betsy shook her head, smiling. "He always comes to our rescue when we need to make changes."

"We've talked to Wyatt, and he is willing to work with us on this project, at a reduced rate."

"Okay, we could certainly afford to pay Marella a little extra until we could afford to hire someone to help her." Jenn's mind was racing with ideas. "What's your plan for how we pay Michelle?"

"When Ellie and I talked to her after the interview, Michelle mentioned that she already had a real estate license for this state." Betsy continued.

"Yes, while based in Atlanta, the real estate company she works for has offices in about every Southern state. She's sold real estate all over the South."

"Michelle indicated that she might continue to do some real estate work, even if she got the job with us." Betsy paused, taking a deep breath. "I think she would be willing to work on a strictly commission basis, a larger commission than we might normally pay, while we are getting this project up and running."

"That doesn't surprise me. Michelle has done *very* well selling real estate in the last few years. I'm sure they have a sound nest egg. I also think that I know my daughter-in-law well enough to surmise that she might want to be a partner in this business venture, and I think that would be an excellent idea." Jenn leaned back in her swivel chair, almost losing her balance and laughing at herself in the process. "This is exciting, ladies. You two are fabulous. I suppose that you've also run this idea by Mel, since she's our local tourism guru."

"I hope that you aren't mad that we've talked to her." Ellie looked at Jenn, sheepishly.

"Absolutely not! I think you and Betsy have done your homework and presented a fabulous well-researched idea. I obviously have some smart and savvy women around me who have a lot of determination and drive." Jenn jumped up from her desk. "I love it!"

"We're so happy you feel that way, Jenn." Betsy picked up her files. "Would you like for me to go ahead and offer the full-time position to Sutton?"

"Yes, that will be fine, Betsy. Use the salary we discussed as a starting offer. Do you have a potential commission structure to offer Michelle?"

"Ellie did some research and we've run some numbers. We thought that might be something you would want to discuss with Michelle directly."

"I can do that. She and Foster are planning to arrive in Serendipity next week or the week after. Hopefully, if Sutton accepts our offer, we can get her on board within a few weeks."

"That would be great." Ellie rose, gathering her tablet and other files. "We appreciate you allowing us to be a part of this decision-making process."

"That's what teams do; they work together toward a goal."

Jenn heard the buzzing of her phone. She'd been so interested in the discussion with Betsy and Ellie that she forgot it was still in her purse.

"We will leave you now and begin to put this plan into action." Betsy followed Ellie to the door. "I'll email you updates on our progress and send you links electronically to the research we've done about the commission structure. Thanks, Jenn. I'm as excited about my role with this newspaper as I've been in a long time."

"Happy to hear it!" Jenn gave them a big smile before they closed the door.

"Wow! That was an inspiring meeting." Jenn began digging in her purse. "I've got to find that phone."

After taking everything out of her bag, Jenn finally realized that, for some reason, she'd put it inside her makeup case. Shaking her head, she brushed off some powder and saw that the missed call was from Renee. There wasn't a message, so Jenn called her sister back.

"Hello, my sister." Renee answered on third ring. "I've interrupted your busy day."

Immediately, Jenn did not like the tone of Renee's voice. It was emotionless.

"You are never an interruption. I'm sorry that I couldn't take your call. How are you feeling?"

"Do you have a few minutes to talk? If not, I'll call you when you get home tonight."

"Talk to me, Renee. I've had my last meeting of the day." Jenn bit her bottom lip. A feeling of fear began to grow.

"I went to the doctor today."

"Oh, I thought your appointment wasn't until later in the week."

"It was. I received a call first thing this morning from one of my doctors asking me to come into the office today. Jenn, the cancer was not contained in the colon. It has spread and they want me to begin treatment as soon possible."

"Oh, Renee." Tears filled Jenn's eyes.

"I'm going to be brave, little sister. My doctor feels confident that we can kick this stuff to the curb with a couple of rounds of chemo followed by some radiation."

"Absolutely!" Jenn wiped tears from her cheeks. "I will come and drive you to your treatments."

"Well, I was planning on your helping me with that. Only I was thinking about taking them in Serendipity. If that is okay with you?"

"It's fine with me. What does your doctor think?" Jenn furrowed her brow. Her mind was racing.

"It was my doctor's idea. She already knew that I was considering staying with you as I recovered from the surgery. She checked into the treatments offered at the Cancer Center of Serendipity. I can have all the treatment she's planned right there."

"Okay. Will Neil be coming with you?"

"He'll bring me to Serendipity and stay a couple of days. I've told him that he should go back to Raleigh and keep working. He's been juggling a lot over the past couple of weeks. There are several big projects that need Neil's guidance. I've told him that I want some beach time with my sister. That will be better medicine than the chemo."

Jenn was silent for a moment, absorbing the shock of Renee's news.

"I'm okay, Jenn. You know I've been through worse. I had a feeling that this battle wasn't over."

"The ocean air, the relaxing sound of the waves, and the sand between your toes will be just what you need to make your treatment successful. I'm happy to hear that your doctor feels so confident about you taking the treatments here. This is still going to be a recovery, Renee." Jenn's tone was direct and positive. She wished she could see Renee's face.

"I'm assured that I will not be hindered from drinks with little umbrellas or sampling our mother's vino stash."

"Paisley always emphasized that anything made with grapes was medicinal." Jenn chuckled.

"Mother knew best!" Both Renee and Jenn spoke simultaneously.

"I'm going to take the best care of you." Jenn felt tears returning. "We are going to face this bravely together."

"I hear too much emotion in your voice, Jenn. Even if I lose my life in this battle, it will not be my worst day. You must know that. Battling cancer pales in comparison."

"You're stronger than you know. I'm proud of you, Renee. Come let me help you."

"I'll be there on Friday with more luggage than Neil wants to carry."

"Friday? This Friday?" Jenn's mind raced. She couldn't remember what was on her calendar for Friday. It didn't matter.

"Yes. Is that a problem? My treatment starts on Monday. Do you want me to wait until then?"

"Absolutely not! I was just trying to remember what day today is. I've been so busy. This week has been a blur. We've been hiring new people for the advertising department."

"That sounds exciting. I want to hear all about it. I'm going to let you go so you can have as much free time as possible before your big sister invades. It will be like when we were growing up. This time, you can borrow any of my clothes that you want."

"Text me when you and Neil get on the road on Friday."

"I will." Renee paused. "Thank you, Jenn."

"I love you, Renee. We are going to get through this together."

CHAPTER TWELVE

Sinclair

SINCLAIR HAD BARELY FINISHED dialing the number before his call was answered.

"Serendipity Sun, this is Doris, how may I assist you today?"

Hearing the woman's cheerful greeting, Sinclair smiled. There was no one quite like Doris Hudson.

"This is Sinclair Lewis."

"Sinclair, I heard you were back in town. We appreciate you becoming one of our newspaper's newest and largest advertising clients. I'm sure our readers will be interested in buying a new vehicle from one of our town's all-time best athletes. I understand that you have rekindled a friendship with the lovely Melinda Snow. It warms my heart to see the smile on her face. You make sure you keep it that way. Who would you like to speak with today?"

"Hello, Miss Doris. I look forward to stopping by the office and giving you a great big hug. Our family has not forgotten the kindness you extended to our folks during their last years. Mom was always telling me about the delicious food you would drop off. You were truly a blessing to them. I thank you."

"It was my pleasure, Sinclair. It filled my heart with joy to help such good people. I miss them."

"Me, too. If you don't mind, I'm returning a call from Lyle Livingston. I think he wants to do a story about this old jock."

"It will be a great one. I look forward to it. One moment and I will connect you."

While he waited, Sinclair remembered the younger version of the person who was about to come on the line. Lyle Livingston was a legendary high school athlete in his youth. All the girls wanted to date him. All the boys wanted to be him. Sinclair frowned, remembering the serious motorcycle accident which ended Lyle's college athletic career. Most people expected Lyle to pursue a professional career in sports until that fateful crash.

"Sinclair, thank you for returning my call." Lyle's greeting was friendly and direct. "You and I are living proof that athletes can make a successful life after their glory years pass."

"I don't know about that, Lyle." Sinclair chuckled. "Most people would probably say I'm just an old car salesman who finally found his way home."

"After buying the largest dealership in a fifty-mile radius, I'd call that successful. From what our advertising department tells me, your account helped my entire staff's job security. I should probably be calling you Mr. Lewis."

"Not unless you want me to remind everyone of your high school nickname."

"Ugh. I scowl as often as I can to avoid that."

"From what Mel tells me, there's no hiding that smile."

"Well, I guess that's true. I got the name honestly, because I'd rather have a smile on my face. So, do you have time for me to interview you today over the phone?"

"Yes, I've cleared my calendar for the next hour."

"I was thinking about sending our sportswriter, Shaun Hardy, to take a couple of photos of you. Thought you might enjoy chatting with him a little."

"That sounds fine. He's Tom Hardy's son, isn't he? His family owns the hardware story?"

"Yes. I forgot that you might have known Shaun's family. Okay, let's get down to some questions."

For the next forty-five minutes, Sinclair basically recounted his life story to Lyle, from his youth as a star athlete to working his way up in the car dealership business.

"I've got one last question for you, Sinclair."

"I can't imagine what it might be. You've covered about everything."

"This one may be more personal than you want to answer."

Lyle paused. Sinclair felt his neck starting to tense up.

"This is a series of articles about people who've come back here after many years away. Everyone has a different reason or circumstance. I've got to ask yours. Why did you come back to Serendipity, Sinclair?"

Sinclair rubbed his forehead, letting out a deep breath.

"I did some foolish things in my youth."

"We've all got some of those in our past." Lyle chuckled.

"I did one foolish thing that changed every aspect of my life. One choice gave me the two most important people in my life, but, in the process, it took the love of my life away from me. So, if you want to know the real reason I came home after all these years, it's because I wanted a second chance. I probably don't deserve it, but I had to try."

"That's a mighty good reason, Sinclair. I don't know if you want me to put that in the story."

"I'll let you be the judge of that, Lyle. For anyone who reads the story and knew me then, it will make sense. For anyone who doesn't know, maybe they will think I'm a better man for trying."

"I know our situation has probably moved faster than you would like." Sinclair began talking after the server put an appetizer on the table between him and Mel. "I guess I'm anxious. I feel like we've lost so many years, I don't want to lose anymore."

"This is a nice place." Mel looked around the outdoor restaurant. "I guess Serendipity doesn't have an exclusive right to all the beautiful sunsets. This view is gorgeous."

Because Mel was going to be busy working during a festival that was being held all weekend in Serendipity, Sinclair suggested that she meet him on Thursday evening at a restaurant in the coastal community where his dealership was located.

"All my staff said this is a local favorite. Apparently Big Al is still the main cook."

"Truth in advertising. There's really a 'Big Al' at Big Al's." Mel took a bite of a hushpuppy. "Yum! Al knows how to make a hushpuppy."

"I don't want to scare you off by being overly anxious."

"Talking about being anxious also counts as anxious." Mel raised her eyebrows while taking the second bite of her hushpuppy. "If this crab dip is as good as the hushpuppies, you might should be worried about losing me to Big Al."

Sinclair did not respond. Even though he'd only been around Mel again for about a month after over thirty years of estrangement, he realized that some of her behaviors were the same as the young woman he knew long ago. If she didn't feel comfortable talking about a topic, Mel would make a joke.

"Did I tell you that Lyle Livingston interviewed me yesterday?"

"No, I remember Jenn talking about the series of articles that they were planning that would focus on individuals who had left Serendipity in their youth and now returned. The first article has already run. It was about Jenn."

"Yes, I read it. It was a good article. Lyle told me that the next one is going to be about someone who is about ten years younger than us who came back to be a surgeon here."

"Oh, that would be Prisha Mehta. Her grandfather was Dr. Gupta. He was a pediatrician when we were growing up."

"Yes, I remember him."

"That will be a good article, too. Prisha worked in Europe for a while. She's had an interesting life." Mel stopped talking while the server placed their food in front of them.

"Can I get you all anything else right now?"

"I'll probably need some more tea in a few minutes." Sinclair nodded at the server then returned his gaze back on his food. He wasn't going to continue to make idle chitchat. He'd let Mel lead the conversation.

"I know that you think I'm dodging your questions." Mel put down her fork before she took the first bite of her entrée. "Yes, you are being a little anxious. That is normally my role. I don't know how to act with you doing it. I think it's time that I say some things that I need for you to understand."

"Okay." Sinclair set down his silverware and focused on Mel.

"This has all happened so quickly. You move back to town. We meet again. Then suddenly, we are dating. It's been a whirlwind. I think I've been too shocked to say the things I've been carrying around in my heart since we were teenagers."

Sinclair gave Mel a forced smile. He remembered that Mel's neck would get red when she was mad. Her neck was getting red.

"There's no sense in rehashing what happened all those years ago. We both know the story. There are probably not too many details that have been left out. I know that you married Dana and settled into family life." Mel held up her hand to stop him from speaking. "I know that is a simplistic way of describing your life since then, but I would imagine those are the main things you've been doing."

"Basically. Everything I did centered around taking care of my family."

"It shows. I met two mature individuals the other day. By the way, that was too early for me to meet your children. It was an example of you being too anxious. They might be curious. I was not ready. I don't want to be put into that position again."

"I understand. I'm sorry. For what it's worth, they both said they enjoyed meeting you."

"Is everything okay with your food?" The server suddenly appeared at their table and was refilling their glasses of iced tea before Sinclair realized the young man was there. "It doesn't look like either of you have touched your food. Is everything okay?"

"Everything is fine. We ate too many hushpuppies before the entrees were served." Mel quickly responded. "We were taking a little break. We need to start eating, Sinclair. This young man will send Big Al out to check on us."

Mel and the server exchanged a laugh before he walked away.

"Let's eat our food before it gets cold and enjoy the sunset. We can talk about this later."

"I don't care about this food, Mel. I want you to tell me what is in your heart."

Mel chewed the bite of food she had already put in her mouth while staring at Sinclair. Her gaze was intense. Sinclair could almost feel it. That scared him. He didn't feel any love in that gaze.

Setting down her fork again, Mel took a deep breath. A slight smile crossed her face before her eyes met Sinclair's.

"I cannot begin to tell you the number of times throughout the last three decades that I imagined what it might be like to sit across a table from you and pour out my heart. Often, my scenario was filled with getting revenge, breaking your heart, casting you aside, while some wonderful man waited a few feet away to whisk me off my feet."

"There's no doubt I would have deserved that scenario." Sinclair frowned.

"Other times, I was running into your arms, immediately forgiving you, picking up right where we left off, and living happily ever after."

"I love that one!" Sinclair felt an ache in his heart.

"The thing is I never imagined what did happen. I wasn't prepared for the reality of you showing back up in my life one day and what I'm feeling."

"I'm almost afraid to ask this. What are you feeling, Mel?"

"I don't feel the anger and incredible sadness that filled my mind and heart for so many years. I suppose it's like the stages of grief. You get past those early stages. You go on to numbness and acceptance." Mel paused, from her expression she looked to be in deep thought. "A lot of people have said that I've used what happened between us as an excuse not to love again. I suppose there is some truth to that. No one wants to have their heart broken a second or third time. I think it goes deeper than that. Somewhere in my subconscious, I think I rationalized that I didn't deserve to be loved. My younger self was convinced that there must have been something wrong with me that made you cheat."

"Absolutely not!" Sinclair's voice was a little too loud. "You were perfect. You *are* perfect. I was stupid, arrogant, and foolish."

"I'll agree with the stupid and foolish part. I'm not sure about arrogant. I couldn't see much through the hurt back then. I thought it had to be my fault. I got over that feeling a few years later."

Mel looked at the tables around them. Sinclair followed her gaze. He saw couples and families, laughing and enjoying their meals. From the way the people were dressed, Sinclair imagined that most of them were on vacation—a fun trip to the beach.

"I've spent my working life, Sinclair, luring people to Serendipity on vacation. Week after week, year after year, I see carloads of people arrive from hundreds and thousands of miles away. They are here to soak up some sunshine, play in the ocean, and eat seafood. But you know what the number one reason they come is?"

"Because of Serendipity's sunsets. I've seen your advertising materials." Sinclair laughed.

"There's truth in that advertising, but it's really a hook. All these people sitting around us and the thousands more like them go on vacation to make memories with people they love."

"I suppose you're right."

"Now, don't get me wrong, I've been on plenty of vacations in my life. I enjoy travelling. But in my adult life, I've not gone on even one family vacation. I don't have those memories. The biggest reason why is because somewhere along the way, I became afraid of commitment. I know I'm talking in circles, but I'm trying to find a way to put into words how I feel about the potential for you and me. It wasn't a straight path from the summer after our senior year until today. There have been many curves and detours."

"I'm listening." Sinclair reached across the table, squeezing Mel's hand before quickly releasing it.

"Not to say that every man I've dated was husband material, but several were caring gentlemen who I probably could have built a family with and been happy. Something always stopped me. It wasn't entirely the love I still carried for you. It was the confidence I didn't have in me. So, when you ask me how I feel, I'm not sure it's much different than I've felt all these years in between. I wake up in the middle of the night thinking about that. I say aloud what I keep turning over in my head—'but it's Sinclair.' It doesn't seem to matter. I think I'm broken inside. I'm not sure I can be fixed."

Mel looked down at her food. Sinclair watched Mel pick up her fork and begin to eat her meal with a vengeance. She didn't make further eye contact.

"The lady appears to be enjoying her food." A few seconds later, the server appeared at the table. "Can I get you something else, sir?"

"The food is fine. Thank you."

Mel continued eating, not looking up.

"Mel, I think I understand what you are trying to say. I don't think you're broken though. You've been scared and apprehensive. I want to assure you that I will do everything in my power to make up for the years we lost."

"That's the thing, Sinclair, we can't get back those years. I've got to make peace with that. I truly want to find a way to open my heart up enough to close the door on the past and give the future a chance. In order to do that, it's going to take a lot of forgiveness."

"I hope you can forgive me, Mel."

"It's not just you I need to forgive. I've got to forgive myself."

"I don't understand." Sinclair searched his mind, trying to figure out why Mel would need to forgive herself. "What do you have to be forgiven for?"

"The biggest mistake of my life."

Chapter Thirteen

Jenn

"I'm sorry to call you this late, Randy. I've been so busy that it is already nine o'clock and I'm only halfway through my to-do list for today."

"Sounds like you need to slow down and rest."

Randy's voice was a welcomed sound to Jenn's ears. Since her return to Serendipity, she realized his soothing tone had become a calming force in her life. She needed to hear that sound after the last two days.

"I don't think rest is going to be on my agenda for this weekend."

"Uh oh. Sounds like something has happened."

"It has. Everything seems to be happening at once. While I would love to pour out all the details to your listening ears, I'm afraid the abbreviated version will have to suffice if I'm going to get anything else checked off my list today."

"Maybe we'll have a few minutes alone after dinner tomorrow night."

Jenn hated to cancel their plans. Randy was hosting one of his former police officers who was in town to testify at a trial. Randy's caring self was also trying to help the young man get his life back on track. That included arranging for the young man's former girlfriend, a local girl, to have dinner with them on Friday evening. Jenn knew that her absence would leave a hole in the dinner conversation.

"I'm afraid that's why I'm calling. There's been a new development with Renee. It's a mixed bag of news. The bad news is that her cancer was not contained within the colon. It was more widespread. Her doctors are ordering treatment to begin right away. It sounds like they think an aggressive approach can get a handle on it."

"Oh, Jenn, I'm sorry to hear this. It sounded like the surgery would be the extent of it. I know you were looking forward to having Renee visit during her recovery."

"The visiting part is still happening. That's why I can't come tomorrow evening. Neil is bringing Renee on Friday. Her doctors have arranged for her to begin chemotherapy treatment on Monday at the cancer center here."

"That is a new twist. I'm sure it will help Renee to be with you. Remember something, Jenn. You are back home now. There's a legion of people who will step up and help you care for Renee. You've got a new business that I know you need to focus a good deal of your time and energy toward. Let us help you. I'm sure that Doris and Mel can recruit people who know Renee to help take her to treatments and assist with meals. You can certainly count me on the list for both."

"Renee would love having her own personal security detail in the form of Serendipity's Police Chief."

"It would be my pleasure. I've always wished that I hadn't been halfway around the world when her son was abducted. I would have gone to Raleigh and volunteered for the search."

"Randy, Renee has been so strong for so many years. When she told me about this diagnosis, she said that no matter how this battle ended, it would not be the worst day of her life. My heart breaks every time I think of that precious boy. This may sound crazy, but I can't help but wonder if this cancer hasn't fed on the anguish of the last twenty years."

"Has it been that long? It does not seem possible."

"Yes, when I visited them the other day, Neil mentioned that the twentieth anniversary of Jonah's disappearance was coming up. He thought it would be good for Renee to be in Serendipity when that day came. Now, it's going to probably coincide with the first or second week of her treatment."

"It's hard to say how that will affect her. Renee's obviously a strong woman to have endured what life has handed her already. I'm glad she's got one strong sister here by her side."

Randy's comment made Jenn's thoughts go to her sister Amber. She hoped that Neil had some updated news regarding Amber's progress in rehab.

"Please forgive me for leaving an empty seat at the table tomorrow night. I know that you wanted me there to help keep the conversation going between that young man and Megan."

"Don't worry about that for a second. I know they will both understand. I can keep a conversation going. I'm sorry that you won't be able to meet him. I think Fairfield is a good young man. Hopefully, I can help him figure out what's holding him back from continuing his career in police work."

"I have no doubt that you will be able to get to the bottom of the situation. Between your wise counsel and Megan's influence on the young man's heart, I have no doubt that he will be living in Serendipity again in no time."

"We shall see. At the minimum, we will get Edwin Greer the testimony he needs to keep another criminal off the streets. This will be a busy weekend for me with having a house guest, but don't hesitate to call me if anything comes up that I can help with when Renee and her husband move in."

"It will only be Renee who is staying. Neil is going to bring her on Friday and head back to Raleigh after her first treatment on Monday. Have you ever met Neil?"

"I don't believe I have. I was already in the Army when Renee got married. I remember Mom sending me a newspaper clipping of the wedding announcement. Once I was back here, your mother often spoke fondly of Neil. Hopefully, I will have a chance to meet him while Renee is staying with you."

"I believe that you two would get along splendidly." Jenn looked at her watch. "I wish we could talk longer, but I've got several things to do before I head to bed. Thanks again for understanding."

"No thanks needed. It cannot be helped. I think I just heard Fairfield pull into the driveway. Text me when you can over the weekend. I will do the same. Goodnight, Jenn.

"Goodnight."

While she was talking to Randy, a text from Foster came in. Jenn hadn't updated her children about Renee's latest news. She would try to do that before Renee and Neil arrived on Friday.

"That was quite a cryptic text message, Foster." Not understanding what Foster's short message meant, Jenn decided a quick phone call would probably save time.

"I'm sorry, Mom. Michelle and I have been trying to finish packing and wrapping up loose ends so that we can get on the road Sunday morning."

"Get on the road?" Jenn thought it would be another week or more before the sale of Foster's home was finalized. "I thought the new owner had a death in his family."

"He did. It turns out that he wasn't so keen on staying extra days after the funeral. Apparently, the man's father had a second family, and they don't get along too well. He called yesterday morning and said he would be here on Friday to make everything final. Michelle and I have been working nonstop to pack up the rest of our personal stuff. Crazy thing is that Michelle will be closing on two other properties tomorrow that she has sold in the last few weeks. The real estate market is wild here. We've barely had a chance to really talk, but I heard her having a conversation this morning with one of your staff. Sounds like she may be going to work for you."

"Yes, my advertising team is excited to have Michelle join them. They have an idea for a new advertising project for Michelle to sell that is related to real estate." Jenn paused, thinking about what Foster had just said. "Did you say you are planning to leave Atlanta on Sunday morning? Does that mean you will arrive that night?"

"Yes. I hope that's okay. We are buying that condo I told you about, and maybe another one, but we haven't closed on it yet. We were hoping that the timing would be better so that we could move directly there."

"It's not a problem for you guys to bunk here for a while. I need to fill you in on something though. I was going to try to have a group phone call with you and your sisters tomorrow morning, but I'll go ahead and tell you now. You might want to sit down."

"Oh no, what's wrong, Mom?"

"Your Aunt Renee has gotten a further diagnosis. It appears that the cancer has spread, and her doctors want to begin treatment immediately.

It's been arranged for her to begin chemo on Monday here in Serendipity. Renee and Neil are arriving tomorrow."

"Oh, Mom, I hate hearing this. We were hoping that the surgery had taken care of all the cancer. How is Renee taking the news?"

"You know Renee, she's one tough woman. Foster, I'm sure she has all the emotions including dread and fear. To her though, nothing will ever be as hard as losing Jonah. Even cancer pales in comparison."

"Hopefully, the same strength that has gotten her through that horrible loss will also help Renee overcome cancer."

"That's the type of attitude we all need to have."

"I'm happy that the timing of our move will allow us to be close by to help you and Renee. One goal of this move for us was to have more flexibility in our lives. We will be happy to use that flexibility to help people we love."

"That's a wonderful sentiment, Foster. I'll warn you though; flexibility has a way of disappearing quickly when you begin a new life. I love living here, but the short weeks I have lived in Serendipity have been crammed full of adventures I never even dreamed could occur."

"I'm learning that can be the theme of life sometimes."

Jenn suddenly heard through the phone what sounded like something crashing.

"Foster, is everything okay there?"

"Yeah, Mom." Foster laughed. "Buster knocked over a stack of boxes. Luckily, it was mostly office stuff. Hopefully, there wasn't anything breakable in there."

"I better let you go." Jenn pictured the big adorable male Collie dog that Foster adopted while he was still in college. "I'm going to have to remind Jasper that his buddy Buster is coming to town."

"Thanks for calling, Mom. I'll text you when we get on the road on Sunday."

"Sounds good. Good luck with all the closings for you and Michelle tomorrow."

When the conversation was over, Jenn plopped down on the couch, looking at the list of tasks she'd assigned herself earlier in the day.

"What was I thinking? If Mel were here, she would tell me that I didn't need to do half of the things on this list."

As if on cue, Jenn's phone buzzed with a call. Mel's name blazed on the screen.

"I suppose this is what best friends do." Jenn answered the call.

"Call each other?"

Jenn could hear the questioning tone in Mel's voice.

"Right before you called, I was imagining what you would say to me if you were here."

"Stop cleaning! Your house isn't dirty!"

"Something like that was what I was imagining." Jenn lay down on the couch as she laughed.

"Your sister Renee is arriving tomorrow. The same person you shared a bathroom with during childhood. You do not need to impress her. She is coming for your care and attention. Renee will not be looking for dust bunnies."

"I know. It's part of my persona to want everything to be perfect."

"Jenn, there's Martha Stewart perfect and there's real people perfect. Your sister is real people. In her case, she's had too much experience dealing with the harsh realities of this life."

"There's my smart friend bringing me back to reality. Is that why you called?"

"Not really. I wanted to tell you about my own brush with reality this evening at dinner with Sinclair."

"Oh, I forgot. You went to meet him for dinner. What was the name of the restaurant?"

"Big Al's. What I ate of the food was delicious. That business should be advertising in your newspaper."

"I'll make a note of that. I'm a little confused regarding your comment about the food. Why didn't you eat?"

"Because you and I are best friends and we have similar personality traits, only in different situations. You obsessively clean and straighten rooms that aren't dirty. I obsessively worry about conversations I had decades ago."

"What?" Jenn heard the words, but her tired brain could not translate what Mel was trying to tell her.

"Sinclair asked me if our relationship was progressing too quickly. I took what could have been a simple 'yes or no' response and delivered a college dissertation. I felt like I needed to reveal some of my current feelings. I probably shouldn't have told as much as I did about the past."

In that moment, Jenn realized that nothing left on her list was even half as important as the person who was talking. Jenn headed to the kitchen, pouring the last glass from a bottle of wine on the counter.

"I'm sure it's not as bad as you imagine. Tell me all about it."

"Aunt Rachel, this is Jenn."

"Oh, my goodness, you are calling mighty early on a Friday morning. Who died?"

The snark in her aunt's voice would normally have made Jenn laugh. Unfortunately, the news Jenn was about to share with her late mother's sister was serious.

"I wanted to let you know that Renee will be arriving today."

"That's wonderful! I'm happy that it will be working out for her to visit while she's recovering from her surgery. I must insist that you both come for lunch within her first week here. I'm not getting any younger; I need to see my nieces."

"Well, there's more to Renee's visit than recovering."

"Oh, please don't tell me that she and Neil are splitting up. That's always been my fear after Jonah was taken. Losing a child is one of the worst things a couple can go through."

"No, their marriage is fine as far as I know. Neil is bringing her here later today. Aunt Rachel, I have some additional news about her health." Jenn paused. The silence on the other end of the phone made Jenn wonder if her aunt was holding her breath. "Renee's cancer is more extensive than the doctors first thought."

Jenn heard the gasp Rachel was holding in. She could almost envision the woman clutching her heart.

"Her medical team is approaching her treatment aggressively. It will begin on Monday. She will start with chemo at the cancer center here in Serendipity."

"The same facility where your father took his treatments."

Everyone in the family remembered the weeks and months that Marshall Halston spent going back and forth taking treatments for his multiple bouts with cancer. Even Rachel helped transport her brother-in-law. They were all so full of hope. The ultimate outcome was heartbreaking.

"Despite how it turned out for Dad, the Serendipity Cancer Center is the best in the region. We've got to all work together to keep Renee's spirits high and not dwell on our past experiences there."

"Absolutely! Renee's strength is boundless. This battle will be no harder than ones she's fought before."

"Renee said something similar when she told me about the latest diagnosis. It's hard to imagine something as tough as cancer being the lesser evil in one's life."

"It's a cruel reality. Jenn, please tell me what I can do to help."

"I know that Renee will want to spend time with you. Let's see how her first few treatments go. I have no idea if the treatment will make her sick. I believe there have been some positive advancements in how doctors treat the sickness side of it."

"Yes, I have several friends who've gone through extensive cycles of treatment in recent years. From their experiences, it seems that there are more effective drugs to help patients feel better during the process. I hope that's the case for Renee."

"I would imagine that she would love to spend some days with you, either at your home or here at mine. Let's see how the first week goes and we will make some plans."

"That sounds good. In the meantime, I will discuss this with Doris. I know that we have some mutual friends who help with transporting cancer patients to their appointments. You are busy with a new business. You cannot be expected to take Renee every day. We can organize drivers. I can think of at least a couple of them who know you and Renee from your childhood."

"That would be wonderful. You also are probably not aware that Foster and his wife are moving here."

"Doris mentioned that the other day. That was surprising news. I don't fully understand this world of remote work, but if it gives the opportunity for loved ones to be closer, that's a positive development."

"I agree." Jenn glanced at her watch. "I just wanted to take a few minutes to update you, Aunt Rachel. I promise I will do better to keep in touch with you. Life has been a whirlwind since I moved back."

"I understand, my darling girl. There's no sugarcoating it, life has been throwing you too many curveballs. You are made of hardy stock. The strength of your dear mother is coursing through your veins, too. Never forget that. I know that I am a poor substitute, but I'm here for you, just like my beloved Paisley would be."

Jenn felt a lump of emotion form in her throat and her eyes filled with tears. The wound of her mother's sudden passing was still fresh in her heart. *Oh, how I wish Mom was here.*

"She's right beside you every day, Jenn. She will be holding Renee's hand."

Rachel's on point comment was just what was needed to push Jenn's emotions to a point that demanded releasing. After a hurried goodbye to her aunt, Jenn allowed the pain in her heart to come pouring out of her eyes. *It was time.*

Chapter Fourteen

Randy

"I'm sorry that your friend had to cancel, Chief. Is she a special friend of yours?"

Randy's former patrol officer, Joe Fairfield, leaned against the counter in one corner of the kitchen while Randy chopped the final vegetables to go into the tossed salad he planned to pair with grilled steak and chicken kabobs and baked potatoes. It was a simple meal, but it was a safer choice since Randy knew nothing about the eating habits of his guests.

Looking at the clock on the stove, Randy saw that it was another twenty minutes before Megan Whitman was supposed to arrive. That would give him some time to surmise if Fairfield's time with Edwin Greer had successfully prepared the young man to testify on Monday.

"Jenn and I grew up together. We lived on the same street throughout our entire childhood. Up until recently, it had been over thirty years since we've seen each other though."

"Wow! That's a long time."

"Life has a way of doing that. Jenn went off to college. I went into the Army. Both of us came home for visits, but our paths never crossed. I've been surprised that I didn't run into her through the years since I've been back in Serendipity. I suppose Jenn's visits to her parents were brief and focused. She probably didn't stray far from the family home."

"It's nice that you've known people for so many years. I don't really have any long-term friends. We moved around a lot when I was growing up. The town where my mother lives now is the one that we put down roots in the longest. That's only been since my father died."

Randy decided to take that information as an opening to find out more about the young man's background.

"What happened to your father, if you don't mind me asking?"

"He drank himself to death." Joe bowed his head, taking a deep breath. "There's no reason for me to mince words with you, Chief. My father was not a pleasant man. My mother and I have had a rough life. Mother always made excuses for him. She said that he drank a lot because of what he experienced when he was in the military overseas. After I became an officer, I did some of my own investigating into his past. He was never in the military. That was just my mother's way to make excuses for his abusive behavior. I just hope and pray that I don't have any of those genes in me."

Bingo! It was all starting to make sense. Joe Fairfield didn't think he was worthy of being an officer. Randy would keep asking questions and hope there was a possibility to convince the young man otherwise.

"You need to remember something, Fairfield. Children aren't responsible for the actions of their parents. I'm not going to say that genetics aren't a powerful part of determining who you are, but the heart of a person is what drives his or her actions. My experience with you so far has shown me a man with a good heart."

"That means a lot to me, Chief. I appreciate that. For the last few years, I've tried to tell my mother that we need to put him behind us.

There's a fear in her heart that she can't release. I saw it when I was back home these past few months. It's like he's still there in the house. I can't ever remember a time when she wasn't afraid. It's killing her physically. Mentally, that fear took her long ago."

"I'm sorry about that. I can hear the love you have for her in your voice."

"She always protected me from him. I don't know, maybe I'm crazy. As I was growing up, it seemed like he was punishing her for me existing in their lives. Maybe he didn't want me to be born. I've often wondered if maybe he wasn't my biological father. Truthfully, I've hoped he wasn't. I know that's a bad thing for me to say."

"You're not the first man I've heard say those words. The Army is full of men and women who had hard childhoods. You've got to dig down deep inside you and focus on the good. That's the stuff that will make you have a strong and happy life. Let the past stay there. Keep your eyes on the future."

"Yes, sir." Joe shook his head affirmatively. "Mr. Greer says he thinks I'm ready for court on Monday."

"That was my next question. I know that Edwin's preparations probably reminded you of a rough day at the police academy. He's a tough prosecutor with a strong record of convictions. Edwin doesn't mess around when it comes to preparing for questioning. He wants officers to be ready for any questions that the defense attorney might throw at them."

"He grilled me good. I testified in another case while I was still living here. It was one of his assistants who handled that case. That one was a breaking and entering case. It was fairly cut and dry. This case is a little more complicated."

"Yes, I've reviewed the files. It appears that my officers did their job when the incident occurred. That makes the prosecution easier."

"My sergeant was a stickler about following protocol and clean paperwork. Cutting corners doesn't make anyone's life easier."

"That's exactly right. Clean case work leads to justice being served." Randy glanced out the window, seeing a small car parking in the driveway. "You are about to get a reprieve from your personal justice because a lovely young lady has arrived to have dinner with you."

"Dinner with us, Chief. She's probably here to stay in good graces with Serendipity's Police Chief."

"Young man, Megan has no reason to need my good graces. She was visibly upset when I first spoke to her about you. If you're smart, you'll be on your best behavior and try to win her back."

"Yes, sir." A visibly nervous Joe dried the palms of his hands on the front of his jeans.

"Don't just stand there. Go let her in the house."

Randy shook his head, watching Joe quickly move toward the door. Staying in the kitchen, he continued working on last minute preparations, giving the two a little privacy for their reunion.

"Hello, Chief Nave."

Hearing Megan's sweet voice, Randy grabbed a kitchen towel, wiping his hands as he turned to greet her. The young woman wore a summer dress in bright yellow. Her shoulder-length sandy-brown hair was pulled back away from her face. Randy glanced at Joe. He was beaming from ear to ear.

"Welcome, Megan. I'm so happy that you could join us this evening." Randy smiled at the nervous young woman.

"I appreciate your invitation, sir. I was sorry to hear that Ms. Halston couldn't join us. I met her a few days ago."

"Jenn mentioned to me that she'd met you. She sends her apologies for not being able to join us. Jenn's sister and brother-in-law arrived today, rather unexpectedly. I hope you're hungry, Megan. I've prepared a simple meal, but there's plenty of it. Since the weather is nice this evening, I thought we could enjoy our meal out on the deck."

"That would be nice, Chief Nave. It seems like I never have time to get to enjoy the ocean view much. I think people who don't live in a coastal town think all we do is sit with our feet in the sand and look at the ocean. But if you live inland, weeks can go by without you even getting within view of the ocean. At least it's been that way in my life."

"You are right, Megan." Randy handed Megan and Joe each a platter of food before heading out the door with an empty platter. "I'm fortunate that I live on the beach now. I remember when I was growing up in Serendipity though my beach visits were few and far between. Even as a teenager, I was either working or at a sports practice. Go ahead and sit down at the table. I'll grab the food off the grill."

"I have a blurry memory of being at a beach when I was small." Joe set the platter he was carrying on the table next to the one Megan had placed there. "I had never been back again until I came for my interview to work for you, Chief. All those years though, I dreamed of living at the beach."

"How much time did you spend at the beach when you were working here?" Randy handed the platter of steak and chicken kabobs to Megan before he sat down.

"Every day I was off, I was at the beach. The way our shifts were that wasn't as often as I imagined. Maybe I should have become a lifeguard."

Randy watched Megan laugh and caught the two of them lock eyes. *These two have got it bad.*

"I'm going to try to convince Joe this weekend that he needs to re-apply to be a patrol officer here in Serendipity. What do you think of that idea, Megan?"

Randy kept a stoic expression even though Joe's eyes were big as saucers. He imagined the young man might be mentally sending him a few choice words.

"I was sad when Joe left, Chief. I think it would be wonderful if he moved back here." Megan looked down. "If he wants to be a police officer again."

Randy nonchalantly glanced at Joe. He was surprised to see his brow furrow and a frown where a smile should be. Obviously, something was troubling the young man. Randy was determined to get to the bottom of that subject before Joe returned home.

"Well, Megan, it's not any officer's favorite job duty, but perhaps Joe will be reminded about what he enjoyed about being an officer while he is back in Serendipity for a few days. Keeping company with a lovely young lady like you must be high on that list."

Watching Megan's blushing reaction, Randy changed the subject to chitchat about things going on in Serendipity and asking Megan about her job at the bank. By the time dinner was over, Randy realized that Joe had contributed little to the conversation. He wished that Jenn had been there. Perhaps, she would have been able to pull Joe into the dialogue.

Randy suggested that Joe take Megan for a walk on the beach before she left. It was a beautiful evening. After Randy quickly loaded the dishwasher and put the remaining food away, he took a beer out to the deck and watched the sun set from his most comfortable chair. Relaxing evenings were few and far between, he might as well enjoy it.

Almost an hour later, Randy was dozing when he heard laughter. Randy opened his eyes and sat straighter in the chair a few seconds before Megan and Joe appeared on the deck. Both looked relaxed and happy.

"That was a lovely suggestion, Chief." Megan stopped in front of Randy's chair. "It's been a long time since I've watched the sun set with sand between my toes. Mel is right about it being Serendipity's welcome mat."

"She is indeed. I forgot that you are good friends with Imogene. I suppose you hear a lot about what the Visitors Bureau does to bring travelers to our town." Randy stood up. "Can I get you two something to drink?"

"No, thank you. I've got to be getting home. I will be working in the morning. The bank is open half days on Saturday. It's my turn to work. I'd like to thank you again for asking me to spend the evening with you and Joe. Dinner was delicious."

"You're as welcome as you can be. I hope to see you again soon."

Megan smiled before turning to walk down the deck steps to her car. Joe glanced at Randy before following her. Randy couldn't read his expression. A few minutes later, Joe closed the door behind him, joining Randy in the kitchen.

"Thanks for dinner, Chief. I think I'll turn in, if that's okay."

"Sure, I thought we might watch the game for a while, but if you're tired, go ahead and hit the hay. If work doesn't sidetrack my plans, I thought you might like to go out on the boat with me tomorrow and fish a little while. Do you like to fish?"

"I can't say that I ever remember going fishing." Joe lingered in the doorway that led to the hall where the bedrooms were located.

"You've never been fishing? Young man, you've been missing one of the most relaxing forms of recreation ever created. What did you spend your childhood doing?" Randy shook his head, shocked.

"Moving. I spent most of my childhood trying to remember what street I lived on and what my teacher's name was."

Joe's monotone reaction surprised Randy. He remained silent, hoping that if he left the door open, Joe would reveal more about what made him tick.

"You know they do a fairly extensive background check when you go into the police academy." Joe took in a deep breath, rubbing his forehead. "One of the instructors had us write down all the schools we had attended. I thought maybe it was either to see how truthful we would be or test our memory. So, I made a list of all the schools I could remember attending. I didn't know all the names of the schools. I just remembered something different about each one. When my list was finished, there were seventeen schools on the list before I entered high school. Some of the guys I was in training with thought I was joking. Most of them had only been to one elementary school and one middle school."

"That's certainly a lot of different schools. Did going to so many schools make learning harder?"

"It didn't really. My mother made sure that I was strong in the basics. She didn't have much education herself, but she made sure that I learned to read and write. Everywhere we lived, we got library cards. I still have all of them in an old shoebox. We would read together every night. That helped me as I jumped from school to school. We spent a lot of time learning the fundamentals of math. When I got older, I taught her about algebra and geometry as I was learning it."

"It sounds like your mother is a smart woman."

"To most people, she is not. She is shy and backward. She appears scared of her shadow. Her shadow was my father. There were reasons she was afraid. That's not the woman I saw though. She read at least a hundred books a year for herself and read with me each night. She read a dictionary the way most people would read a magazine. Her mind is strong with knowledge. I wish her spirit had the same muscle."

"If I may ask, why did your family move so often?"

"Sometimes it's hard to understand a situation even when you are living in it." Joe slumped down in the chair that was across from Randy. "My father always seemed to be running from something. I don't know what it was. That's part of the reason I wanted to become an officer. I wanted to have a life that I didn't have to run from. In the years since he passed, I've tried to find out more about him. It's kind of like he was a ghost, in a way. There are few records that really lead back to him. We only lived in places we rented. They always paid cash for what they purchased. I guess that's not too unusual, but it doesn't leave much of a trail. That's kind of what my childhood felt like." Joe rose from the chair. "I appreciate you listening to my sad story, Chief. I appreciate everything you've done for me. I think I will go to bed."

"Happy to have you back in Serendipity. Megan seemed happy to see you again, too. Maybe between the two of us, we can convince you to give our town another chance."

"Good night, Chief."

Randy sat in his chair for a few minutes, after Joe went to bed, scrolling through some emails on his phone. One was from Edwin, confirming that the testimony preparation session with Joe had gone well. Randy hoped that nothing prevented him from being in court on Monday so that he could see firsthand how Joe handled himself on the stand. The young man's past obviously weighed heavily on him. It seemed to create a barrier from the life Joe wanted to lead. The conversation made Randy think of his own son. Despite the divorce, Randy knew that Bryson's childhood had been nothing like Joe's. His life with Randy and his mother, and later with Bryson's stepfather, was stable in all the ways that Joe's was not. He couldn't help but wonder if there were unanswered questions that Bryson had about the lives his parents had led. Randy would ask him about that on their next fishing trip. Until then, he'd see if tomorrow he could help the young man staying in his guest room figure out the next phase of his life.

Chapter Fifteen

Mel

"I THINK THERE'S BEEN a larger crowd at the festival this year than last. What do you think, Mel?"

Imogene's question jarred Mel out of the deep fog of thought she'd allowed her mind to wander into. It was the last day of the three-day event. Early mornings and late nights of not only staffing the information booth, but also making sure all aspects of the festival were going smoothly, made for a tired mind and body.

"I think you're right. We won't know for sure until we tally the ticket sales and revenues, but this feels like the first lull we've had in three days. I guess that targeted video advertising on social media paid off."

"I'll say. I will enjoy writing up the grant report with the data showing increases in attendance and revenue." Imogene resumed typing on her laptop. "I do enjoy my numbers."

Mel yawned through a tired smile. She wished for the energy of Imogene's youth. At the end of the festival's third day, the young woman looked as fresh as she did the day before the festival began. All Mel could think about was sitting in the Jacuzzi tub in her bathroom with a large glass of something cold. She'd lived in beach humidity her whole life. For some reason, it seemed hotter in recent years. Perhaps it was the hot flashes which curiously increased in intensity as the temperature had risen. *Getting old sucks.*

"I hope he doesn't break her heart again."

For the second time in the last few minutes, Imogene pulled Mel out of her exhausted thoughts.

"What?"

"I'm talking about Joe Fairfield. He and Megan are getting ice cream from that vendor across the street."

Mel looked across the street. The couple had stopped by the Visitors Bureau booth earlier in the afternoon, but Mel hadn't talked to them. She'd been busy doing a live interview with a television reporter. Catching only a glimpse of Joe then, she thought something was familiar about him. She couldn't put her finger on it.

"I remember Joe from when he lived here. He looks different to me."

"He had a moustache and beard. It was the first thing that Megan mentioned when she called me after their dinner date the other night at the Chief's house."

Mel walked outside of the Visitors Bureau tent to get a better look at Joe and Megan. She could only see Joe's profile. He reminded her of someone. Shaking her head and stretching, Mel looked at her watch.

"I think we can start packing up our extra boxes. Thankfully, we don't have too many remaining."

"Especially after you had to go and get more from the office yesterday." Imogene began pulling boxes out from underneath the display table. "I will be sure to note how many of each brochure we've used this weekend in my follow-up report."

"Let's also add some of the most frequent questions we received to our facts sheet. I'm surprised at how many people were looking for real estate information and where to find electric vehicle chargers."

Mel picked up a box and walked to her vehicle that was parked on the grass behind their booth space.

"I get the real estate question almost daily at the office." Imogene came up behind Mel with another box. "The electric charger question is a newer one. I was glad to see there is good information online about that."

"Just goes to show we need to always be ready for new types of questions. Some of the newspaper staff have mentioned about creating a regional real estate guide. Jenn will be happy to hear that people are frequently asking about such information."

Mel moved a few things around in the back of her SUV to make room for the table and tent when it was time to take them down.

"Mel, were you expecting Mr. Lewis to stop by? I think I see him walking in this direction."

Taking a deep breath, Mel's thoughts returned to the dinner she and Sinclair had the evening before the festival began. She knew why Sinclair was there. Quite frankly, she was surprised that he hadn't attempted to talk to her sooner. Sinclair would want to know what Mel meant when she told him she had to forgive herself for the 'biggest mistake of her life.' It was a secret that she'd held in her heart for too long. It was a sliver of knowledge that no one else knew, not even Jenn. Mel partially held herself responsible for what had happened between Sinclair and Dana on that trip all those years ago. Maybe if she confessed that to Sinclair, it would relieve some of the responsibility she'd felt.

"What a festival this has been!" Sinclair came walking around the tent to where Mel was standing.

"Oh, have you been enjoying it?" Mel turned around, putting a smile on her face.

"I have." Sinclair lowered his voice. "Regina and her husband came yesterday, and we spent the whole day here. I made sure that we kept a respectable distance away so that we wouldn't run into you. I didn't want you to feel uncomfortable."

"Thank you. I'm happy that you and your family had a good time. Imogene and I were just saying that we think there was a record attendance." Mel moved back toward the tent, turning to Imogene. "I think we can go ahead and finish packing up. Everyone will be moving toward the pavilion to watch the fireworks. Imogene, didn't you tell me that your sister and her children were coming for the fireworks show?"

"Yes, but I told them I would be helping you take our booth down and moving our stuff back to the office."

"That's not necessary. We can pack it all up and unload it tomorrow. We'll have all day to put everything away. I bet Mr. Lewis will help me get the tent down and packed. Can you do that, Sinclair?"

"Absolutely! It would be my pleasure."

Sinclair's beaming smile tugged at Mel's heart. It reminded her of his expression after winning a baseball game.

"Problem solved. You've worked extremely hard this weekend and I appreciate it." Mel handed Imogene's purse and tote to her. "You did *all* the preparation work for this event. I can do this part. You go run along and find your sister and those adorable nieces and nephews. They've missed their Aunt Imogene."

"Thanks, Mel." Imogene smiled. "I appreciate you helping us, Mr. Lewis."

"You are going to have to stop calling me that. You can call me Sinclair."

"I'll try. See you in the morning, Mel."

Imogene disappeared into the crowd of people walking toward the pavilion. Mel could see the deep orange of another beautiful sunset growing darker on the horizon.

"This tent is easy to take down—" Mel spoke, turning around to find that Sinclair already had the canopy off the tent and was folding it. "I guess you've done this before."

"Only hundreds of times." Sinclair chuckled. "You will probably find it shocking to learn that both of my children were athletes. We helped with a lot of fundraisers to raise money for uniforms and such. That's a lot of tent pitching."

"I should not be surprised." Mel felt a little melancholy, imagining a younger Sinclair encircled in small children, coaching or selling hot dogs. "I appreciate your help."

"Earlier this afternoon, I thought you and Imogene might need some help taking down your booth. You've both put in some long days at this festival. I imagine you've put in a lot of time preparing."

"We are involved indirectly with some of the festival's committees. Our main contribution is the advance promotion of the event and running this information booth. The real backbreaking work is done by a legion of volunteers."

"Maybe I will volunteer to be one of them next year. At the minimum, I will offer a business sponsorship." Sinclair laid the tent poles in the back of Mel's vehicle. "Do you want to go by your office and unload this?"

"No, it will be easier for Imogene to do that tomorrow. She can take things out one at a time and put them away. She's very organized. I'm not allowed to put things away." Mel laughed. "She does a fabulous job. I try to stay out of her way."

"Good employees are hard to come by. When you find one, it's best to let them do their own thing." Sinclair closed the back door of the SUV. "Are you hungry? We could go get a bite to eat."

"I've eaten too much festival food this weekend. I think I need a shower, a bowl of cereal, and my bed. I appreciate the invitation. Thanks for your help, Sinclair."

Mel began to walk around Sinclair to get to the driver's side of the vehicle. Gently, he took hold of her arm, stopping her.

"You know I've got to ask what you meant the other night. It's been keeping me awake since then."

Mel moved backward out of Sinclair's grasp. She wasn't ready to tell her last secret. Mel needed to talk it through with her best friend first. Jenn was busy with Renee moving in and beginning cancer treatment.

"I know that I shouldn't have dangled that piece of information in front of you. I should have kept it to myself."

"I understand that it may not be something you want to reveal. I hope you can learn to trust me enough to share it with me. I gathered that it is obviously something that has to do with us."

"It has to do with me. It affected us. I will think about it. It may be a deal breaker in any future we might have."

"There are no deal breakers from my point of view." Sinclair started to reach for Mel again but stopped himself.

Mel felt years of emotion rise inside her again. All this time, it had been easy to focus on what Sinclair had done to end their relationship. Mel pushed any other possibilities to the back of her mind.

The crackling sound of distant fireworks drew their attention in the direction of the sky lighting up over the ocean. It reminded Mel of another summer night long ago when she and Sinclair sat side by side at an older version of the pavilion that was full of people tonight. She could almost sense the same memory going through his mind.

"If we could just talk to the kids we were when we last watched fireworks together." Sinclair's words confirmed what Mel imagined. "I'd tell them to slow down and not be in such a hurry to grow up. Maybe then, we would have had a lifetime of memories together, instead of apart."

Mel almost gasped at the truth of Sinclair's words. *I've got to get out of here.*

"Thanks again for your help."

Mel did not look in Sinclair's direction. Instead, she jumped into her vehicle, immediately starting the engine and putting it in gear. Only when she was a safe distance away did she dare to look into her rearview mirror. A distant moon was barely shining enough to show Sinclair still standing in the same spot, watching her drive away. The tears came, still flowing when she reached her own driveway.

"How did Renee's first treatment go?"

It was late Monday evening before Mel attempted to contact Jenn. Her day had been full of responding to emails and other messages which had been pushed to the backburner in the days before the festival. True to form, Imogene had everything organized or put away by lunchtime, even with the Visitors Center being full of people staying over in the area for another day or two after the festival.

"I believe everything went as planned." Jenn responded to Mel's short text with a phone call. "Renee and Neil met with her new doctor and then Renee had the first chemo treatment. Neil left shortly after they returned to the house, so I've been working from home this afternoon."

"Oh, I thought Neil might stay a few days." Mel stretched out on her couch with Princess Mia snuggled beside her. The pooch had been missing Mel during the busy weekend.

"Apparently there is a major contract that is being signed tomorrow morning. The meeting with the lawyers about it has been moved twice already because Neil was with Renee in the hospital. He was concerned that a third delay might put the deal in jeopardy. Neil told me that it is the biggest contract they've had in several years. I told him that I could handle taking care of Renee."

"I'm sure that juggling such a big company while his wife has been ill has been tough on Neil."

"I think work is what keeps Neil sane. Dad would be proud of how far Neil has taken his business."

"There's no doubt that your father would be proud." Mel scratched Mia behind the ears. "How is Renee feeling?"

"After Neil left, I got her to eat a little soup. She's been sleeping ever since. I think tired is going to be a consistent but expected byproduct of her treatment and everything that led up to it. We learned that from our father's battle with cancer. Thank you for checking on her. How did the festival go? All the reports I've heard say that it was a record-breaking success. That must make you and Imogene two exhausted ladies."

"The weekend was a busy one. Despite the long days, it's rewarding to see the crowds of people in attendance. It means that our marketing is working and that the festival is continuing to bring in visitors and revenue. Your team will be happy to know that real estate was a hot topic. The planned development of the area is news that is reaching beyond the locals. I think the emphasis on a real estate publication and website that Betsy and Ellie are developing will come at an ideal time. Imogene is going to add real estate as another topic that viewers of our website can request information about. That will also help us to develop a database of addresses to send the link to for your new real estate website whenever it is ready."

"That sounds fabulous. We appreciate that."

"It's obviously something our visitors want to know more about, and we need help to fill that need."

"Is there anything that *you* need to talk about? I know you called to check on Renee, and I appreciate your concern. However, my bestie radar is sensing that there's more to this phone call."

Mel should have known that she couldn't hide anything from Jenn. Her 'bestie radar,' as Jenn called it, was always keen, even when there were hundreds of miles between them. Now that they were both in the same town again, it was razor sharp.

"We do need to have a talk when we both have time. It can wait though. You need to handle all the guests who are checking in to your oceanfront bed and breakfast. Have Foster and Michelle arrived yet?"

"No. Everything was finalized on Friday with the person who bought their home. They decided to take their time driving the moving van here since Renee was also arriving this weekend. They departed Atlanta on Sunday after staying a couple of nights at a hotel and tying up some lose ends. Then, they stopped to visit a college friend along the way. I expect them to arrive on Wednesday. They will stay here for a few days, but they will be getting the keys to their condos on Thursday."

"Condos? As in plural?"

"Yes. They bought two in the same building. They are going to do a little remodeling, then live in one and rent the other as a monthly rental."

"That's smart. There are many visitors who like to come and spend a month. What about Claire?"

"Claire is planning to head in this direction. I wonder if she might initially rent the other condo that Foster and Michelle bought. I don't know if she will want to buy any real estate right now. She might change her mind about living in Serendipity."

"It's funny. I'm sure that your kids enjoyed visiting here as they were growing up, but I don't remember them ever mentioning that they were interested in living here."

"That's true. All of them have always seemed to prefer city life over a small town like Serendipity. I guess this new world of remote working is giving opportunities to explore some different possibilities." Jenn sighed. "When I moved here, I didn't expect to have my children so close by. My life has been a series of curveballs this past year. I think I will try to catch these that are coming my way. Claire and Foster have always been forcefully independent. I don't expect them to need their mother much once they get settled."

"Can Emily be far behind?" Mel giggled, picturing the feisty college girl.

"Emily will not like missing all this family action, I'm sure. But she's deep into carving out her own life niche. I think she will just show up for tanning visits."

"Tanning visits, that's catchy. Maybe I should use that in Serendipity's marketing."

"It won't go too well with your whole sunset brand, I'm afraid. Not much tanning occurs while the sun is setting. I think I might have heard some movement in Renee's room. I think I better go check on her. I plan to work from home tomorrow. You are welcome to come visit after work, if you would like."

"That sounds like a good idea. I'll text you tomorrow afternoon and see if you think Renee is up to a visit."

"Perfect. Thank you for checking on us."

After the call ended, Mel remained on the couch, thinking about all the aspects of Jenn's life that had changed in the past year. It was a wonder that her friend was able to keep a semblance of sanity with all the change. Mel had long kidded her friend that she was part cat.

"Jenn always lands on her feet. I can't imagine that she planned to have so many lives at one time though."

CHAPTER SIXTEEN

Jenn

"DID YOU GET THE license plate information?"

Jenn was surprised to see that Renee was already up when Jenn entered the kitchen the following morning.

"What? I don't understand."

Despite being tired, Jenn's sleep had not been sound. She needed a strong cup of coffee before she could have a coherent conversation.

"I'm hoping that you wrote down the license plate of the truck that ran over me yesterday. From the way I feel, it must have been a tractor trailer. I want Chief Dreamy to arrest the driver." The tired scowl on Renee's face did not stop her from raising an eyebrow with her last comment.

"Oh, sister dear, I was hoping that you might have a few days before you started to feel the effects of your treatments. Were you sick during the night?"

"No, I didn't throw up, if that is what you mean. I slept quite well. That bed is heavenly. I woke up about an hour ago with a splitting headache though and my entire body hurts."

"Are those symptoms that the doctors told you to expect?"

Jenn retrieved a bag of dark roast beans from the cabinet above her coffee maker. She stopped herself considering the noise the grinding would make. Jenn put that bag away, opting instead for some pre-ground coffee from her collection.

"There are pages and pages of information about potential symptoms. I opted for a little mystery with my treatment and stopped reading after the sentence that said, 'every patient reacts differently.' The bottom line is that they are injecting me with poison to kill the bad stuff. It may kill some of my good stuff, too, and it will most definitely make me sick."

"Did you take any pain killers for your headache?" Jenn prepped the coffee maker and pushed the button to begin brewing. The aroma from the ground coffee alone began to awaken her senses.

"Yes, I took the maximum dosage allowed for three days." Renee's expression remained pained and stoic.

"Renee." Jenn gave her sister a stern look.

"This is not going to be any fun if I can't be my usual snarky self." Renee stuck her tongue out, in childhood fashion. "I took two of the maximum strength pain relievers because I have a maximum strength headache. I took that dosage an hour ago. I haven't seen any real change in the magnitude of pounding my head seems to be enduring."

"The coffee will be ready in a few minutes. How about I start on some breakfast for us?"

Renee grimaced, holding her head with her hands.

"I've got some delicious brioche bread to make some French toast with fresh strawberries and some Maplewood bacon. I know my sis loves her bacon."

"The French toast part sounds great. I don't know if I can stomach the smell of bacon. I'd really hate to ruin my love affair with my favorite breakfast meat by having to revisit it later." Renee put her hand over her mouth.

"Okay. No bacon, no problem. Do you think the smell of cooking in general is going to bother you? Maybe you could have your coffee out on the deck while I'm cooking."

"That sounds like a great idea. I'm sure the ocean breeze will be soothing and relaxing." Renee rose from her chair. Moving toward the door to the deck, she bumped Jenn as she walked by her. "I'm glad I'm here with you. I appreciate you taking in your big sister. I think I'm going to need you."

"I hate the reason, Renee, but I welcome the opportunity to help you. The longer I am here, the more I understand that Serendipity is more than the name of our hometown. I keep doing these quite normal things and something else entirely comes along and changes the direction I thought I was going in."

"I wouldn't call my cancer a happy accident, but, somehow, I think you are right. I feel like there's going to be something good come out of this experience. It might be as simple as deepening my relationship with my sister. I do so need her in my life."

Renee didn't give Jenn a chance to respond. She kept walking toward the door.

Jenn's heart swelled with love and concern. She bit her bottom lip to keep from starting to cry. The rollercoaster of emotions that her life had been on during the last year was only one layer under the tough independence Jenn had so carefully crafted for her life. There was no doubt that Renee could penetrate that shell. Maybe there was going to be some mutual healing occurring during Renee's recovery.

"That sounds great, Doris. I had forgotten all about the meeting with our company attorney. Renee is feeling much better this afternoon. After we had breakfast and almost two pots of coffee between us, Renee's headache disappeared. We took a short walk on the beach and then she took a nap. She's deep into reading a book on the deck. I know that she will be thrilled to see you and Aunt Rachel. I'll see you at three o'clock."

"Did I hear the words 'Aunt Rachel' and 'three o'clock' in the same sentence?"

With her back to the deck, Jenn didn't see Renee come inside.

"Yes. I hope you are okay with that. I'd forgotten that I have a meeting with my attorney about some newspaper business. That was Doris on the phone, reminding me about the meeting. She said that she would love to bring Aunt Rachel over for a visit while I go to my meeting."

"I don't need a babysitter every minute of the day, Jenn." Renee retrieved a pitcher of iced tea from the refrigerator, pouring herself a glass.

"I understand. I don't plan on staying with you all the time. I just thought it might be good to at least be with you for the first forty-eight hours after your initial treatment. You've not had chemo before; you could have an adverse reaction. Doris volunteered to bring Aunt Rachel over. I think she's anxious to see both of us."

"You're the one who is in trouble though. You've been here months and months and not visited her."

"I've been here weeks and weeks. I have talked to her on the phone since she called us at your house."

"I'm sure that doesn't count as a visit in Rachel Frederick's book." Renee chuckled. "It would be a wise move on your part for this visit to be on your own turf. The stately Frederick house is full of the guilt of our ancestors. Rachel is the Queen of that since Grammie Elana is gone."

"I don't think either Mom or Rachel have ever come close to the level of guilt that Grammie could inflict. As strong as that was, you know what was even stronger?"

"Grammie's love. Mom's love. Aunt Rachel's love. We need some of that. Bring on the visit. I'll score extra points with Aunt Rachel while you're off to your meeting, *and* I'll be sure to thoroughly question Doris regarding what she knows about you and Chief Dreamy."

"This is not fair. I've opened my heart and home to my sick sister and she's conspiring against me."

"I would more aptly describe it as leveling the playing field and investigative reporting. I know you understand that last term. I'm going to *interview* Doris."

"There's zero chance that you will get your own column in the *Serendipity Sun.* Nice try though."

"I seem to recall that Lyle the Smile asked me out once while we were still in high school."

"I don't think Neil would be too happy about you accepting Lyle's invitation forty years later."

"It wasn't forty years ago!" Renee eyes darted back and forth, searching her memory. "Crap! It has been that many years. I surrender. It's the chemo talking. What time is it?"

"Two-thirty."

"I have just enough time to take a shower. Aunt Rachel is expecting to see two fine Southern ladies. If I can't feel like one, I can at least look the part."

The lilt in Renee's voice was unmistakable as she sashayed toward her bedroom. Jenn could feel the presence of their lovely mother, Paisley Halston—the ultimate Southern lady. *Everything will be okay.*

Less than an hour passed before Doris' little blue Subaru pulled into Jenn's driveway. Watching from the kitchen window, Jenn caught the first glimpse of her beloved aunt as Rachel's tall frame emerged from the small vehicle. A lump caught in Jenn's throat. While Paisley and Rachel each had their own distinct looks and features, there was a sisterly similarity that could not be denied. Somehow the resemblance to Jenn's mother was stronger now that her mother was no longer in view.

"Are they here?"

For the second time that day, Renee came up behind Jenn without her noticing. This time Jenn jumped.

"They've just arrived." Jenn turned around, gasping at the difference in Renee's appearance. "You clean up good, Sis."

Renee had not been joking when she told Jenn she would be bringing too much luggage. What was an empty closet in the guest room Renee was staying in was now full of lovely clothes. Renee was currently wearing linen pink capris paired with a flowing fuchsia blouse. She'd pulled her hair up with a clip on the back of her head. Her natural-looking makeup was flawless. She looked well.

"There was something about looking good and feeling better in the cancer propaganda they sent home with me." Renee sneered. "You look like you're preparing to go and testify."

"I'm giving a deposition. It's about something that transpired while I was buying the newspaper. It's not a court case, but there must be a deposition for legal purposes."

Renee's mention of testifying made Jenn think of Randy. She wondered how the court case had gone.

"They are probably almost at the door. I've got to warn you. Rachel is looking a lot like Mom today."

"I was thinking about that while I was in the shower. I was struck by that same feeling at Mom's funeral. I saw a certain expression cross Rachel's face and it was just like Mom. We must keep a stiff upper lip. She'll think something else is wrong otherwise."

"Hello. Hello." Doris' cheerful voice filled the room as she opened the sliding door from the deck. "Brace yourself, ladies. You are being invaded."

A relaxed feeling came over Jenn. It was a feeling she had come to love. Being in Doris' company made Jenn feel peaceful. There was no doubt that Doris was an integral part of the newspaper's operation. The work she did was perfection. But it was her aura that Jenn valued the most. She exuded peace and tranquility. Everything would be okay if Doris was in the room. Jenn likened the feeling to the satisfaction of comfort food.

"Get out of my way, Doris Hudson. You are standing between me and my beloved flesh and blood."

Rachel's commanding presence swept into the room not unlike the way Scarlett O'Hara did in *Gone With The Wind*, minus the hoop skirt and petticoats, of course.

Always looking like she stepped out of a fashion magazine, Rachel was dressed in a comfortable but tailored powder blue pantsuit. A large flower broach rested near her left shoulder. Her silver hair looked like it had been styled at a beauty salon that morning. She was in stark contrast to her best friend's typical 70s-like fashion. Doris' pantsuit was brown and orange with a design that might make you dizzy, if you stared at it too long.

"Oh, my goodness, Renee. You are nothing but skin and bones. You've lost so much weight." Rachel pulled Renee into a rib-crushing embrace.

"I've been on the cancer diet, Aunt Rachel. It's all the rage. Surely, you've seen it featured on the talk shows."

Jenn did not miss that Renee's snarky tone still had a tired sound to it. She remembered that tone in Renee's voice from the early months and years after Jonah was taken. The signature sassiness her sister was known for could not conceal heartache, exhaustion, and fear.

"Don't use up all your honey hugs on Renee, Aunt Rachel." Jenn snuck in Rachel's pet word for her embraces.

"Now, Jennie Girl, you know that Aunt Rachel always makes extra honey hugs before she comes to see her favorite nieces." Rachel held up her hand when Jenn approached her. "Although, I should withhold all of yours since you've lived here six months without visiting me."

"Now, Aunt Rachel, you know it's not that long."

"It's been *too* long. Here my best friend gets to see you practically every day since you moved back and this is the first time I've laid eyes on you, except for that scandalous photograph that everyone is talking about."

"Yes. *That* photo!" Renee exclaimed, making herself wince in pain. "Doris, I think that should be the main focus on our chat this afternoon."

"Help me, Doris. There's obviously not going to be any allegiance from my next of kin. I'm counting on you to at least be on my team." Jenn glanced at her watch. "I'd love to stay and hear every second of this conversation, but duty calls. Doris, I appreciate you and Aunt Rachel coming over and visiting with Renee. I will try not to be gone too long. I was planning on stopping and getting us all some Chinese food from Peking. I would love for the four of us to have dinner together."

"That sounds lovely, Jenn. We weren't expecting to stay for dinner though." Rachel joined Renee on the couch. "We don't want to be a bother."

"I insist. It will be great fun for us to have a meal together. I'm certain that we all would enjoy a good dose of the most delicious Chinese food in Serendipity. Doris, there's a notepad on the counter with the entrées that Renee and I would like to have. I've also left their takeout menu so that you and Rachel can make your choices. I will text you when my meeting is over so that you can call the order in."

"That reminds me. Doris, I forgot that I left the cake in the backseat of your car." Rachel frowned. "I'm so forgetful these days."

"A cake? A special Aunt Rachel cake?" Renee clapped her hands like an excited child.

"The One and Only Orange Blossom Special." Rachel tilted her head back, cackling in laughter.

It was a familiar scene. Rachel sitting in the home of her beloved sister, laughing and telling stories. Jenn's heart caught with the sadness of who was missing. In that moment, she realized this was the first time Rachel had been in this house since her sister Paisley suddenly passed away. Jenn never thought about that and how hard it must have been for her to visit.

"It's the yummiest cake in the world. Please go retrieve it from your car, Doris, before something happens to it."

Renee's dramatic reaction to the cake being left in the warm car was comical. Jenn knew that the delectable dessert, which combined orange cake with orange sherbet, coconut, whipped cream, and mandarin oranges, would not survive for long in the late summer sun.

"No worries. It's in a cooler, of course." Doris rose from her chair. "I'll walk down as Jenn leaves and get it."

"I hope you all have a delightful visit. Please try to not discuss me too much. Renee is a far more interesting topic." Jenn gathered her purse and files before heading to the door. "Renee, if you think of anything you need, text me, and I will pick it up."

"Hope your meeting goes well." Aunt Rachel smiled. "Attorneys can be such pains in the caboose when they are on the opposite side of the table. I hope yours is the conductor of this meeting."

"He will be, Aunt Rachel. Mr. Crewe seems to oversee whatever situation he is in."

"Ah, yes, I've heard of him. Excellent reputation for being a hardnosed litigator."

Once Jenn and Doris were down the outside steps, Doris stopped Jenn before they reached their vehicles.

"I'm so glad that circumstances have allowed for Rachel and me to visit with Renee this afternoon. Rachel has been so worried ever since she heard about Renee's emergency surgery."

"Life seems to be just a crazy whirlwind these days. I appreciate you taking care of things at the office. I believe that we will be able to work out some volunteers that can help with transporting Renee so that I can be in the office more." Jenn looked at her watch. "I've got to scoot, if I'm going to get to Mr. Crewe's office on time."

Jenn jumped in her vehicle and focused on safely getting to her meeting on time. Mentally, she briefly ran through the list of questions she was told would be included in the deposition. Stopping at a traffic light before the right turn to the attorney's office, Jenn caught a glimpse of Randy's police vehicle as it crossed the intersection in front of her. Randy didn't see her, but the person in the passenger seat turned in her direction as the vehicle went by. There was something very familiar about the young man. He was probably one of Randy's officers.

"Maybe it's the young man who came here to testify." Jenn spoke aloud, pondering for a moment. The blow of a horn behind her made Jenn realize that the light was now green, and it was time to make her turn. She wished there was time for her to follow Randy and apologize to the young man for missing dinner the previous Friday. Seeing the office building where her meeting was located, Jenn's thoughts returned to her immediate responsibility, and she parked her vehicle in the first available spot.

"I cannot remember the last time I was this full." Renee set her fork down on the almost clean plate in front of her, relaxing in the deck chair. "As can be seen from my weight loss, I've not had much of an appetite in recent months. I could not resist Peking's delicious sesame chicken though. I bet it's been a decade or more since I've eaten there."

"That was one thing that was always missing about a visit back home to see Mom and Dad. Mom always wanted to cook for us, so we rarely ate at the local restaurants we loved growing up." Jenn took the last bite of her entrée.

"Except Dippers. We always made room for some homemade ice cream from Dippers." Renee rubbed her stomach. "I'm happy that I opted to wear loose pants this evening."

"It's been delightful enjoying this meal with this beautiful view." A serious expression crossed Rachel's face. "I cannot count the number of times I've sat on this deck with your mother or your grandmother and revealed the secrets of my heart."

"We like secrets." Barely a second passed before Renee's response. "This generation wants to know all the Frederick and Halston secrets. Jenn and I may have missed some since we've lived away from here for so long."

"Secrets come with responsibility, my dear. Some of them are best left in the past."

Jenn watched a silent communication pass between Aunt Rachel and Doris. There could probably be a book written with all the stories that lifelong friendship held. Paisley Halston was never too forthcoming when it came to revealing the secrets of her sister's life. Doris likely carried most of the same information in her mind and heart. Jenn doubted Doris would be any more telling than Jenn's mother. Loyalty ran deep when it came to Rachel Frederick.

"For all the chatter we've had during this dinner, we never landed on the meeting you went to, Jenn." Doris slyly changed the topic of conversation. "Did it go well?"

"It was relatively painless, I suppose. As painless as it can be when you are being filmed under oath."

"Filmed?" Rachel's voice rose with her question. "In my day, there would be a stenographer feverishly recording a legal proceeding, but the recording would be with ink and paper, not a videoing device."

"Your day has not completely passed. There was a young man in the room who was frantically typing every word on a laptop. Unfortunately, there was also a camera aimed at my face that recorded my nervous answers."

"It was merely a formality regarding old newspaper business, correct?" Doris stood up and refilled each glass of iced tea.

"Yes. It had to do with some work that was supposed to have been done on the building before the real estate transferred to me. The work was delayed with an agreement that it would not hold up the transfer. It was specialized work involving the replacement of some brick on the rear wall of the structure. The contractor has been slow to finish it. The attorneys for both sides are using this deposition process to 'encourage' the work to be completed sooner rather than later."

"It's unfortunate when people do not naturally keep their word and must be forced to do so." Rachel sat up straighter in her chair. "Unlike them, I am a keeper of my word and vowed to make my beloved nieces their favorite cake, if I was ever so fortunate as to be in the same room with both of them again."

Jenn swore her aunt could have been a character from a children's fantasy story with the Cheshire Cat grin which now resided on her face. The expression on her face was purely mischievous with a Southern lady flair. *Alice In Wonderland Meets Gone With The Wind.* Jenn almost laughed aloud at her thoughts.

"No, I can't possibly eat another bite of food. I ate too much Chinese food." Renee moaned dramatically.

"Fiddle-dee-dee, Scarlett." Jenn chuckled at her private joke. "You knew full well of the existence of the cake before you put the first bite of dinner in your mouth. Despite my current role as your caregiver, I am not going to miss out on the orange lusciousness of our favorite cake because you are playing the 'full card.' Let there be cake!" Jenn rose from the table with her right arm extended above with dramatic flair.

"Paisley would be proud of her middle daughter standing up for her cake rights." Rachel clapped her hands.

"I'll serve it." Doris chuckled while she began picking up the dinner plates.

"Shall I make some coffee to go with it?" Jenn cleaned up a few other items on the table that would no longer be needed.

"Coffee would be splendid." Rachel handed her empty tea glass to Jenn. "A fine complement to the cake's orange richness."

"This visit has been so good for Rachel." Doris spoke once she and Jenn were alone in the kitchen. "I know that you girls have certainly grieved your mother's passing and the suddenness of it. Rachel's sadness has been deep. As different as she and Paisley could be, there was an unbreakable bond between them. It went beyond sisterhood. Paisley stood beside Rachel at one of the most trying times of Rachel's life. She helped Rachel make a decision that put both at odds with their own parents. They dared to stand up to Elana."

"Stand up to Grammie?" Jenn whispered, as if the long-dead matriarch could hear her. "I cannot imagine it. What on earth was it about?"

"The bonds of friendship can be as strong as sisterhood. I cannot reveal the situation. I can only say that Paisley's support was steadfast, and it sustained Rachel as she moved forward with her life." Doris opened the refrigerator, picking up the beautiful cake by the base of its pedestal plate. "Their bond became even stronger after your father passed. I don't think that Rachel ever imagined that Paisley would pass before her."

Jenn desired to question Doris further but knew this wasn't the time or place. Jenn's mother would not reveal the secrets she held for her sister. Rachel's best friend would not reveal such either.

The sunset began its show of colors as the four of them took their last bites of cake and sips of coffee. There was silence around the table. The satisfaction of good food and familial love was enough.

"You're up early again. I expected you to be sleeping in after yesterday's excitement."

Rising before seven the following morning, Jenn found Renee sitting on the living room couch with a photo album on her lap.

"My body doesn't know what is going on. It's had doses of chemicals to kill villainous disease and the exquisite deliciousness of that heavenly cake, all in the same week. I've already brewed the coffee. Get a cup and join me."

"The aroma awakened me from my own slumber. I've already poured a cup." Jenn set her steaming cup on the coffee table in front of where Renee was sitting. "Are you taking a trip down memory lane this morning?"

"I'd forgotten that the family albums were kept inside this table. Since this furniture was staying here, I don't think we even opened this since Mother passed."

"I guess not. We can certainly divide these photos, if you like."

"I think they should stay here for now. I can visit them. I've found some hidden gems in these albums. Hilarious. Embarrassing. Unforgettable." Renee turned the page of the album. "Look at my pretty sister laughing with Neil on our wedding day. My goodness! Were we ever that young?"

Jenn studied the photo, remembering the special day and the joke she exchanged with her new brother-in-law. Jenn's eyes grew big as she focused on the image of a young Neil. He'd worn a beard and moustache for so long, Jenn had forgotten how he looked clean-shaven. It was like he was a different person. Yet, there was something quite familiar about the young man in that photo. Jenn was distracted by the sound of Renee's phone buzzing on the table.

"There's my Romeo now. Checking on me." Renee moved the album to the table, picking up her phone to answer the call. "Good morning, darling."

Taking her cup of coffee, Jenn made her way to the bathroom to get ready for the day. While Renee was taking her treatment mid-morning, Jenn would go into the office and meet with Lyle Livingston about an upcoming special section in the newspaper. After her shower, Jenn found her phone, still charging, on her dresser. A text message from Foster conveyed that he and Michelle would be arriving the following day. A voicemail from Claire gave the news that she would be travelling to Europe in a week on an art buying trip with her boss. Jenn frowned, seeing a missed call from Simon. *I don't have the time or patience for him.*

While waiting on Renee to get ready, Jenn answered multiple emails from Betsy and Ellie regarding aspects of the new real estate website that they were working on with Marella and her web designer brother. They were determined to have a skeleton of the future website in place before Michelle joined their advertising team. Jenn was impressed with the enthusiasm and creativity that everyone was bringing to the table. The project could be the new product that gave the *Serendipity Sun* the financial stability it needed.

"I'm ready! Let's get this party started." Renee appeared in the doorway dressed in a bright yellow sundress with a floral orange sash at the waist. "Do you like my outfit? At my first appointment, I noticed that most of the other patients were dressed in comfortable, yet dreary, looking clothes. That's not my style. I want to be the most fashionable person in the chemo room."

"Maybe we should stop at one of the tourist stores and buy the other patients some sunglasses. Because my big sis is going to light up the room. Let's go."

The cancer center was located on the opposite side of Serendipity from where Jenn lived. The ride gave her the opportunity to tell Renee what she knew about the status of some of the long-term businesses along the way that Renee might remember from their childhood. Jenn was surprised to learn that Renee had kept up with local businesses better than Jenn would have expected through conversations with their mother and reports from Neil about local construction.

Back at Jenn's office, she found that Alice was at the front desk. Doris was at a doctor's appointment. Taking advantage of the limited time she had, Jenn immediately asked Lyle to come to her office to discuss the editorial for the next special section. A brief update from Betsy told them the projected advertising revenue that was expected to be sold which would help Jenn and Lyle determine the number of pages the section would be. The meeting was brief since Lyle was working on an early deadline for the next edition.

"Happy to see you back at your desk." After her meeting with Lyle concluded, Jenn found that Doris had returned. "Thank you again for bringing Rachel to visit with Renee. I thoroughly enjoyed our dinner conversation."

"Renee looks much better than I expected after all she has recently been through medically. Rachel never stopped talking about the two of you all the way home. It was good for her to have such an enjoyable visit the first time she returned to Paisley's home. What time do you have to pick Renee up from her treatment?"

"I dropped her off at ten-thirty. She said to come back in two hours, unless she texts me differently. Apparently, Renee is also meeting with a nutritionist today about a suggested diet. That may mean we need to go grocery shopping on the way home. I better get back to my desk and make the most of the next thirty minutes."

Checking her phone to make sure Renee hadn't texted, Jenn found a text from Randy asking how things were going with Renee. It reminded her of seeing him the previous afternoon on the way to the deposition. Her thoughts drifted to the young man in the vehicle with him.

"Oh...Oh...Oh, I know who that young man looks like!"

Jenn stood up from her desk the same moment as a text from Renee came in.

"I've got to call Randy! He probably doesn't have time to talk to me right now. I've got to go to pick up Renee. Why does everything happen at once?"

Running out the door, Jenn waved at Doris. Her mind was going in a dozen directions. She must have made the trip on autopilot because about fifteen minutes later Jenn found herself pulling in front of the cancer center. Renee was hard to miss, sitting on a bench outside the front door in her bright yellow outfit.

"The nutritionist says that I should only have potato chips and vodka. It's my new diet." Renee got in and closed the door.

"Good to hear. That means I don't have to go grocery shopping. We have those items at home."

"I told the nutritionist that you would be happy."

"Your attitude is encouraging."

"I've decided to be a bright spot in this situation, in more ways than one." Renee took a deep breath. "You know me, I never meet a stranger. I talked to some of the people taking treatment around me today. They told me their stories. Some have had several battles with cancer. I don't say this too often, considering what I've had to deal with in my life. But, all things considered, I'm quite fortunate to have lived this long and had such excellent health."

Jenn reached over and squeezed Renee's hand. She knew what a hard statement that was for Renee to make. Maybe the same strength that carried Renee through the loss of her son would help her battle cancer.

"I forgot to tell you that I had a phone call from one of my old friends from high school yesterday while Doris and Aunt Rachel were visiting. Her name was Violet. Violet James then. I'm not sure that I caught her last name now."

"I think I remember her. You two were majorettes together."

"Yes, that's right. She goes to church with Doris and found out that I am staying with you. She wants to come over and visit this afternoon."

"Do you feel up to that?"

"I think so. She's a cancer survivor herself and has offered to take me to any or all my treatments."

"That's very kind of her. Have you been in touch with her any since high school?"

"I've seen her a couple of times through the years. I've not been good at keeping up with people. Violet and her first husband were some of those who came to Raleigh and helped search for Jonah. Sadly, I sort of put a block up on those people after the initial search ended. I couldn't face them. Violet's husband was a police officer and was killed in the line of duty. Mom let me know when that happened. I did make the effort to go to his funeral. We've been in touch off and on since. She remarried about two years ago."

"Your friendship with her has a complicated story."

"It does. I do feel comfortable with her though. She understands what it is like to go through treatments. Thankfully, I don't have too many friends who've faced this battle."

"Violet's is certainly welcome to come visit any time. If she wants to take you to some of your treatments, that would be a great help."

"That's what I thought. I appreciate you being willing to rearrange your whole schedule for me. But I also know you've invested your life savings in this business venture, and you don't need to mess around with that. So, I think we should let my old friend help us."

"Sounds like a good plan."

"Violet has offered to bring dinner this evening. You are welcome to join us, but perhaps you'd like to have dinner with Chief Dreamy since you had to cancel on him when I arrived last Friday."

Jenn's pulse quickened at the thought of seeing Randy. She'd missed spending time with him. She also wanted to ask about the young man who'd been visiting this week.

"Well, I wouldn't want to interfere with your friend time with Violet." Jenn tried to sound casual. "It would be nice if I could offer to take Randy out to dinner since I did cancel."

"Stop trying to sound nonchalant, little sister. I grew up with you, remember? I know all the things you do when you're trying to hide something."

"What do you mean by that?" Jenn continued looking straight ahead.

"You would never be good at playing poker. You tap your fingers on something when you are trying to be deceptive." Renee laughed. "You're doing it right now on the steering wheel."

Jenn rolled her eyes and moved her hands to the bottom of the steering wheel. "It's great having a sister who knows you so well." Jenn briefly turned in Renee's direction and stuck her tongue out.

"Let's pull over at the grocery store. There are a couple of things that the nutritionist suggested I eat. I'll run into the store while you text Chief Dreamy."

"You don't plan to call Randy that when you next see him, do you?" Jenn turned into the parking lot of the shopping center.

"I most certainly do. You better hope I don't decide to call you Mrs. Dreamy in his presence."

"You wouldn't dare." As soon as the words were out of Jenn's mouth, she knew they were a mistake." Jenn parked the vehicle, resting her head on the steering wheel in defeat.

"I most certainly will now." Renee opened the door and carefully got out of the passenger seat, cackling like a witch as she walked toward the store.

Jenn decided to make the most of what little time Renee would be in the store, opting to call Randy instead of texting. "If he's not available, he'll let it go to voicemail."

"I hope this isn't an emergency. You never call before texting." Randy answered on the second ring.

"Hi, Randy. It's not an emergency. I just have a few minutes to talk and didn't want to waste any time texting you first. Is this a bad time?"

"It's never a bad time for you to call me."

"I picked Renee up from her second chemotherapy treatment a few minutes ago. We've stopped at the grocery store so she can pick up a few items that her nutritionist suggested she include in her diet. It also happens that a friend of hers has offered to come over this evening and bring dinner for Renee. I thought that if you weren't busy, I might could buy you dinner as an apology for cancelling on you last week. I hate to ask so late and I don't want to presume that you might not be busy. This may be a bad idea." Jenn took a deep breath.

"What do you really want to talk about, Jenn?"

"What? I don't understand. I was asking about having dinner."

"You always talk very fast when you are nervous. That usually means you are leading up to asking something else."

"I don't do that."

"Yes, you do."

"Since when?"

"Since you were five, probably. Maybe earlier, I can't remember back farther than that."

"Oh, dear. I am surrounded by people who know me too well."

"You've returned to your hometown. This is your life, Jennifer Halston."

"I do want to have dinner with you."

"And?"

"And I want to ask you about something else."

"I'd love to have dinner with—"

"Randy, I've got to go. Something is wrong with Renee."

Jenn dropped her phone, jumped out of her SUV, and ran in Renee's direction. Her sister was walking toward her with a wad of paper towels on her face. Jenn could see red seeping through the material.

"What happened?"

"I've just got a little nosebleed." Renee briefly removed the towels from her face. There was blood running out of her nose.

"Tilt your head back. Maybe we should call an ambulance." Jenn put her arm around Renee, helping her continue to walk toward the vehicle.

"Don't be silly. It's nothing. This is probably a side effect that's on Page 39 of the symptoms list I didn't read."

"If you won't go to the ER, we are at least going back to the cancer center."

"It's not necessary, but I will concede to go there. I hope I haven't gotten blood on my pretty yellow outfit."

Ninety minutes later, Jenn and Renee returned home to find two vehicles in the driveway.

"I forgot to call Violet. It looks like Randy is here, too. That is a somber reunion." Renee picked up her purse.

"Somber reunion? I don't understand." Jenn parked the vehicle.

"Randy was Violet's husband's police partner. That limp Randy has is from the night that her husband was killed in the line of duty. They caught some guys in the act of robbing a jewelry store."

"I didn't know."

"Violet, I'm so sorry that I didn't call to let you know we were going to be late." Renee got out of the vehicle. "I had a little mishap."

"It's no problem. Randy told me that something had happened. We've been worried." Violet walked to Renee. They gave each other a gentle hug.

"Hello, Chief. I didn't know that you were aware of my little emergency." Renee gave Jenn a wide-eyed look over her shoulder.

"I was on the phone with Randy when you came out of the store. I threw my phone down and ran in your direction." Jenn dug in her purse. "I'm not sure where my phone is now."

"When you find it, there will be a dozen messages and missed calls from me." Randy walked toward Jenn. "When I couldn't reach you, I went to the ER. Then I came here and found Violet. I was about to retrace the route to the cancer center when you pulled up."

"I'm so sorry. Renee had a nosebleed. It scared me to death. She refused to go to the ER. I convinced her that we would circle back to the cancer center. They checked her out. The nurse said it was not an uncommon side effect from chemotherapy but that we didn't need to be too concerned at this point."

"I tried to tell Jenn that it was nothing to be concerned about. She is such a worrier." Renee began to climb the steps to the deck. Violet followed behind her with a cooler.

"Worry is a common side effect of being a caregiver." Jenn went back to her Jeep. "I've got to find my phone." After looking on the floorboards and under the seats, she finally found it in the back seat.

"Found it!" Jenn rose from her searching position, retrieved her purse, and closed the vehicle doors.

"Listen, Jenn, you've had a lot of excitement in the last few hours, maybe I should head on home." Randy began backing up toward his vehicle.

"Oh, I thought we were going to have dinner."

“I thought so, too. But maybe you want to visit with Violet.”

“I don’t know Violet. I’ve not seen her since Renee was in high school. She’s offered to take Renee to some of her treatments. Since she’s an old friend of Renee’s, I’m going to take her up on it. She seems like a nice person who has gone through a lot.”

“Yes. She has been dealt a bad hand on more than one occasion.” Randy took a deep breath, looking down at his feet.

“I didn’t know until Renee told me that you worked with Violet’s husband.”

“Jake was as fine an officer as they come. We were doing our jobs and the worst happened. The criminals got the upper hand of the situation and took the life of a good man.”

“That’s when the injury that caused your limp happened.”

“I was shot in three places—hip, calf, and shoulder. Jake took one fatal shot to the head. It’s a night I’ll never get over, no matter how many years pass. I wish it would have been me who took that fatal shot.”

“I wish neither of you were shot. I appreciate every officer who risks their life to protect others. I wish we didn’t live in a world that needed it.” Jenn looked at the phone she was still holding. “Eleven missed calls. You must have really been worried.”

“I heard you say that something was wrong with Renee and then it sounded like the phone hit the ground. That’s an alarming scenario for a police officer.”

“I’m sorry. It was scary. Thankfully, it turned out okay. Now, I owe you for cancelling plans and alarming you. Let’s go have dinner somewhere. My treat.”

“Are you sure you don’t want to stay with Renee and Violet?”

"Absolutely! They are probably going to babble all evening about their glory days as majorettes. I lived with Renee then. It would be a rerun."

"Okay, if you insist. Why don't we both drive? I'm technically on call this evening."

"Let me run in and tell Renee. I'd like to try that new Italian restaurant that's a few miles south of here. I think it's called Table for Two."

"Sounds romantic." Randy raised his eyebrows. "I'll go ahead and get us a table."

"Perfect. I'll be ten minutes behind you."

Jenn ran up the steps. If she was quick, she could freshen up a little. Once inside, she found Renee and Violet eating at the table in the kitchen.

"Hello. It looks like Peggy brought you a homemade dish. It smells delightful."

"There's plenty here, Jenn. You and the Chief are welcome to eat with us." Violet smiled briefly. "Randy is a good man. He's grieved himself something fierce over what happened to my Jake. They were doing their jobs. The criminals got the best of them."

"I'm so sorry for your loss, Violet. I didn't know anything about the incident until Renee told me today."

"I'm surprised Randy hasn't told you the story. I heard that you two were dating."

"Randy and I are old friends. I've enjoyed getting to know him again, but our time together has been limited. I noticed that he was injured, of course. I hadn't asked him how it happened." Jenn continued to walk through the kitchen. "Since Violet is visiting with you, Renee, I am going to go ahead and have dinner with Randy as we planned. I'm just going to run back to my bedroom and quickly change clothes."

"She has a date with Chief Dreamy."

Jenn did not stop to acknowledge Renee's comment. She told Randy that she would be ten minutes behind him. She wanted to stay as true to that as possible. It was already later than she'd planned to meet him.

Jenn quickly freshened up, picking a comfortable pantsuit to change into with a lightweight sweater, in case the restaurant was chilly.

"Where are you having dinner?" Violet asked before Jenn could get out of the door.

"At a new Italian restaurant a few miles south of here. It's called Table for Two."

"I've heard about that one." Violet continued talking. "All of the seating are tables for two. It's quite the date night place."

"Jenn has a date with Chief Dreamy." Renee was sounding like Jenn's teenage sister. "They should have dated when they were young. I bet they would have gotten married."

"Again, Randy and I are old friends. I've got to go. It was great to see you again, Violet. Thanks for everything you are doing for Renee."

Jenn turned around to open the sliding door.

"What time should I expect you home, young lady? Sunrise?" Renee giggled.

"I'll be home by ten, my darling sister."

"You are mighty quiet for someone who seemed so anxious to talk to me about something."

Jenn looked up from her plate to find Randy staring at her. They'd made chitchat as they ate their salads with too much bread while waiting for their entrees. The nosebleed incident with Renee had thrown Jenn's thought process off track, almost making her forget what she so desperately wanted to talk to Randy about. Jenn took a deep breath.

"I don't like the sound of that. I sure hope you aren't going to tell me that you are reconciling with your ex-husband." Randy's look was too serious.

"Not in this lifetime." Jenn rolled her eyes. "Although, since two of our children are going to be living here soon, Simon might decide that's all the incentive he needs to come visit. I think there should be a law on the books that states an ex-husband can't visit within fifty miles of his former wife for a certain number of years."

"Ouch! I'm an ex-husband, you know. I liked visiting my son."

"You would be an exception to that rule. You are an exception to most rules." Jenn closed her eyes, shaking her head. She couldn't believe she'd said that aloud. Now, she had to change the subject. "I saw you the other day when I was heading to Mr. Crewe's office to do a deposition for a case involving the newspaper. You crossed in front of me at a stoplight. There was someone in the vehicle with you. I think it might have been the officer who was staying with you. I can't remember his name."

"Fairfield. Joe Fairfield. That was probably on Tuesday after the trial was over. I drove him to court that day. Poor boy was a nervous wreck. He did a great job testifying though. Edwin won the case."

"Happy to hear that. Is he still here? I wondered how things went between him and the young lady at the bank."

"Joe spent time with Megan over the weekend. I think they attended the festival on both Saturday and Sunday. I believe that he went to see her before he left to travel home. There's certainly a spark between the two of them. He and I had a couple of long talks about why he left here. I've invited him to reapply with my department. He's promised to let me know his decision within a couple of weeks. I've got to start filling these open positions. My team has been shorthanded for too long."

Jenn remained quiet, repeatedly twirling her spaghetti around her fork without taking a bite.

"Jenn, please tell me what is concerning you. You've barely eaten and seem lost in thought."

"Randy, I'm afraid to say the words aloud."

"Why? First and foremost, I am your friend. I want to help with whatever is troubling you." Randy reached across the table, taking Jenn's hand in his.

"It is not something that has to do with you and me. I have no complaints about our relationship. I appreciate you understanding that I want to take it slow."

"My only worry is that some other guy will come along and whisk you off your feet before I ever have a chance. Someone who can offer you a life I cannot."

Jenn saw real concern in Randy's furrowed brow. She wondered if he had somehow learned of Parker Bentley's advances toward her. Serendipity was a small town.

"There is no one I want to be with other than you, Randy. There. I've said it. Perhaps that makes us even. You've kissed me in the middle of downtown. I've admitted what I've held in my heart since the moment we reconnected."

"Those are welcomed words. I am happy to hear them. I do not believe they are what you are so concerned about. Does it have to do with Renee?"

"Well, as a matter of fact, it does. It could. It might. It's a long shot though. That's why I am even afraid to say it. Oh, what a wonderful possibility it could be. How heartbreaking it will be if it is not. And it's probably not. It would be a miracle."

"My head is dizzy from listening to you go round and round. Give both our minds a break and spill it."

"Okay." Jenn took a deep breath, reaching for her purse and pulling out her wallet.

"Are you ready to go?" Randy looked down at his plate. "We haven't finished eating. There is no way that I am letting you pay for this dinner, by the way."

"No, I'm not finished. I want to show you something." Jenn dug around in her wallet. "I am paying for dinner."

"We'll argue about that later." Randy took another bite of his manicotti.

"I want to show you this photo." Jenn took a moment to stare at the photo before she placed it in front of Randy.

"Wow. How did you get a photo of Joe Fairfield? It looks like it might have been a school photo, maybe senior year. When he worked for me before, he had a moustache and beard. He really has a baby face without it."

"You've thought the same thing I did when I saw Joe in your vehicle as you drove by me. This isn't a photo of Joe Fairfield. You are right about it being a school photo. This young man was in his sophomore year of college. It was the year he first met Renee. This is my brother-in-law, Neil Davenport."

"Holy smokes! What's the term when someone has a twin? Joe is Neil's doppelganger. They could be brothers."

"These are the words I'm so afraid to say aloud." A swell of emotion cursed through Jenn's body. Before she realized it, tears were running down her face. "They could be father and son. Oh, Randy, it would be a miracle."

"Jenn, I understand what a horrible ordeal it was for your family for your nephew to be kidnapped. That was a long time ago."

"Almost twenty years." The words came out in a sob.

"I don't want to ruin your hopes, but it is highly unlikely that precious little boy lived more than a few months after he was kidnapped. The types of people who kidnap children don't normally keep them alive."

"I know. It's a one-in-a-million chance. I've tried to talk myself out of even mentioning it. But you see from this photo how incredibly strong the likeness is between them. It's been years since I've seen Neil clean shaven. When I first saw the glimpse of Joe, he looked familiar. I couldn't place who he reminded me of though. This morning, Renee was looking through some old photo albums, and I saw this photo. It hit me like a ton of bricks. I would never have slept tonight if I didn't talk to someone about this. I obviously can't mention it to Renee."

Randy picked up the photo again, staring intently. "Again, please do not get your hopes up. It's a longshot at best. Rest assured though. I'm going to thoroughly investigate Joe's background and find out if there is any way he might be related to Neil."

"Oh, thank you, Randy. I knew that I could count on you."

"Can I keep this photo?"

"Absolutely."

"I think it's time that we got the check and call it a night. I've got a big day tomorrow." Randy waved to their server.

"Oh, what do you have to do?" Jenn picked up her purse, preparing to leave.

"I'm going to start working on this immediately. I'll clear my calendar and take a trip back to the western part of the state. This time, I'm going to meet Joe Fairfield's mother and hear the story of her son's life."

"Oh, Randy, thank you."

"Don't thank me yet, Jenn. There's no guarantee that this story will have a happy ending."

"I understand. But there's a tiny possibility that it might. That's a thousand percent more than Renee and Neil have had in twenty years. I've got to continue to believe that we might see our precious Jonah again. I love my sister too much to do anything else."

About the Author

Attributing her limitless imagination to growing up as an only child, Liza Lanter enjoys creating heartwarming fiction with characters who instantly seem like friends and have bonds that feel like family. Every aspect of her life has involved writing of a non-fiction variety. Her heart is most at home spinning yarns of a fictional nature.

To sign up for Liza's newsletter and learn more about
her writing adventures,
visit www.LizaLanter.com.

Visit the Liza Lanter author page on Amazon
at www.amazon.com/author/lizalanter

Visit the Liza Lanter Facebook page
at http://www.facebook.com/lizalanter

Did you enjoy this book? You can make a big difference by leaving a short review. Honest reviews help convince prospective readers to take a chance on an author they do not know. Thank you.